THE
STUFF OF
MURDER

THE STUFF OF MURDER

AN OLD STUFF MURDER

KATHLEEN MARPLE KALB

LEVEL
BEST BOOKS

Author Photo Credit: Steven Kalb

First edition

ISBN: 978-1-68512-516-5

Cover art by Level Best Designs

This book was professionally typeset on Reedsy.
Find out more at reedsy.com

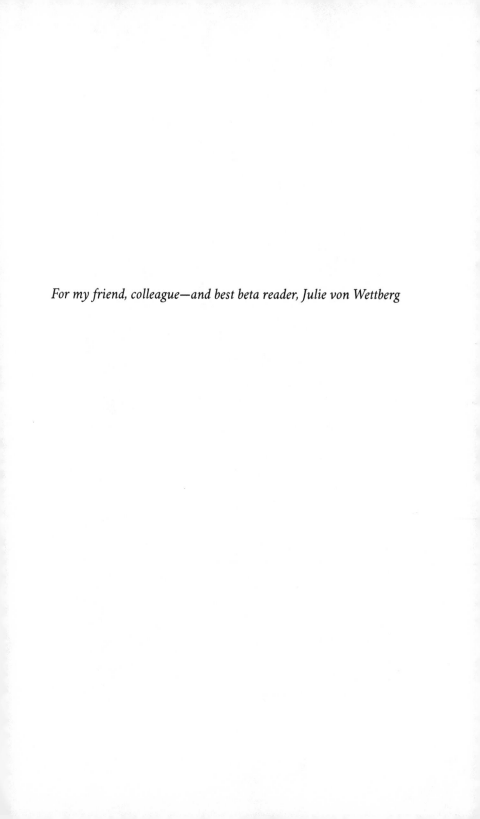

For my friend, colleague—and best beta reader, Julie von Wettberg

Praise for The Stuff of Murder

"I received an ARC copy of *The Stuff of Murder* in return for an honest review. And I'm delighted to be able to say, this was one of the best books I've read this year.

"This is a thoroughly enjoyable modern murder mystery with a likable, diverse cast of characters and a town that has a charming sense of community. An additional plus for me was the addition of a young character with Type 1 diabetes, and as the parent of a 9 yr old with the same, the descriptions of diagnosis and general life with T1D were accurate, positive and at one point, brought tears to my eyes.

"The mystery is neat, well plotted and fun and there's a dollop of romance that fleshes out the main characters nicely. Another nice touch is the way the history and especially social history of the town is brought into the life of the characters and the mystery plot. If you have an interest in history this will be an especially nice read.

"In short, I'm already looking forward to book 2."—Geraldine Byrne, author of the Irish Music Shop and Caroline Jordan Mystery Series

The Stuff of Murder checks all the boxes of a great, modern murder mystery. A strong lead with a diverse supporting cast, Kalb's latest is a charming read for mystery fans.

"Dr. Christian Shaw is the head of the Unity, Connecticut, Historical Society, serving as a consultant for a movie shoot in town. When the star of the movie plunges from the synagogue pulpit, his murder quickly becomes the focus of small-town life.

"As a fan of Kalb's Ella Shane series, I was eager to meet Dr. Shaw. I must say, Christian has one of the strongest voices that I've come across in a long time. As I read, I often felt like she was sitting beside me, guiding me through her life. She sifts through suspects and motives with the care of a historian and the sarcasm of an *SNL* writer. Her modern, sharp wit was a very enjoyable experience. I learned so much from Christian as well. These pages are peppered with fascinating information about "stuff." And kudos for gifting the reader with a different type of investigative procedure. This is the first time I've encountered a prosecutor as the principal investigator that an amateur sleuth contends with, and Joe Poli was a surprising delight. I loved the teamwork between Christian and Joe, and the case offered plenty of twists. The culprit takedown scene is one of the most memorable I've read—I loved it!

"I also must commend Kalb for the diversity and inclusivity she brings to Unity, CT. Christian is surrounded by kind, warm, welcoming people from all backgrounds and walks of life, and it was really lovely to see a community like this in a cozy mystery. Kalb also isn't afraid to call out the social injustices we unfortunately still see in our world.

The Stuff of Murder is a fun, charming series debut, full of smart characters and an even smarter mystery."—Sarah E. Burr, author of the Trending Topic Mysteries, Book Blogger Mysteries, & Glenmyre Whim Mysteries

"So many fun characters in this book! Aside from the fact that it's just a really good murder mystery in the "cozy" sense of the word, it's also got a charming and refreshing group of characters that round out the story. I really hope there is another one of these, because I found myself wanting to live in the town with these folks."—Brian, first Goodreads review

Chapter One

Unholy Mess

Everybody loves a good public shaming. Nowadays, we do it on social media, but back in the day, people showed up at the center of town or at church to do it the old-fashioned way, face-to-face, or maybe whip-to-back. It's plenty of fun for the shamers, old or new school, even if not much for the shame-ee.

Well, until somebody gets hurt. Or worse.

Just ask everybody who'd come to Congregation Beth Shalom that pretty day in May for the thrill of seeing a movie star and a big dramatic scene…and got way more than they bargained for. Did we ever.

It was supposed to be fun, spending an hour or so observing the streaming service crew shooting a prestige production (*very*) loosely based on *The Scarlet Letter*. Brett Studebaker, who'd been the crush of choice for many of the locals and not-so-locals when we were teenagers, was hoping to revive his career as the Reverend, and this was his climactic meltdown at the pulpit. Yeah, I know. See what I mean about loosely based?

I was in an out-of-the-way spot with some of my best buddies: Rabbi Dina Aaron, EMT Captain Tiffany Medina, and Garrett and Ed Kenney, hoping we could wring a little enjoyment out of a shoot that had become a serious pain in the *tuches* for the whole town. Not to mention all of us, individually and severally. Though I was probably the only one who was actively praying for the crew to leave. My friends are much nicer than me.

Studebaker patted the priceless Bible on the pulpit, licked his finger, and turned a page, then changed his mind, *licked again,* and put it back. I winced as if he'd slapped me. In the hope that he'd treat the Book with care, I'd told him the truth: it was an irreplaceable seventeenth-century piece that had survived a terrible ocean voyage, five or six wars, plus fire, upheaval, and tragedy in two different families. No one was really supposed to handle it without gloves. Now his spit was on it.

Probably should have just lied and said one of the local witches had cursed it.

I winced again as Studebaker took a swig of what I really hoped was water from a metal tankard that he'd grabbed from the Historical Society dining room, then fussed with his cravat some more. There'd been three emails about that blasted cravat just this morning. I'd forgotten how aggravating consulting was—and resolved yet again to stay with my day job running the Society and its living history museum, just a few steps from the synagogue.

Until about ten years ago, what we know as Beth Shalom was the Congregational Church, an absolutely perfectly preserved mid-eighteenth-century sanctuary that was on the National Register. The temple was looking for a new home when the dwindling *goyim* were looking to sell, and the town fathers and mothers wanted to keep the building in use. And that's how a Reform synagogue ended up in the prestige spot on the Green in Unity, Connecticut, the very definition of a classic New England town.

It was a truly lovely building, and just as I picked up a little consulting here and there, Dina brought in a few extra shekels for the building fund with the occasional documentary shoot, concert, or lecture event. The town had never hosted a real movie before, though, and we'd all quickly come to the conclusion that it was way more trouble than it was worth.

From the Green outward, the center of town was clogged with trucks and trailers and mess for weeks. We didn't even get much of an economic boost, because our perfectly nice local inn and our two absolutely magnificent Italian family restaurants weren't fancy enough for the movie types. All we got were a few measly techs and lower-level production folks.

We were thoroughly sick of it all before we even got to this big scene, thankfully the last shoot in town, even if there would be a lot more work back in Hollywood. They were doing several major sequences on location first, and then finishing the rest of the film on a soundstage. I had the feeling that had a lot to do with keeping Brett Studebaker happy and at home. Well past his action-hero prime, he was apparently hoping to show a new side of himself as a serious actor, but didn't want to be far from his cushy life.

The only side I'd seen in my limited contact with him was arrogance, that mug being a prime example. He saw it on a tour of the Society museum, proclaimed, "That's the Reverend's tankard!" and scooped it up, carrying the thing like Gollum with his Precious, even as I protested. The fact that he was apparently incapable of hearing a female voice saying *no* worried me a little.

The tankard actually worried me more.

I was left hoping that the thing really was pewter—as it appeared to be—and there wasn't anything weirder than lead in the alloy, because something funky could definitely have happened back in the days of silversmiths' hearths. Not that lead wasn't bad enough. I assumed that he'd be done with the shoot and the piece before any serious metal poisoning could take hold. But still, every time he drank from it, I shuddered. I shuddered more when my smartphone beeped with the email notification. Studebaker had a million tiny questions, and it was my job to answer them all, since I was the ranking, and paid, expert on stuff.

Literally. I'm a duly accredited authority on Colonial, Early American, and nineteenth-century household items and personal property, i.e., stuff.

Stuff (in the less elevated meaning) was about to hit the fan right about then, as Brett Studebaker started his scene in the pulpit, a marvelously carved old wooden box looming more than ten feet over the sanctuary floor. He'd seemed normal enough when he climbed up the windy little staircase, but now it was getting weird. He hung onto the edges of the pulpit, writhing and shaking the whole thing with his bulk, his piercing blue eyes glassy, his far less than authentic salt-and-pepper mane disheveled. Method acting, I figured, though I'd thought that was out.

The movie crew didn't seem bothered by it. They barely even noticed. The camera and sound operators, and the small army of support people who made it all happen, gave no hint of particular interest or concern at Studebaker's behavior.

The director, a geeky guy with bad retro glasses, had been the screenwriter too, until the original one left in some kind of last-minute creative dispute a week before the shoot. As had become his habit, he sat there looking terrified about what he was putting his name on. Some people step up when life comes for them. Other people curl up in a ball and hope it doesn't hit them too hard. It was pretty clear which one he was.

Clustered around the director's chair was a much smaller group of guys (and they *were* all guys) who seemed to be neither terrified nor disinterested...but at least kind of paying attention. Mostly middle-aged, all dressed in some variation of California casual, they looked pretty bored, too. The producer, Greg Holman, an older guy with dead eyes that I'd talked to a few times, seemed to be the most bored of all.

About the only one who was really focusing on Studebaker was his assistant, a swaggery little bro who treated everyone who wasn't a potential groupie with disdain. I figured he was pretending rapt interest because he had to.

Still, I realized, as Studebaker took a big, ragged breath, it was showtime, and I supposed we might as well enjoy it.

"Fly from me, demons!" he shouted.

"I'm just an old Lincoln scholar," Garrett, originally my academic mentor and now the dad I should have had, observed quietly, "but I'm pretty sure that's not Nathaniel Hawthorne."

"It's not." I swallowed a giggle and nodded to the director. "It's that guy. He's the screenwriter, too."

Ed snorted. He's a former state trooper, not an academic, so he doesn't have to be as diplomatic as his husband. "Nothing worse than some mope in love with his own words."

Since Garrett still wrote the occasional journal article (under what he archly called his maiden name, Koziekiewicz) and tried out lines on Ed, there might just have been a teensy bit of subtext there.

"*Shah!*" Dina hissed, using her grandmother's much nicer way of saying shut up. Her grandmother had probably looked just like her too, a tiny, ferocious redhead. "Enjoy the show."

"And tear it apart later," Tiffany said, a wicked gleam in her amber eyes.

Dina's serious rabbi mien slipped a trace. "Yes. But behave now."

Garrett pulled his round face into regal and serious lines and adjusted his wire-framed glasses. Ed sighed and stepped into his default at-ease stance, still looking like a cop, tall, spare, and always alert.

Tiffany and I carefully didn't look at each other and kept our gaze on the pulpit. We were on the floor near the front, just far enough away to be out of the shot, but much closer than most of the spectators, who were in the balcony over the sanctuary, ranged on the side benches so the camera could shoot from above.

"Loose me, ye demons!" Studebaker cried out, this time looking as if he were really in pain. He let out a deep, awful wail, hanging onto the sides of the pulpit and rearing back, almost howling like a wolf.

The mostly-accurately costumed pilgrims in the pews, almost all college kids from New Haven, gasped and murmured in character. The locals, up in the far reaches of the balcony, just shook their heads. This may be New Haven County, Connecticut, but it's still New England, and we don't go in for histrionics. A couple of the older ladies, docents at the Society, were muttering something. I had no doubt it was about what an absolute mess the streaming service was making of Nathaniel Hawthorne's perfectly lovely book.

I was equally sure I'd hear about it later.

Studebaker looked down at the amazing Bible, a gift from a now-dispersed founding family that normally occupied a special case in the Society foyer, and put his hands flat on the pages, almost clutching at them. I could see a crinkle in the thick paper.

My stomach twisted. I took a deep breath and tried to tamp down my anger.

Method acting, hell, show some respect for a sacred object that's survived about three centuries more than you have, fool. Garrett patted my arm. He's not a mind-reader, but it's close sometimes.

"Forgive me, my Lord, for I have sinned..." howled Studebaker, thankfully moving his hands off the Bible to the pulpit edges again, then running them down his face, and now really starting to thrash around in simulated agony.

The tankard rocked. I feared a splash, but apparently, he'd swilled enough of whatever it was, we were at least spared that danger.

He thrashed some more.

Something creaked.

Dina, who still had nightmares about the certified restoration contractor's bill for the last time they shored up the pulpit, never mind the disrespect to the building, bit her lip. She was furious, too.

I bent down and whispered to her: "Bill him for the repairs. I will if I have to."

A muscle in her jaw twitched. "Don't think I won't."

"Oh, forgive me..."

Don't think so. He didn't need to expect any absolution from me—or Dina, not that rabbis really do that.

"Pleeeease!"

Studebaker ripped his cravat away and pounded the pulpit as he howled, his face turning a strange shade, his orangey makeup suddenly standing out.

"Um, is he having a seizure?" Tiffany whispered. "Should I do something?"

"Method acting, I think." I hissed back.

"Weird old white guy stuff."

Ed coughed in a way that meant he was stifling a laugh. So did Garrett. They're not exactly the usual old white guys. Tiffany gave them a sparkly little eyebrow raise.

"My Lord, My Lord, what have I done..." Studebaker continued wailing, warming to his theme and alternating between pounding on the pulpit and thrashing. The whole thing, box and stairs and supports and all, a good ten feet above us, was shaking.

I glanced back to the pilgrims, who seemed to be stunned into silence—but clearly still in character, and to the spectators in the balcony. Most of them now just looked bored, though a few, like Mae Tillotson, were watching with considerable interest.

Mae volunteers at the Society, and while she's eighty if she's a day, she likes a fine-looking man. I suspected that transfixed expression had as much to do with the fact that there was a pretty nice expanse of rather manly Studebaker chest visible with the cravat gone.

If I hadn't known what a jerk he was, it might have been worth a look. But I've always had a hard time separating a guy's hotness from the rest of him.

"I have sinned!" shouted Studebaker. His voice cracked on the last word, and he let out another horrible nonverbal howl. His face had a strange grayish cast now, which was a little off – I'd have expected him to be red from exertion.

"You *sure* he's acting?" Tiffany whispered, reaching for her radio.

"Ninety percent?" I hissed back.

"Sin!" Studebaker cried. "Sin! I am a sin-"

He suddenly stopped on that last syllable, looked down at the congregation for a moment, then reared up on the pulpit again, letting out another of those horrific wails. Then he thrashed around one more time, knocking over the tankard – this time almost splashing the Bible. Finally, apparently struggling for breath, he took his hands off the lectern and fell away, almost as if pushed by some unseen force.

Demons, maybe? Maybe angels, protecting that Bible, thanks.

It probably made an awfully good picture.

Right until he hit the pulpit door. His weight carried him straight through it and his height over the stair rail, which might have caught the much smaller men who built the church. It was only when Studebaker landed with a sickening wet crunch ten feet below, just behind the *bima*, that we realized this wasn't the movies anymore.

Chapter Two

Before These Witnesses

Tiffany, of course, was on him in seconds, putting out the call to her ambulance crew and getting right to work. I had my infant and child CPR certification, but I knew I'd be more harm than help, so I just stayed with the rest of my friends and waited.

None of us were delicate flowers, but this was pretty shocking. I swallowed hard and tried to think about anything but the fact that my insides really wanted to become my outsides. Dina kept her face calm, but there was a tension in her posture I rarely, if ever, saw. Garrett and Ed reacted like the old-school standup guys they are, protectively closing ranks around the two of us, a quiet but definite announcement that anyone who wanted us would have to come through them.

As Tiffany and her minions put Studebaker on a stretcher and rolled him out, Ed warned us that we were going to be stuck at the scene for hours. That was fine, as long as it wasn't *too many* hours. With Tiffany occupied, I was going to have to pick up her daughter Ava as well as my son Henry. It had happened before when there was a situation, and it would happen again. One of the benefits of being able to set my own schedule a little.

I take my lunch hour at school pickup time, about two-thirty, and then bring Henry, often Ava, and maybe another friend or two to the Society, where they do homework, read and often wander around exploring for a couple of hours. It works.

It would be about the only thing that worked that day. I knew what it meant when a couple of Ed's former State Police colleagues went through the crowd, taking our names, "Just in case we need to contact you."

I had been married to a reporter long enough to hear what they were really saying: that they'd be calling once the docs pronounced Studebaker.

At least we were stuck at a scene that was comfortable, familiar, and close to home. I'd left Shoreline Connecticut State University to take over the Historical Society when the post-Garrett tenure committee brushed me off after seven years of blindingly hard work, capping a decade and a half of fighting my way into academia. My area of study, I was told, was too specific and not important or interesting enough in a small state college context. Never mind that my bosses had been perfectly happy with my take on Early New England social history right up until they had the choice of hiring me or a guy who'd been making the rounds for his headline-grabbing book on the Founding Fathers' sex lives.

I was better off at the Historical Society anyway. It was within walking distance of my little house and Henry's school, making mornings a lot easier. Garrett and Ed were one street away from the Green, meaning plenty of family coffees. And Dina was two steps away at Beth Shalom. We were like one of those old-school sitcoms, only with a good bit more diversity. Plus, it paid me decently well to do what was really my best thing: working with stuff.

As in the things we use: clothes, cradles, skillets and plates. Anything we handle in the course of daily life—like the metal tankard Brett Studebaker kept swigging from, despite my repeated reminders that there were no product safety laws in the 1700s. It's all way more intimate than names and dates; it's the actual things people held in their hands and used in their daily work. I'm not one of those supernatural types, but I do often feel a tinge of some kind of energy when handling something that people used decades or centuries ago.

I'd never say it out loud, but I sometimes get a little echo when I'm putting a wedding dress on a mannequin or hanging up a cooking pot on the big hearth in the Society's amazingly intact eighteenth-century kitchen. Just a sense I'm not the first person who's been here.

It was hard to boil the feeling down to dry academic prose, parsing the importance of household objects in social history and making it all sound desperately serious when what I really wanted to do was set the table with plates that were already priceless family heirlooms in the 1700s, or open a trunk full of clothes that hadn't been touched for a hundred years. I don't have to justify it to anyone now—it's my job.

These days, I get to spend my time making the fourth-grade field trip giggle about chamber pots and showing wide-eyed teenage girls the teeny-tiny kid gloves their great-great-grandmothers wore. Once in a while, I pick up a little consulting work, advising visiting crews on authentic set decoration or exchanging a few emails with some Hollywood production assistant about what embroidery snips a Regency maiden would use (yes, really happened!). And a Scotch-Irish girl from the Rust Belt never turns down honest work.

Even if it usually ends up being more trouble than it's worth.

It sure had with Brett Studebaker, who was far too important to actually talk to me but was more than happy to appropriate that tankard. I got the assistant to make him sign for it and reminded the star once again I had only an approximate idea of the alloy, some kind of pewter, so there was no guarantee there wasn't some terribly dangerous impurity in it. No one other than me seemed particularly worried by that.

What Studebaker *was* worried about was detail. He wouldn't waste face time on someone as insignificant as a consultant, but he email bombed me with questions about literally every aspect of his character's life. Not just what kind of socks he wore, but in what order to put them on (before the shoes). Did he splash his face with water after shaving? (yes, unless he wanted a face full of hair bits all day). Did he leave most of his clothes on during his illicit tryst on the edge of town—and how did he accomplish that? (too cold and risky not to, and he figured it out).

That last one hadn't been good enough, and after a couple more rounds of oblique suggestions as to how one might work around button-front breeches and a very long shirt (a lot of men at the time didn't wear underwear as such, they just tucked the shirt end around everything—yeah, I know, ick!), I finally drew him a diagram. After that, he moved on to other things.

Not that I much cared. The check cashed the same, and it wasn't about me at all.

What is about me: my name is Christian Shaw. I'm the director of the Historical Society, and by the way, pretty good with old weaponry, too—summer internship at Old Williamsburg. I'm the proud mother of third-grader Henry Glaser. If you call me Chrissy, you will live to regret it. Christian is a very old Scottish female name, which my family apparently thought would make me stand out. They didn't need to worry—I'm six foot one with flaming red hair and, as they said back home, a mouth on me. Most people who know me well and don't call me Mom call me by my full name. Or try to—it's Southern Connecticut, and a lot of people swallow the T.

T or no T, you'd be surprised how sexy a weird ancient name sounds coming from a hot guy on a sweet summer night... I know I was. Not an issue now. My husband, Frank Glaser, was a newspaper reporter, back when we still had them. He interviewed me about life before air conditioning on a slow Monday in July because I was the only person the PR guy at Shoreline State could find. A week later, after the story ran, he asked me out to dinner at his favorite Chinese place, and that was the end of that. We got eight good years—including Henry's first six—before Frank was driving to the scene of a fire, overworked and sleep-deprived as always, and hit a patch of black ice that spun him into a pole.

Dina, Garrett, Ed, Tiffany, and my other good friends saved me. The first year or so, there was never a time when there wasn't someone within reach, cooking dinner, picking up Henry at school when I had to deal with legal stuff, just handing me a cup of tea or glass of wine, and sitting with me for a while. I can't ever give that back, but I make sure to take care of everyone around me as best I can.

Today, somebody close to Brett Studebaker was going to need it.

I might have to care about his demise in more than the John Donne "no man is an island" way, damn it.

Chapter Three

Ladies of the Pen

T he Staties released us just in time, and I sped-walked to Phyllis
Wheatley Elementary. It was a pretty day, and any other
time, I'd have enjoyed the warm air, sunshine, and blooming
flowers. Unity has that classic Old New England look, with Town Hall,
Beth Shalom, and the Library on the Green and the historic houses
on the side streets. Garrett and Ed live in one of them, a clapboard
saltbox that Garrett bought for cheap when he started at Shoreline
State thirty years ago. Ed does all the handy outside stuff, and Garrett
happily holds his ladder and tends the garden. It works.

So does my life, though I'd never have expected it to. Not because of
Frank's death. Life is uncertain, and terrible things happen. You have
to keep moving for the people who need you, even if you think you
can't. No, the surprise in my life is a good one: how much I love being
Henry's mom.

When I was working my way through degrees and starting the
tenure track, I never thought much about having a child. Never really
expected that any man I'd meet in my current world could love a girl
from Mars. Mars, Pennsylvania, that is: classic Rust Belt Appalachia,
and everything most folks here are grateful to fly over. Growing up

the daughter of a divorced single mother before that was cool, I always knew I was getting out. As an adult, I doubted anyone understood the knife edge you live on when you're the one who does.

Frank Glaser didn't, but as a Jewish reporter from the Bronx, he was an outsider in other ways. He got close enough. We genuinely liked each other before we loved each other, and we were both astonished by how much we adored Henry. More, I was amazed at how much I just simply enjoyed parenting.

I know the really hard-core feminists like to call it making beds and wiping butts, but the bed and the butt belong to the center of my world, so what's the problem again? Caring for Henry and making sure he grows into a good man is the most important thing I'll ever do. Especially since I don't have Frank to help me.

I miss him every damn day.

Thank G-d (I do my best to follow the Jewish commandment against using the Lord's name even though I'm not legal) for Garrett and Ed. Garrett, who was a gay smart guy in Akron about three decades before I was a smart girl in Mars, took me under his wing when I arrived at the History Department at Shoreline State, and eventually became surrogate family. I'm the daughter he never had, and he's the dad I should have had. Not that Garrett wants to be reminded he's so much older than me.

Ed was Security Director at Shoreline State for a few years after he retired from the Staties. He'd been married to a woman years ago, and, after she died, stayed very close with his son and daughters. And spent a lot of time thinking about who he was and who he wanted to be when he didn't have to meet the unfortunately fossilized expectations of the State Police at the time.

So, when he met Garrett, he knew exactly what to do. He asked him to coffee...and Garrett said no because he'd had his heart broken one too many times. At the time, I was filled with all of the happy hormones of cuddly new motherhood, and I did something I honestly never do: I meddled. I pushed Garrett into changing his mind – and out the door to go see Ed.

The rest, as they say, is history.

Probably not the Civil War kind that Garrett still writes about, though.

One street past Garrett and Ed's is the little converted carriage house that Frank and I had bought soon after we married. It's nowhere near as old as the Historical Society or Beth Shalom, but it's still built to last, with a big living area in the front, a small kitchen tucked in one side, a half-bath on the other, and then two cozy bedrooms at the back with the full bath between. We were talking about looking for a larger place when first-grader Henry was getting bigger and busier...and then I was really glad we hadn't.

The school is vintage, too, but not the same kind of vintage as much of the neighborhood. It's a 1960s-era special, one split level, with a traffic circle and portico, two separate playgrounds, one for the little ones and one for the big. The energy, of course, comes from those kids, and it's amazing. They bounce like popcorn on the way into the building in the morning, and fly out the doors in the afternoon, climbing all over each other, giggling at potty jokes, and telling some terribly exciting story from their day.

In the pickup pen, the area where the moms and grandmas (and a few dads and gramps) meet the cherubs at day's end, there's a little less uniformity of amazing. Some, like Tiffany and Lidia and Ruby, the matriarchs, are indeed wondrous. But then there's Sally Birdwell. The princess of the PTA, Martha Stewart acolyte, part-time real estate agent, and full-time one-upper, whether in person or on her immaculately curated social media feed, she was an enduring irritant to those of us who consider it an achievement to make it to wine o'clock.

And wouldn't you know it, as I sped toward the door, Sally was the first one there. The sight of that tiny, perfect woman always made me feel insanely inadequate. More so today, as she preened in a hot-pink shift dress and heels, her spray-tan still smooth from a week in Cancun—couple getaway, obvs!—her silky black hair falling in perfectly ironed waves, and of course, the best no-makeup makeup job money and time could buy.

I know, I know, people can only make you feel inferior if you let them. But it's hard not to let Sally.

We've already established that I'm huge: six-one, life-stress thin, but not especially dainty of frame. And that my hair is red, an unruly medium-length puffball of curls. None of that bugs me—we are who we are.

What does make me nuts, and usually only when Sally's around, is that I am not, and never will be, one of those stylish, sexy women men adore and other females emulate.

Over the years, I've worked up a comfortable, affordable, and professional uniform, and while it's definitely mine, no one will ever mistake me for anything but a scruffy tomboy, if I can call myself that these days. I usually wear a men's vintage oxford (great fabric and long enough arms), some kind of schoolboy-style blazer, whether vintage or not, and skinny pants, finishing with low-top sneakers. There's always a sparkly pin on the jacket, and some bright lipstick on me, so I look girly enough. But definitely not stylish or sexy.

Sexy isn't a consideration these days anyhow, of course. Back in the day, I always had one dress and spikes for date night with Frank, who loved me in heels and didn't care that they made me tower over him. It's not really that I *want* to be sexy and cute like Sally. I just wish I didn't feel enormous and ugly around her.

Well, hell, I thought as her bright brown eyes landed on me, I'm here now.

17

"Christian!" She chirped my name almost close to correctly—Sally talks so fast and breathlessly she doesn't have time to swallow a T. "Was it really awful at the temple?"

Her eyes gleamed with the sort of unholy glee that you see on lookie-loos at three-alarm fires. Pretty is as pretty does, I reminded myself. "It wasn't fun, for sure."

"Is he dead? I heard he fell ten feet and-"

"Last I heard, they were still working on him at Yale. It's too early to speculate about anything."

"Sure." She would have been happy to speculate about all sorts of things, I knew, but since I wasn't playing, she moved on. "Is it true that somebody slipped something in his drink?"

"Everything I've heard was that it was a terrible accident." And whatever I'm thinking is none of your damn business.

"Oh." She pursed her shimmery nude lips as much as the fillers would permit. "Well, I wonder if it was some kind of #MeToo thing. You know those movie stars."

My antennae, as I call the good sense of people that I'd always had and sharpened with Frank's help, went up. "Did you hear something?"

"Not really. But someone like that stuck at a hotel in New Haven for weeks…there might just be a jealous husband around somewhere."

"Could be."

"I know what Malcolm would do if some visiting movie star made a play for me…" She shuddered extravagantly, making me wonder if she'd taken one of the same method acting classes as Studebaker.

"Yeah, you never know." I nodded. "I imagine the authorities will look into it."

"You might want to tell Rabbi Aaron to talk to a lawyer, too."

"Why?" I asked, allowing the syllable to linger cautiously.

"Well, it happened on the temple property, of course. Those movie people will sue anyone over anything. Malcolm's firm did some

18

forensic accounting in a lawsuit over someone tripping on the sidewalk in New Haven for an ad shoot once."

Her husband Malcolm is a CPA and, one can only assume, a saint. Either that or Sally brings other things to the marital table we do not want to think about.

"I hadn't thought about the liability issue. I assume the production company would be on the hook." I shrugged. "It never comes up in any of my consulting contracts, of course."

Sally's mouth tightened a little. I couldn't resist reminding her that one of us had actually worked on films, and it was not her. "Well, she might want to just informally ask her lawyer."

"What's so serious?" An Italian-accented voice rang out behind us, followed immediately by one with a more urban flavor:

"Talking about that mess at the temple today."

Lidia and Ruby, the grandmas, had arrived.

Lidia was tiny, everybody's mental picture of an adorable *nonna*, with curly salt-and-pepper hair, sparkly brown eyes, and a winning smile. Ruby was the regal one, with her still-smooth ebony skin, crown of braids, and striking light-green eyes. Plus, as usual, an immaculate little girl holding her hand, proudly walking to meet her big brother.

Both were women with whom one did not mess. Lidia had once driven up the sidewalk to an open parking space because rude parents in the traffic circle had refused to move over for her. Ruby, after a boy called her grandson a slur he could only have heard at home, had very calmly escorted the mother from the playground to the principal's office to talk it out *right now*, thank you!

Needless to say, the kid and his rotten mom never used that word again. Oh, and people behave better in the traffic circle, too—not that it matters as much.

Sally is a little bit afraid of them. I'm not, since they like me, partly because I'm a few years older than most of the moms, but mostly because people who came up hard recognize each other and stick together.

"Hey!" I said, turning. "You didn't make the shoot."

Both had talked about it, but I'd suspected that neither would have the time, because of their childcare schedules. Lidia had two grandchildren at different schools, one elementary, one middle—and Ruby had toddler D'Andrea in addition to her third-grade grandson. In both cases, they were watching the kids for daughters whose spouses worked too and enjoying the great fun of being able to hand over the little angels at the end of the day.

"Busy, you know." Lidia shrugged.

"Heard it got freaky." Ruby's expression was mostly sympathetic, but just a little curious too—nothing like Sally had been.

Before I answered, I bent to greet D'Andrea, and as usual, she gave me a grin and then ducked behind her grandma's leg.

I nodded as I pulled up. "Yeah, it did. Studebaker went nuts and fell through the pulpit door to the floor."

Both women winced.

"How is he?"

"Did he make it?"

I shook my head. "Doesn't look good, but we don't know anything. Tiffany's crew took him to the hospital, so I'm picking up Ava."

"This is going to be a mess for the town," Sally sniffed, cutting into the conversation in her usual imperious way.

"Seems pretty bad for Studebaker," observed Ruby.

"His family, too," added Lidia.

"I don't know them. I do know what this is going to do to our property values." She shook her head. "Having that horrid movie crew in town was bad enough, but now a murder?"

"We don't know if it's even a death," I pointed out. "Never mind what kind of death."

"Do you really think he fell out of that pulpit by accident?" she asked waspishly.

Lidia and Ruby, who were well used to the ways of Sally, stifled laughs and whatever unkind comment they were thinking.

"I think I will let the authorities determine that." I managed to keep my voice cool.

The universe, or possibly just the gym teacher, Mr. Holly, showed mercy at that moment, and he appeared, opening the door to the school lobby and allowing us into the building to sign for our various kids.

Ruby and Lidia shot me glances over Sally's head as she signed with her own fancy pen, her beige acrylics making a little plasticky scrape on the paper. Just another day at the ranch.

Well, except for the murder. Yeah. Between me, myself, and G-d, I was pretty damn sure about that.

Chapter Four

Family Night

The great thing about parent life is that it carries its own weight. No matter what horrible thing has happened, once the kids are on the scene, you have to meet their needs and get them ready for the next day. From the moment Henry and Ava came blasting down the hall, Brett Studebaker and what I presumed to be his untimely end were on the back burner for a while.

The main controversy in my daily life at the moment is Henry's persistent refusal to pronounce the name of the eighth planet correctly. It's Ur-AN-ous, but my sweet little cherub has discovered that Ur-ANUS gets a big laugh, so he brings it up at every opportunity.

That's life with an eight-year-old.

I was talking to Ruby and Lidia, keeping my back very deliberately to the hall, when I was tackle-hugged from behind. He's going to knock me over someday, but I've got a little while to figure that out. He's big like my side of the family – already nearly five feet tall and sturdy—but it's too much fun to let my boy surprise me. I ruffled his dark curls and smiled down into his sparkly hazel eyes, so like Frank's.

The way I always do, I greeted Henry with: "What's your number?"

And as happens most of the time, he reeled off the reading from the

Dexcom with a grin. It was good, and he knew it, so that was the end of the discussion for now. Conversation on the walk back was all about the new third-grade project, a big mural celebrating kindness. When we got to the Society, he and Ava tore into the turkey sandwiches I'd kept in the mini-fridge behind my desk, finished their homework, and went exploring. All good.

I haven't mentioned this until now because it doesn't rule our lives, but it's worth knowing. Henry has Type 1 Diabetes. He was diagnosed a year ago after showing all the classic symptoms – thirst, weight loss, fatigue. When it happened, it was strange and clearly serious, and I was terrified, fearing I might have to bury my baby as well as my husband. It's the one thing that would break me.

This will sound weird, but I was actually relieved that it was something manageable, if not curable. When you've feared the worst, something merely life-changing is not nearly as big a deal.

We live by the numbers, and the carbs, and there's a fair amount of calculation involved. There's also a fair amount of pain for Henry, some of which I have to inflict. Even though, thankfully, now that he has a pump, there are no daily injections of insulin, parts still have to be replaced and attached regularly. Not to mention occasional finger-sticks for blood testing when his Dexcom meter doesn't give a clear indication. It's not always pleasant. We manage.

As far as Henry's concerned, it's just part of his life. He actually has more trouble with his photographic memory, because that makes him see the world a little differently than other kids. The diabetes is just something to deal with. I take my cues from him.

That afternoon, I was very glad to spend a couple of hours keeping one eye on homework and the other on the annual effort to kid-proof the second-floor bedroom for the fourth-grade visit. The longer I could skip thinking about probably violent death, the better.

I wasn't the only one. Tiffany appeared as Henry and I were

buttoning up the building for the night, making sure there was food and water out for the Society cat and that everything was as it should be. Aside from a few apothecary bottles someone had taken down from the shelves near the ceiling of the eighteenth-century kitchen, all was well. I had no idea why the docents might have been looking at old rat poison and beauty tonic, but the ladies were into all kinds of oddball art projects, and it could be anything.

Not worth worrying about right then.

I had a big slow cooker full of Henry's favorite beef stew, and Tiffany and Ava didn't have dinner plans. Jorge, a firefighter in New Haven, was on a long hitch and wouldn't be home that night. They'd met on the job, but wanted to live in a smaller town with better schools, and Tiffany liked being closer to Ava. It meant a lot of girls' nights, but it also meant they both had good jobs with excellent benefits.

Girls' night often included the guys, too. After the day we'd all had, I wasn't really surprised when Garrett called as I set the Society alarm, announcing that Ed had baked honey wheat bread. I told him it would go great with the stew, and the party was on.

So, we piled into Tiffany's Jeep for the short drive back to my house.

As for why she was so late, it was exactly as I suspected. They had just wanted to be sure they'd done everything they could for Studebaker, and the EMTs had to stay to do paperwork because it was probably going to be a death. As indeed it was by the time Tiffany got back to Unity.

She'd just gotten the word as she walked up to the Society, and told me, quietly, once the kids were buckled in and back to discussing how they planned to trick out their cars the next time they played their favorite driving video game.

"Is it a homicide or an undetermined?" I asked. I'd picked up the technical lingo from Frank.

Tiffany growled at a bigger SUV that Hollywood stopped at the four-way intersection, rudely plowing ahead of her, then sighed. "I'm guessing undetermined for now. Did you hear something?"

"No. Just gossip."

"Me too. I can tell you he wasn't breathing when I got to him, but as for why, that's going to be up to the M.E."

"It looked like a bad head injury."

"That may have been part of it. But a head injury is no guarantee of breathing problems." Tiffany shook her head. She wasn't going to give much detail because even—maybe especially—Brett Studebaker had confidentiality rights. "I just hate head injuries. Unless it's a minor little bump, things can get really bad, really fast. Or, worse, linger on. If they don't hit the brain stem, basic functions sometimes continue for a long time even if the rest of the brain is dead." She shuddered. "It can be pretty horrible."

I nodded. "That's when families have to start making the hard choices."

"Yeah."

She left it at that. I didn't pursue the conversation, and she knew why. Just about the only merciful thing about what happened to Frank is that it was fast and definitive. I'm told he probably felt the wheels go as the spin started and nothing else. It's soothing in its way.

"Anyway," she said with a wry twist to her mouth, "It's going to be a mess. We spent hours on the paperwork."

"Ugh." I nodded. "For the investigation or the lawsuit, or whatever."

"Whatever. Thanks for doing pickup."

"Glad to. Henry loves a good playdate."

"Still appreciate it, Christian."

I probably don't have to tell you that my very precise friend pronounces my name without so much as slurring the T, never mind swallowing it. But you might want to know why.

Her mother, Yadira Medina, is about as fond of swallowed T's as

25

one Barbara Ann Shaw is of "yins," the common second-person plural in Western PA. We are both the daughters of mothers who did well enough for themselves by the standards of their time—a nurse and a teacher—and who expected far more of their girls. And we were both steeped in perfect manners, speech, and demeanor before we were old enough to protest.

Dina, in case you're wondering, is the Westchester Jewish version of this same thing. It's why we are all such good friends, despite disparate backgrounds, callings, and lives.

Once you realize that someone has exactly the same things on her soundtrack, it's impossible not to have a bond.

Tiffany turned into our driveway, and the kids unclipped from their booster seats before she even stopped.

"C'mon guys," I said. "You know better."

Two little mumbled sorries.

"Just don't do dumb stuff." Tiffany gave them her motto and a smile as they jumped out and headed for the door. Garrett and Ed, with their dog and a wrapped loaf, were just turning down the street.

An hour later, we were all ranged around the living room, Ed in Frank's old easy chair, Garrett opposite him in the vintage wing chair that I'd picked up at a house sale, and Tiffany and I sharing the couch with Cookie, Henry's tuxedo cat. Cookie, christened for a certain monster, believes he is the lion protector of the house. In fact, he is a large ball of furry love who will snuggle and purr with almost anyone who gives him attention, as long as they understand that they are not and never will be his person.

He pretends Garrett and Ed's dog, a huge red mutt named Norm, simply does not exist. Norm returns the favor, sitting at Ed's feet and dozing happily.

The stew and bread, and most of the leftover Girl Scout cookies, were gone, and the kids had ditched the icky adults for a little game time on the computer on my desk by the bookshelf. It was their favorite racing game, admittedly not educational, but certainly not harmful, with cars trying to outsmart sharks and sea monsters.

The grownups had coffee, even though it wasn't going to help anyone sleep. Not that anyone would be sleeping well anyway.

"Heck of a day," Ed said.

"No kidding." Garrett reached for one of the last two Thin Mints, drawing a mild glare from Ed, who worried about cholesterol, but taking it anyway. "Was it just terminal overacting?"

Tiffany took the other Thin Mint with a grin. "Could have had a heart attack. He's in the right age cohort."

I nodded. "True, and he didn't exactly live a disciplined life when he was young."

"All that Hollywood partying and misbehavior."

Ed chuckled. "You two are so cute."

We turned on him, glaring in unison.

"You kids don't know the kind of trouble that people can get into when they're young and then still lead clean and healthy lives after."

Garrett exchanged a mysterious smile with his husband. "I think they're talking about drugs, Ed."

"Same difference. Whatever he was in his teen idol years wasn't necessarily who he was today, and it may or may not have killed him."

"Fair enough," I said. "I don't know much about what he's been doing in the last—I don't know, twenty years?"

"Me either." Tiffany looked at the empty cookie plate and sighed. "But my sister will."

"Yeah?"

"She watches all of those Hollywood TV shows. I'll call her in the morning. Right now, I want to relax a little and then get some sleep."

"Second that motion," Ed said.

"Passed by acclamation," Garrett agreed.

Everyone cleared out with plenty of friendly goodbyes and hugs, as usual, even though we practically live in each other's pockets. We've all had enough losses to know that you have to prize the people you love while you can.

Tiffany and Ava took off first, in the middle of a back-and-forth over whether Ava really needed a new glitter lip gloss palette. Substitute Hot Wheels Monster truck set, and Henry and I could have been having the same talk.

Garrett, Ed, and I lingered at the door for a few minutes as we always did.

"This could get kind of interesting, Christian," Ed said as he leashed up Norm.

"Interesting, how?"

"Not sure. But when someone like that dies, it draws all kinds of attention. And there's something hinky here."

Garrett and I froze. Even Norm looked. *Hinky* is cop (and sometimes reporter) slang for that creeping feeling that something nefarious is going on. On the very rare occasions Ed uses the word, it is a big deal.

"Any idea what?" Garrett asked.

"Nope. Just something doesn't feel right." Ed shrugged. "I'll figure it out."

We nodded. I knew Ed's sense of crime was a lot like that little buzz I get when I handle old things. It's not really supernatural, but it's not entirely rational, either.

After we hugged, Garrett kept his hand on my arm and made very careful eye contact. "You okay?"

Meaning, was I feeling any echoes from Frank's death, and did I need any extra care and feeding? "I'm fine. Surprisingly fine, actually."

"Good. You need anything, you call."

"I will."

Norm tugged on the leash then, giving us all a chance to move on with a chuckle. I knew they'd "happen" to be around the Society or the neighborhood more than usual over the next few days...and that was just fine by me.

After I got Henry showered and tucked in, I picked up my book, wine, and phone. Dina had texted me during the goodnights, and I called her.

"Just wanted to make sure that you two are all right," she said.

"I'm holding up fine. What about you?"

A strained, bitter chuckle. "Still here. Police were in the sanctuary into the evening collecting evidence. It's kind of disconcerting to see a bunch of men in blue, even ones with good intentions, climbing all over everything, considering."

Five thousand years of ugly history there. Not to mention whatever specific horrors lurked in Dina's family tree. I knew there were great-aunts and -uncles who weren't here who should have been. I didn't know the details, and I would never have been intrusive enough to ask.

"Had to be hard to watch. Are you—?"

"Ben's poured me a nice glass of wine, and we're going to watch a couple of terrible sitcom reruns. I'll be back to my usual sunshiny self by morning."

The combination of irony and resolution left no doubt.

"I'm having a nice glass of wine, too. But I'm reading about underwear."

As I'd hoped, Dina laughed. Really laughed. "What?"

"Reviewing a new pop history thing for an old pal at a journal. She couldn't get to it, and knew it's in my wheelhouse."

"And?"

"So far, barely accurate—and way too hung up on the sexy stuff. Those split pantalets had nothing whatsoever to do with romance...and everything to do with primitive bathrooms."

29

Her laugh expanded into a full-out howl. "Thanks, Christian."

"Well, it's true."

"I don't doubt that it is. I'm also really glad you shared it."

"If you really need a laugh, ask Henry about the eighth planet."

"Why?"

"Just ask him." I chuckled. "Save something for later."

"Never know when we might need it."

"Exactly."

Studebaker was the lead story on the local news app, and I wondered if that was going to be an issue for us in Unity, but the simple question was all I had the brain space to offer at that moment.

I would have to find energy for it soon enough.

Chapter Five

Not Poli's Wonderland

The next morning, after drop-off at Wheatley, I was bringing a little order to the Society parlor, smoothing out a wonderful old chenille floral afghan crocheted by some long-dead woman with a terrific eye for color, when a person walked into the foyer. It wasn't Garrett or Ed because they always announce themselves, and it was too early for Dina, who was leading the morning minyan. I figured a nervous first-year teacher working on field trip planning. We were a week or so before the big fourth-grade visit, after all.

If you've never safely herded three dozen nine-year-olds through an eighteenth-century house, it's a little daunting. Even if you have.

Maybe the cops, though, considering everything that happened yesterday.

"We don't open until ten," I called. "Please make sure the door is closed."

I heard the heavy swish and click and then a few footsteps, stopping just before I walked in.

Standing in front of the empty case that normally held the seventeenth-century Bible was a very tall blond man in a very nice

31

dark blue suit. Not the cops.

Probably not a teacher, either.

We had enough McMansions in Unity for me to recognize the suit as high-end tropical wool in a designer make, though it was also clearly not new...so he might be a real old New Englander, the buy good and keep it type. Whoever he was, he was—or had been—very well off.

There was something familiar about him from the back, and when he turned, I recognized him immediately, to my mild embarrassment. Should have known it would be Joe Poli.

Assistant New Haven County State's Attorney Joseph Poli, to be precise.

No relation, as far as I knew, to the family that had owned the Poli's Wonderland Theatre in New Haven in the late 19th century. But it was an unusual enough name that it stuck in my mind, since the Society had a few show posters from Poli's Wonderland in our ephemera collection.

Prosecutor Joe Poli's face was carefully professional, but his brown eyes were kind. We weren't really friends, but we knew of each other the way you do when you live in a smallish town, and your kids are in the same system. His daughter, then a middle-schooler, had been the Mentor Buddy for Henry's first-grade class.

"Dr. Shaw?"

Nobody other than the occasional hopeful phone solicitor actually uses my title. Yes, I've piled it high and deep, but out here in the real world, nobody cares, and I don't need anyone confusing me with a medical doctor and expecting anything more than antibiotic ointment and a kiss to make it better. I just smiled. "Christian is fine."

Joe Poli shrugged, not ignoring my comment, but also not accepting it. "Old-fashioned, sorry. And you worked hard for that title."

He has one of those voices. Low, warm, the kind of tone that makes you want to just sit there and listen. Probably very good with a jury.

"So did you, Counselor."

We shared a smile, and he nodded to the display case. Pleasantries over, time to do business. "So, I'm looking around a little at what happened to Brett Studebaker yesterday."

"Is it a homicide now?"

"The medical examiner's left it undetermined so far. Waiting for the toxicology and some other tests. In the meantime, I'm doing some informal groundwork."

"Makes sense." I nodded. State Police Major Crimes would probably be the official agency in charge if it became a criminal matter, but considering that there were about three detectives on the squad for all of Connecticut, they'd be happy to have a prosecutor doing some of his own work. "A lot of the stuff at the scene is from the Society. The Bible was there, of course."

He took a moment to read my printed notice that it was on loan to the shoot. "You'll get it back, right?"

"Later today, I hope. Will the State Police release the scene?"

"They already have. I talked to Rabbi Aaron just now. She says hi."

I nodded and took a subtle glance at the big grandfather clock beside him. Nine-fifteen. If I finished talking to him before ten, I could go over and check on Dina. Arrange to get the Bible as soon as possible so she didn't have to worry about it. "Thanks."

"Sure." He looked around a little, glanced to the dining room, which I'd set for a late 1700s dinner a couple of weeks ago. "He came in with a metal mug. Was that from here?"

"Sure was. Studebaker picked it up on a scouting tour of the Society, and decided it was part of his character's business."

He heard something. "Over your objection?

"Well, kind of. I'm pretty sure it's old pewter, so it's not really safe to drink out of...not even water, never mind anything acidic or alcoholic."

"Why?"

"Old pewter is loaded with lead...and might have traces of any number of other things, too."

"Dangerous things?"

"Over time, absolutely. For a sip or two here and there to help someone get into the period...maybe, maybe not." I waggled my hand. "Just because I wouldn't do it doesn't mean that it would be *that* dangerous."

"Get into the period." Joe Poli nodded. "Was it authentic?"

"It was from about the right time as the church and most of the costumes."

"Most?"

"Um, ministers really didn't wear tight breeches like that in the early Colonial period. Nobody did. And women's collarbones were almost never visible outside the home."

"So, why..."

I swallowed a wry smile. "Because this was 'a metaphorical production not limited to a specific time, but striving for authenticity in creative choices to convey the experience of a tragic love.'"

"Is that from the Filmagic press kit?"

"Sure is."

"Yikes. I've already had ten calls from their flack demanding to know when I'm going to announce that it was just a terrible accident."

"Are you?"

"Not anytime soon. There are some things I don't like here."

"Things about me and the tankard?" I asked. Might as well know. Ed could probably find me a lawyer, though I had no idea how much that would cost and-

Joe Poli put his hand on my arm and made very deliberate eye contact. "Absolutely not."

"Oh, okay." I let out a breath I didn't know I'd been holding, as I remembered him paying respects at Frank's wake. He'd done something similar, placing a hand on my arm and telling me I should call him if I needed anything, adding the specificity of police reports, or whatever so that it was clear it wasn't just something you mumble when you're uncomfortable.

His eyes had been serious and reassuring then, too. Safe.

"I didn't mean to scare you, Dr. Shaw," he continued, keeping his hand on my arm, "I'm here to ask for your expertise, not to interrogate you or anything."

I nodded as he pulled back and straightened my spine a little. He was still taller than me. Weird...and nice. "Well, in that case, come back to my office, and I'll give you a good cup of coffee and my thoughts."

His gaze turned slightly cautious. "Really good? I'm New Haven Italian, and if you're just being nice..."

"My cousin in Seattle gets me a coffee club every year." Jimmy had started out slinging lattes at a small local chain in college and stayed with the company as it grew. He considered keeping every close blood relative in good coffee his way of giving back to the universe for making him filthy rich. "I'm assuming you like dark roast, like me."

"Yes, please."

A few minutes later, we were in my office, which is as scruffy and cluttered as my living history rooms are elegant. I cleared a pile of books and metal implements off the better guest chair (research for a new cooking exhibit) and handed him a mug, a Juvenile Diabetes one from some fundraising event, and picked up my own "I Yell Because I Care," a gift from Tiffany.

He looked at his mug. "Your son, right?"

"Yep. My little warrior."

"My best pal in college. These days, he's an architectural engineer—and rappels off buildings to check the facades."

I laughed ruefully. "There is that little need for danger to defy it."

"Yep. But he keeps his numbers good and always checks his harness, so more power to him." He took a sip of his coffee. "Okay, I trust you now."

"I wouldn't lie to law enforcement. Or anyone, really."

"No, but you might have bad judgment."

"Fair enough."

"If your judgment is good on coffee, it's probably good in other areas, too."

I chuckled. "The coffee test?"

"Well, you already pass the book test. I don't trust people who don't read…and since you have a Ph.D., I assume you have some at home."

"Shelves and shelves. Henry, too."

"Good mom. Amber and I did the same for Aly. These days, she has one of those devices…but she still reads."

"Best thing for a kid."

He grinned, "I'm not allowed to call her a kid now that she's in high school, so…"

"Ah. Young adult."

"She claims. She spends the week with Amber in Southport and the weekends with me."

His shrug made it clear he didn't want to say more. I hadn't known he was divorced, and of course, it was none of my damn business. But if the ex was in Southport, it meant she'd remarried—remarried big money. Southport makes Unity's fanciest neighborhood look like a trailer park outside Akron.

"So, how can I help you, Counselor?" I asked, using the lawyerly title since he'd clearly decided he was going to call me Doctor.

"Well, a little more detail on Studebaker and that pulpit to start…and anything else you might have seen in your travels on the set."

"If you're really worried about something hinky, you'll want to take a really good look at the pulpit. I know Rabbi Aaron made sure it was properly maintained."

Joe Poli blinked. Only cops or cop family use that word. "Who's the cop?"

"My—I guess it's easiest to call him my uncle, though we're not blood-related. My mentor's husband. Ed Kenney."

"You know Ed?"

"Garrett and Ed are the dads I should have had. Garrett was my first department chair at Shoreline State, and when he and Ed married, Ed just took me on as another daughter."

The prosecutor's face softened as he drank a little more coffee. "It is really a small world. Ed talked me through a couple of early cases when he was head of Major Crimes, just before he retired."

"That's Ed."

"Sure is. Determined to make sure the right thing happens in the right way."

"Nothing wrong with that," I said.

"Not one damn thing, uh, sorry Dr. Shaw."

"I've heard a word or two, Counselor."

"My mom raised me to be polite."

"I'm sure she did." I returned his smile.

"So, the pulpit."

"The church used to be the Congregational one, but when most of the Christians moved to that big mega-church outside town, they sold it to our congregation."

"*Your* congregation?"

I nodded. "My son is in Hebrew school, and we go to services there. I'm not officially Jewish, but I'm raising him in his dad's faith."

"Nice." Joe Poli wasn't being diplomatic. He was actually interested. "Honoring your husband."

"And making sure Henry knows who he is." I took a breath. "It matters to me, too. I'd convert if I had time for the classes...but in the meantime, we observe the Sabbath and holidays as best we can.

Someday, I'll be the oldest Bat Mitzvah girl ever."

"Interesting. *Choosing* a faith. New Haven Italian, you go to Mass or else. And eventually not at all."

"After everything that's happened with the Church?"

"Yeah. My mom insisted that Aly make First Communion, but after that, even she stopped pushing. And after the divorce, of course..."

I nodded, leaving it there. "So, the building is still an authentic early nineteenth-century sanctuary, and it's been very well maintained. I would have someone you trust take a good look at that pulpit. We don't use it, but because the building is on the National Register, everything has to be in good shape."

Joe Poli nodded. "What about the mug?"

"Actors like bits of business for their character. It was weird, but people do things. I wasn't too worried as long as I got the tankard back at the end—and my consulting credit."

"You get a credit?"

"A tiny line, buried in the final crawl. What's important, as in any business, is that you have a reputation for knowing your stuff and working well with the production."

"Which means what?"

"Providing info on authenticity when asked—and not going crazy when they ignore it."

"Did they?"

"Mostly, they had their own idea about what they were going to do, accurate or not."

"Have you seen that before?"

"I've only done a few actual shoots in my career—I do a lot more consultation by phone and email on particular items—but it's one of the two possibilities."

"What's the other one?"

"Obsessive accuracy. Right after I left Shoreline State, I had a production in New Haven, some Regency romance thing shooting on the Yale campus. Director was nuts. Literally, everything from the undies to the hairpins to the lip-salve had to be precisely authentic. I ended up making rose petal lip salve in my kitchen one night with a three-year-old running around trying to eat the beeswax. Never again."

I chuckled, and then he laughed, too, knowing it was okay.

"I guess 'creative choices' aren't so bad," he said. "What about Studebaker?"

"I exchanged maybe three words with him in person."

"Really?"

"He just bombed me with emails demanding to know about literally every aspect of his character's life. It was annoying because he just wouldn't take no for an answer. Every time I turned around, there he was, demanding information until he got what he wanted. Persistent."

Joe Poli's kind brown eyes narrowed. "Was he—inappropriate with you?"

I burst out laughing. I couldn't help it. The thought of Brad Studebaker coming at scruffy me was just too funny. The prosecutor sat back, shocked.

"I'm sorry," I said quickly. "It's just—I am not exactly a sex kitten, and definitely out of the age cohort for that stuff. If Brad Studebaker wanted a groupie, I would *not* have been it."

"Dr. Shaw, whatever you say, you're an attractive lady, and there are a lot of predators in the entertainment industry."

For a second, I stared at him. I wasn't sure whether to be more shocked by him calling me attractive, or my sudden memory of Sally Birdwell asking chirpily if this were some kind of #MeToo thing. I took a sip of coffee. "I never saw any hint of that."

"You were around the set sometimes. Did you see anything else that might have been suspicious?"

"No." I shook my head. "I really wasn't there that often. And he seemed to pretty much keep to himself. I don't think he was close with the producer or director."

"Did he have an assistant?"

I nodded. "They always do. But it was a young guy. I doubt he knew him well, either. Anyway, if he was up to anything, it probably would have been in New Haven, where he was staying, not here."

Joe Poli took a sip of his coffee, contemplated. "He never married. Tabloids said he liked the Hollywood playboy life."

"Warren Beatty did."

"Until Annette Bening showed him the error of his ways." He shrugged. "I'll have to call some friends in New Haven. Am I presuming too much if I ask you to keep your ears open around here?"

"Not at all, but I doubt I'll be much help."

A wise smile. "Sorry, Dr. Shaw, but you're wrong there. You pick Henry up every day, right?"

"Sure."

"Hang out with the moms and grandmas?"

I supposed Joe Poli might have swept in once in a while when his Aly was younger and checked out the scene. Being male, unknown, and clearly some kind of high-end professional, he probably got plenty of looks, and not one word from the ladies of the pen. I smiled at him. "True. There's a fair amount of gossip and talk. But most of it is just that."

"I know. Still might be a lead in there somewhere. If anything stands out…"

"I'll let you know. Give me an excuse to gossip a little."

"Academics gossip?"

I returned the impish smile with my own. "Academics are the prissiest little gossips of them all, Counselor."

"Except for law enforcement. Word on the street, you know."

"Probably every small insular world—or small town—is that way."

"So true." His eyes sharpened a bit. "And perhaps useful. If annoying."

"It can be." I wondered if there'd been some loose talk during the divorce. It would not surprise me, considering what I'd heard Sally say about other people, though I couldn't say with any certainty if she'd ever mentioned him. I ignore about ninety percent of what Sally says.

Joe shrugged, which with Ed meant that there was something—and he didn't want to talk about it. Reasonable guess it was the same for him.

"Well," I offered, "at least we're not important enough for it to end up on *Hollywood Night*, unlike poor Brett Studebaker."

"There's that."

"Things could always be worse."

"Sure could." Something in his tone made me look more closely at him, and I remembered then why he'd been so kind to me after Frank died. Joe Poli started out as a high-powered corporate lawyer at a firm in New Haven. The guys who rake in huge sums of money by making sure companies pay as little as possible for bad products and worse behavior. He was good, too. Right up until a drunk driver damn near killed his brother and got away because the prosecutor made an obvious legal error.

After that, the hired gun decided he wanted to train his fire on more deserving targets and signed on as an entry-level prosecutor. The reporters' corps thought he was a dilettante and treated him accordingly. Except Frank. Frank, who always knew real when he saw it, gave Joe professional respect.

That was why Joe came to the wake. One standup guy honoring another.

"Anyway, Dr. Shaw, thank you for the coffee and the insight. Both terrific." He put the mug down and checked his watch.

"A pleasure." I understood. Just like me, he was much more

comfortable with other people's disasters. I took one of my business cards from the Victorian card holder, occupying a small clear spot on the desk. "Feel free to call or come by if you need any more information."

"I may take you up on that." He pulled a card out of his jacket pocket and handed it to me. He'd been prepared for this. "I drive right past here on my way to work—I live over on Trelawney."

The McMansion district. That, and the suit, suggested he'd done just fine before trading pay for principle. Not that it was any of my business.

"Well, you're quite welcome."

As we walked out, it hit me that I had really enjoyed talking to him. And looking at him. For the last year or so, I'd been starting to notice there were still a few attractive men in the world, though I had no idea what, if anything, I might want to do about that fact.

But I still had enough radar left to notice Joe Poli watching me with something that sure felt like appreciation, too. I was suddenly and surprisingly glad it was a good hair day and that I was wearing my favorite navy blazer with a wonderful sparkly rhinestone crescent moon pin. Joe Poli held my gaze an instant too long like he wasn't sure what to do.

The thought occurred to me that he might be as rusty as I was.

I probably wouldn't see enough of him for it to be an issue anyway.

As we walked into the foyer, there was an outraged yowl, and a white streak shot down from the stairwell, landing in front of the prosecutor, quickly resolving into a tiny, sleek cat.

"Well, who's this?" he asked in the gentle tone nice people often use for small children and animals, as the cat looked up at him with curious, glittering blue eyes.

"That's Empress Frederick. She's the queen of the house." I laughed in sheer amazement as the cat strode over to Joe Poli and rubbed her head against his ankle. "I'm sorry—normally, everyone is beneath her notice."

"Don't be." He bent down and held out his hand, and Her Imperial Highness sniffed it, then accepted a pet. "She's a sweetheart."

The Empress, who usually ignores all comers unless her food bowl is low, is most definitely not a sweetheart. She more than lives up to the regal example of her namesake, Queen Victoria's eldest daughter, who was perfectly capable of reminding courtiers that she was both an Empress *and* the Princess Royal. Clearly, though, my little royal also appreciated an attractive man. "Um, yeah. She seems to like you."

He grinned up at me. "Probably just smells my dog and wants to send him a message."

"What kind of dog?"

A shrug. "I'm not sure what Cannoli is. He looks kind of like a black mop. Probably part Scottie and part Pom, and who knows what else. Sweetest little creature you'd ever want to know."

I nodded. "Dogs can be."

"Aly's dog went with her and Amber, and there was a pet drive on the Green one Saturday, so…" He petted the Empress again, and she let him. Then, she abruptly sniffed and turned away, the way cats will. We both laughed as he stood, shaking his head.

"Cats," I said. "They do what they do."

"Wish I could get away with a fraction of that."

Another shared laugh.

"Anyway," he said, holding out his hand, "it's been a pleasure."

We shook, and his grip lingered a bit longer than I expected. He had nice hands, long fingers, and neat but not manicured nails, and like a lot of males, including Henry, his body temperature was slightly, and noticeably, warmer than mine.

But his tone was all business. "Just keep your eyes open a little, huh? We don't know what this is yet, and…"

"Will do."

"Call me if anything weird happens. Anytime."

I figured it was just standard caution, the kind of thing Ed would say. I didn't know then that there was a whole lot more weird ahead.

Chapter Six

Sacred and Profane

After Joe Poli left, I still had fifteen minutes to scoot over to check on Dina and make arrangements to collect that Bible. In all honesty, probably a few more minutes, since I only had a couple of docents coming in this morning and a group of embroiderers stopping by on their lunch hour.

Since I use my own hour for school pickup, I've put the word out in town that anyone who wants a personal appointment can skip over on *their* break for anything they might need in the way of info, insight, or just looking at old stuff. You'd be surprised at how many I get. I know I was. Usually, it's crafters and fiber artists of varying descriptions from Town Hall across the Green; there are a bunch of very active embroidery, knitting, and other groups in town, with members who work in the tax or clerk's or council's office.

That morning, though, I was just glad I had a few minutes before the day got interesting.

Dina and her husband Ben live in the top two floors of the old rectory (and so do the twins Sam and Syd when they're home from college), but the ground floor is offices and meeting rooms. On a normal morning, she'd be in her office by now, but this was anything but—and I guessed she'd be in the sanctuary.

There were already some flowers accumulating on the stairs. Cards and a teddy bear or two, as well. No one was there, but it was clear the word was out that Brett Studebaker had posed for his final closeup, and fans were paying respects.

The majestic double doors were closed, but the small side door was open, as it almost always is, so I slipped in to see Dina standing at the back, behind the pews, wrapping her cream-colored waterfall cardigan around herself and staring at the pulpit. She'd sounded upset last night and seemed pensive now.

But when she saw me, she smiled. "Did Joe Poli find you?"

"Just talked to him."

"Nice guy. He wanted to make sure the scene was released and asked if I needed anything."

"He was kind to me when Frank died," I said, knowing she'd understand it was the ultimate endorsement.

She nodded. "I feel better knowing he's overseeing this."

"Me too."

"The scene's officially released, and they have everything they need for now. You can take the Bible back whenever you like." She sighed. "I don't think they touched it at all."

"Lewis and I will come over and get it a little later. I don't want to carry it alone."

Lewis, my assistant, is a nephew of Ruby's. He's finishing his dissertation at Yale and was looking for an understanding employer right about when RoseMarie Marzio decided 85 years of working was enough, and she was moving in with her son in Florida. I'd mentioned it in the pen, Ruby told me about Lewis, and that was that. I was dreading what would happen when he finished the dissertation.

"Makes sense. I always like to have an extra pair of hands when I'm working with fragile things."

"Exactly." I patted her arm. "Better today?"

"Not bad." She sounded more balanced, but not happy. "I have a lot of studying and praying to do."

"Don't we all."

Dina shook her head with the rueful smile she saved for the stupid *shikse*. "No, honey. A death in a sanctuary is a profanation. It might make it unclean, and I may have to call in some other rabbis to re-consecrate it..."

"But he was pronounced at Yale."

"I thought he wasn't breathing when he left."

Of course, she'd have checked with Tiffany. I wondered if what I'd learned in CPR class might help. "That's true, but she had his circulation going again within less than a minute. And it takes six minutes for brain death."

Dina's troubled expression eased a bit. "That's right."

"It doesn't change the fact that something terrible happened here, but I know enough Talmud to know that there's always room for debate...and whether it was an actual death or merely a serious injury that ultimately led to death might be important."

"It is. And the commandment to celebrate the Sabbath takes precedence over almost all else. I need to do a little more research, call my old mentor in the City, but that helps."

I nodded. "Glad I could be useful."

"You're always useful."

"If not ornamental."

We shared a little chuckle. Dina and I like to joke that I'm the 150-percent copy of her. She's just under five feet tall and really tiny, and her hair is almost the same color as mine, though she has lovely waves instead of unruly corkscrews.

"Anyway, it's not going to be a dull day here at the ranch," she said. "Did you see the stuff out front?"

"Makeshift memorial, as the expression goes."

"Exactly. I don't feel right moving it, at least until we start getting ready for Shabbat on Friday."

"We're going to be a pilgrimage site for a while." I shook my head. "It's what people do."

"How they grieve. True. They're really grieving the people they actually know, love, and have lost, but it's not my job to tell them that." Her gaze sharpened on me. "You're really okay?"

"Surprisingly. Too busy not to be."

"Healing is weird. But sometimes good."

"Sometimes."

"You know," she said, a gleam coming into her eyes, "that Joe Poli is awfully nice-looking, and I hear he's been divorced for a year or more."

"I did notice the nice-looking part," I admitted. "He'd never be interested in me anyway."

"I'm probably just being a yenta, but never say never, huh? Even if all you do is notice and flirt a little, it's good practice for when a guy you really want comes along."

A surprising thought: that I might really want a man in my life again someday. More surprising that it could even be true. "Well, today I did give him some coffee and some insight on everything."

"Coffee." Her smile told me what she was thinking.

"The conversation was almost as good as Eddie's coffee. I'm not sure how I feel about that."

"You don't have to be. Be glad that you enjoyed it, and just let things settle." Another one of those moments that I'm keenly aware of Dina's gifts. Understanding people is her superpower.

"Thanks. You're really good."

"That's what Ben says."

Pause. Then she blushed as she realized what she'd just said. We laughed together, that first real, wonderful laugh after something awful happens. The minute it hits that, you will get through it.

"I meant with figuring out what's going on—"

"Okay."

"Yeah, okay."

"Absolutely okay."

We were sharing a nice subtext smile when the old church clock started chiming the hour.

"Whoops, gotta go!"

Dina patted my arm and grinned. "We'll talk more later."

"Coffee pot's always ready."

"Best thing about having you next door."

At the society, Lewis (full name John Lewis Barnes, named for the Civil Rights hero, of course) was standing on the porch reading a book. He's what my grandfather would have called a fireplug of a man, probably three inches shorter than me and sturdy, with a surprisingly young-looking face behind his very serious horn-rimmed glasses. He always wears a jacket and oxford, probably paralleling me, not that I've ever asked, and has absolutely courtly manners.

"Hey, Doc!" He closed the book, a new study of *Birth of a Nation*. His dissertation is on casual racism in early 20th-century life, and G-d knows there's plenty of material for that. "Did your grandma really insist on watching *Gone With the Wind* every time it was on TV?"

"Yeah." I couldn't help squirming a little. "Grandma was a decent human in a lot of ways, but people back home in Mars had a lot of ugly blind spots. Gran thought she was Scarlett O'Hara and had no idea what was wrong with that."

Lewis gave a wry head shake. "Weird world."

"A little better now, I hope." I opened the door.

"Dr. Shaw?"

We turned to see a couple of the movie guys standing on the porch.

One was Chase Maguire, Studebaker's assistant: a young guy with a smarmy smile that he probably thought got him play. The other, Greg Holman, was older, apparently, the ranking money man, though he was called a producer, which sometimes meant a person with a level of creative control. Both were in the jeans, t-shirts, and expensive blazers they apparently thought marked them as important Hollywood visitors.

I didn't have the heart to inform them the real tell was the super high-end hiking boots, about which every single one of us locals had snickered at some point.

"Good morning," I said. "Sorry for your loss."

"Thanks," the assistant replied, carefully pulling his face into sober lines. "Brett was an inspiration. He hired me after I was on the scene crew for *Locked and Loaded*, and I was so lucky to work for him."

"Definitely a good talent. A real loss." Holman's voice was a lot more believable, but his face was too neutral. He was a balding older guy with a basically friendly cast to his features. But something wasn't reaching the eyes.

They were dead. I'm sure they'd been that way long before he arrived in Unity, but it was not soothing.

Lewis tensed a little behind me. He was seeing something he didn't like, and his radar is pretty good, too.

"I don't know if you gentlemen had a chance to meet my colleague," I began, presenting him. "Lewis Barnes, the associate curator of the Historical Society."

They all shook hands, and I watched Lewis's reactions as they did.

"How can I help you?" I asked Holman.

"Well, I thought you should know we're ending the shoot out of respect to Brett, and we'll figure out what to do from here. You'll be paid in full up to yesterday and for all of the email consultations, of course."

"Good to know. Thanks." I nodded. "It's really the last thing on my mind right now."

Chase sighed, then pulled a sad face. "Right? It's so hard to believe."

"A tragic accident, I'm sure," Holman said. "I think the tankard Brett was using went to the hospital with him. The police will probably get it back to you."

I nodded, waited. Something was going on here.

"Did Brett sign a release when he took it?" Holman asked, the cool neutrality of his voice again more unnerving than actual menace would have been.

Only this time, I knew where we were going. While I couldn't stop our star from running off with the tankard, I could, and did, make sure he signed the release and flatly refused to lend any other items, including the Bible, until he had. A few days of consulting work wasn't worth the job that made it possible to raise my son in reasonable comfort and safety. Sorry, Hollywood.

Holman, further up in the tree, probably didn't know what I'd done. Young Chase here had decided the best way to get what his boss wanted—answers to his many, many questions—was to just give in to me.

Holman was probably trying to scare me, though I wasn't really sure why. No matter: that release for objects not only made the borrower promise to return it in exactly the same condition as received or pay to restore it, but it also made any harm that came from its use—*any* use—the responsibility of the borrower. If, say, someone decided to drink from a potentially poisonous old pewter tankard, that was his lookout.

A few years ago, one of the docents had gotten her daughter, the personal injury shark lawyer, to rewrite the release after the Arts Center borrowed an old mending box for an exhibit, and a toddler came *this* close to swallowing a needle. At the time, I had thought

THE STUFF OF MURDER

Amelia was being a pain. More than once, though, I've had cause to praise her name.

As I was doing at that exact moment. G-d shower blessings upon her and the carnivorous daughter. "Well, Mr. Holman, I did indeed. As much as I admired Mr. Studebaker and his work, I could not risk my job, should anything happen to the tankard."

"Or to him?"

I nodded. "Of course, to him. The release was very clear about that."

Holman's face stayed neutrally friendly, but I noticed a faint pink tinge on the skin at the edge of his hundred-dollar white tee.

"It's really a terrible tragedy," I continued, carefully holding his gaze, then turning to young Chase. "May I send you a letter of condolence for his family? I'd just like them to know that he was happy doing work he loved...it might provide some comfort."

The kid wasn't quite sure how to handle good country manners, and he blushed and mumbled an affirmative.

"That's very kind of you, Dr. Shaw," Holman cut in. "We won't take any more of your time right now."

"You do have my deepest sympathies," I said with the grace I'd learned at my mother and grandmother's knees. Lewis added his own condolence in the same fashion as anyone from Ruby's family would.

"Thank you," Holman said, steering Chase to the stairs.

"I only wish we could do more."

Holman snapped at Chase as soon as he thought they were out of earshot. They mostly were – I caught only the words 'release,' 'leverage,' and 'idiot.'

Oh, well.

"That was fun, Doc." Lewis's normally cheerful face was tight and troubled.

"Just weird."

"No kidding. That Holman guy looked like he was from some gangster movie."

"Yeah, the one where they smile and say it's not personal just before hitting you with a shovel."

Lewis nodded, chuckled a little nervously. "That's the one."

"C'mon," I said, patting his arm. "Now that you're here, I need your help."

"What?"

"Time to move the Bible. That's a two-person job."

"Not to mention a treat."

We smiled together. We'd never explicitly discussed it, but I strongly suspected Lewis felt the same connection to objects I did. I *knew* the old Bible had some kind of effect on him. He'd held doors and helped me lay it out on the pulpit before the shoot, and his face was just rapt and magical.

"C'mon, let's glove up. You carry it this time."

"What?"

"I'll get it down and hold doors. You bring it home."

His face lit up. "Cool, Doc."

I smiled. If anything could burn away the menace of the last few minutes – and the ugliness of the last day, it was surely Lewis's joy in handling the Bible.

Gotta focus on the good stuff.

Chapter Seven

Bibles and Bayonets

We wear the same nitrile gloves to handle the really fragile items that Tiffany wears on the job. When I had my first internship, I went in with this mental picture of putting on cute little white cotton gloves like I'd seen some Irish professor wearing in a Nat Geo documentary on the Book of Kells, and I was terribly disappointed. But cotton leaves fibers, and medical gloves don't.

So, Lewis and I put on our snappy purple gloves, his a little tight, mine a little loose, because the Society doesn't want to spend money on two sizes of gloves for two people, and got to it. I climbed up in the pulpit, which would have been weird and scary even if Studebaker hadn't just fallen to his death. It's one of those times that you really realize how much smaller people used to be.

The treads on the stairs were noticeably narrower even than those in the Society house, and I felt them creak under my weight. We were probably too far away to hear the noise when Studebaker took the climb. He'd heaved himself inside at the top; there's no real graceful way to get in, at least not one that has survived to the present day. Not being a major macho star, I sort of crawled onto the floor, planning to very carefully pull myself up by an edge.

I put my hands down for balance near one of the corners, and something jabbed at my fingertip. It didn't break the glove, but it got my attention. It felt like a bit of gravel. Maybe something from the path caught in Studebaker's shoe? I ran my fingers over the wood floor and picked it up. Probably not gravel. It looked like a stone. Some kind of very small clear gem, sparkly enough to be a diamond, though you can't tell the difference from cubic zirconia without good magnification.

In case you're wondering, CZ is perfect; real diamonds, no matter how expensive, are not. Because real things are always at least a little imperfect. There's a lesson in there somewhere.

Not that I had time to process it. Who would be missing a stone? I knew Studebaker hadn't worn an earring...but I remembered the restoration contractors had been a rather hip crew. I wondered if they'd had a little mishap back then. It was near the corner, after all, and could have been there for a long time, just shaken loose by Studebaker's thrashing.

Not important now. I slipped the tiny jewel in my jacket pocket and carefully unfolded myself at the pulpit.

Whoa.

I'm not afraid of heights in any real or serious way. But I do sometimes get a little dizzy when I'm up in a theatre balcony or crossing a pedestrian bridge on an overpass. The pulpit had that effect. Disconcerting.

I'd stood up too quickly, and for a second, everything spun around me. Then I got my focus back and looked down at Dina and Lewis, who were watching me with more than a little concern.

"I'm up. All good!" I called. My voice echoed through the sanctuary. I could have used a room like that in my teaching days. I always hated using a mic—I figure that even when you're doing a two-hundred-person section of Western Civ, you owe it to the students to project if you can—and the acoustics here are amazing. Of course, I'd known that, but there was something about the placement of the podium that amplified the speaker's voice. Damn, those pilgrims knew their stuff.

Dina grinned. "You sound like Moses at Mount Sinai. I may have to use that thing sometime."

I chuckled. "As long as you don't mind the climb."

"I'm happier on the ground."

I looked down at the Bible. It was open to a different illuminated panel than it had been at the Society…and than the director had wanted. We normally kept it at the Sermon on the Mount because it was both beautiful and reasonably neutral. The director, in the only complete sentence I heard him say, observed that it had a nice echo for the pulpit scene.

Now, though, it was the Four Horsemen of the Apocalypse – the Book of Revelation. I hadn't noticed it yesterday, but as I gently closed the Bible, I realized my sight lines were wrong. We'd been on the side of the plain, printed page, so I would never have seen it.

You're probably wondering what on earth Puritans, the people who canceled Christmas because it was too much fun, were doing with a Bible that had illustrations. I don't have a great answer for you. I've managed to trace the family who brought it back to England, and it looks like they didn't start out as Puritans. So, we figure when they turned Puritan, they kept the Bible because it had all the begats, even if it had those evil graven images.

I'm just grateful that they did.

As I picked up the Book, keeping it open to protect the spine, I looked around the sanctuary. It was empty except for the three of us and quiet. A totally different scene than the production and spectator mob of the previous day and quieter than the place had been since the shoot began.

When Lewis and I placed the Bible the night before shooting started, there had been a full complement of production people and a bunch of local lookie-loos moving through, too. I recognized a few docents and maybe even one tiny dark-haired figure in the back.

Yep. It had sure looked like Sally Birdwell couldn't resist playing fangirl.

I'd wondered how she squared it with all of her talk about how bad the shoot was for property values, and then remembered it was Sally. She didn't have to square anything. Except maybe the shot in her Instagram feed.

Lewis climbed up on a sturdy ladder to give him a good reach while I carefully moved over to him. We were just reversing what we'd done two days ago, but it was still a painstaking process. The Book, parchment bound in leather, was even heavier than it looked. I'm not a small or weak woman, but it was definitely hard to manage with the care it deserved.

If you're wondering, Bible reading was a mostly male affair back in the day—just look at the centuries-long debate over whether women were fully human and have souls the way men do—so those tiny Colonial ladies would not have been schlepping the Book around. Even so, they might well have been literate enough to read the key verses, just so their men could interpret them for them.

They would have kept their own opinions to themselves. Or else.

Lewis was reaching up through the open pulpit door, and all I had to do was bend down and lay the Book in his hands. I still held my breath as I did it, and so did he. He stepped back, now moving with the care of a medieval priest in a sacred procession, giving me space to climb down. As I backed off to turn, I took a good look at the door, expecting to see some damage from Studebaker's fall.

Nothing.

Weird.

Now really curious, once I got out of the pulpit, I pushed the door in, and it closed without resistance. I pulled it back and looked. No latch. There was a small mark on the inside of the door that might have been from Studebaker falling, but also might have been an imperfection in the wood. I couldn't tell without a magnifying glass.

It had been open when we placed the Bible, and I didn't remember looking for a latch. It hadn't especially mattered. I cared about making sure the Bible was laid out properly and that it was safe for the night. I'd wanted a security guard, but the unit manager told me he wasn't going to ask Holman for it, though he did promise to have an underling check the security system every hour. I didn't really believe him, and I'd left that night reminding myself that we would *own* that big production company if anything happened to the Bible.

Now, though, the Bible was safe, and we had other worries.

"Did the pulpit door have a latch?" I asked Dina.

"I don't remember." She shook her head. "I know there are some cabinets in the building so perfectly fitted that they don't need latches."

Lewis cleared his throat.

"Sorry. Of course." I nodded. "Let's get back to the Society."

"See you two later." Dina smiled. "Take the side stairs—you don't want to trip on the flowers and teddy bears."

A nervous chuckle from Lewis. "Got that."

Maybe five very tense minutes later, the Bible was back in the case, and we were taking one last look before putting the glass lid down. I was thinking about digging out some antihistamines; during the walk across the Green, my grass pollen allergy had blossomed in all its headachy and sniffly glory.

But first, some appreciation. "Perfect, Lewis. Thank you so much."

He smiled. "It is such an amazing and beautiful thing."

"Really a sacred object."

"Divine inspiration, sure, but all of the people who used it and loved it."

"Exactly."

Lewis leaned in for one more unobstructed look and sniffed. "Hey, Doc?"

Grass pollen, too? I wondered. "What?"

"Did the Puritans use incense?"

"No, why?"

"I smell something on the Bible...I'm not sure—"

I looked at him. I would not have been able to smell it if the thing had been on fire right then, thanks to the lovely grass pollen. I opened my mouth to say something, and we heard a weird little woop-woop noise.

"What?" Lewis asked.

"Town police. They have one patrol car—a Prius with that silly siren. Don't ask."

Neither of us had much temptation to snicker, however, since whether or not the siren was serious, it had just gone past us in the direction of Beth Shalom.

I closed and locked the Bible case, and Lewis and I headed out for the synagogue. We weren't exactly running, but we were definitely moving at a good clip. Dina and an older man were standing on the steps, among the flowers and teddies, both looking troubled.

The man, who was tiny with huge glasses, was Gerry Diamond, a member of the temple board and the morning minyan. A retired accountant, he lived within a short walk of the Green and often dropped by to visit Dina or work on some project. I wasn't surprised to see him pitching in with the floral and stuffed tributes.

What surprised me was the tense expressions on their faces as they gazed down at the steps.

I zipped past Lewis and climbed up to where Dina and Gerry were talking to Unity's only patrol cop on duty. Since it was daytime, it was

Tony DiBiasi, a retired Statie, and friend of Ed's.

"Christian," Gerry said, without the least bit of twinkle. Normally, when we greet each other, there's always some warmly teasing little comment about the rich irony of a woman named Christian raising a Jewish boy and planning her own conversion. So I knew this was serious.

Dina, who was talking to Officer DiBiasi, shot me a quick, tense glance.

They were all standing about a foot away from a dark metal object just under two feet long that had been left on the top step.

"It looks like a machete," DiBiasi, a round fellow who was almost Gerry's age, said. "I can see how you might see it as a threat."

Gerry shook his head. He didn't have to say what he was thinking, and neither did anybody else.

Problem was, that big old blade didn't really look like a machete to me.

"Um, can I take a look?" I held up my gloved hands. "I'm not going to leave prints."

DiBiasi shrugged. "You're not going to hurt it, and it's not going to hurt you."

I picked up the object, which was definitely not a machete. It didn't have a handle, and it didn't have the wide, sharp blade of a machete. It was roughly the same size, but it tapered at the end, and the edges hadn't been sharpened in a long time. It also needed a good cleaning.

No wonder, since no one had probably thought about maintaining it for at least a couple hundred years.

"What is it?" Dina asked.

"Not a machete," I assured her. "And I'm pretty sure not a threat. I've seen this before."

Gerry gave me a puzzled look. "Where?"

Like every female my age, I'd had a bit of a crush on Brett Studebaker in my teens (very, very early teens, of course!), and once I had an idea what the piece was, I was pretty sure what it meant. I turned it on its side and held it up. "In Brett Studebaker's teeth, in *Hero of the Free.*"

Dina looked more confused than Gerry. DiBiasi nodded slowly.

Lewis just snickered. "My grandma used to watch that on cable. I think Denzel had one of his first movie roles in it."

"He did—and he was the only good part of the movie." I shrugged. "This is a Colonial-era bayonet. It's almost certainly a tribute to Studebaker, and not a threat."

Gerry and Dina relaxed a little. I knew how they felt, because the very same knot had uncoiled in my stomach about thirty seconds ago.

"Well, how about that." Gerry peered at the bayonet. "You're right. I saw it during a Mets rain delay last month. Studebaker did run around with something like that clenched in his teeth. Looked painful to me. Silly, too."

"*Hero of the Free?*" Dina actually giggled. "I remember now. We used to watch that on some old video channel in college. Cheesy as they come."

"Yep," I agreed.

"But yeah, I saw the bayonet too." She looked at the thing in my hands, and the amusement faded from her face. "Sure looked like something bad."

DiBiasi nodded. "Can't be too careful, Rabbi."

"Absolutely." Gerry agreed. "Never hurts to keep an eye out for trouble."

"Anyway," Dina said, turning to the officer, "we are all fine here and very much appreciate your help."

"Glad to." He grinned. "Might have to get *Hero of the Free* on Flickies tonight."

"Yeah, well." Dina nodded to me. "What happens to that thing?"

The officer sighed. "It's technically a weapon, but it's so old that it's

61

not really a hazard. You want it for the Society, Dr. Shaw?"

"Sure."

Lewis smiled at DiBiasi. "All donations cheerfully accepted."

"I figured."

"We'll save it and catalogue it as having been left after Studebaker's death," I said. "That's part of town history, too, now."

Gerry shook his head. "So's he."

Chapter Eight

Embroidering the Facts

"Hey, New Hampshire!" Lewis called the joking greeting as the door opened a few minutes after we got back from Beth Shalom.

I was coming downstairs after dropping off the bayonet in the second-floor room where we kept all the military memorabilia. It was mostly World War I and later, but we had some pretty nifty Civil War uniform buttons from a defunct factory nearby and a full uniform from somebody's great-granddad who'd been a Rough Rider with Teddy Roosevelt. Now we had the Colonial bayonet, too.

The two guys from the VFW who kept track of the stuff would be thrilled.

Right now, though, I had a different kind of expert on hand: Faith Stowe, as advertised a Granite State transplant and our best yarn person. She was the one I called when I got to the bottom of a donated trunk and found something like the afghan in the front parlor. If a woman (and it was usually a woman) knit or crocheted it in the last 200 years, Faith would know what it was and how it was made.

Probably be able to fix any damage, too.

While my only exposure to yarn arts growing up was my grandmother's crocheting the occasional hideous throw in neon acrylic, Faith is just the latest generation in a family of women who have always had some kind of project in their laps. Chances are that if she hasn't made a given item, her mother, grandmother, or great-aunts did.

Sometimes, with yarn, they spun themselves from the family sheep.

While Faith's family is legit Old New England, she ended up in Connecticut when her husband took a big job with one of the financial services companies in Hartford. They then moved into the spiffy senior condos in the nicer part of Unity after he retired to be closer to the grandkids.

She's another one of those tiny, adorable women who seem to populate our board, this time in matchy LL Bean sweaters and slacks in soft colors that set off her rosy skin, salt-and-pepper hair, and sparkly pale-blue eyes. Faith's secret weapon was her smile, and it was in full effect as she walked into the foyer.

"Hey, Yalie!" she called back at Lewis.

They're partners in crime and a perfect odd couple, and I'm still amazed that it happened that way.

Like a lot of folks who grow up in Northern New England and/or spend most of their lives in suburbia, she didn't know a lot of black people. It's entirely possible that she'd never spent more than five minutes with an actual African-American man before Lewis. And it showed.

She hadn't realized she was acting scared around him, but he sure did. After a few shifts with her, Lewis stopped by my office and asked what was going on. I was sad it was happening, but really glad that Lewis trusted me enough to bring it up.

So, the next day, I made some coffee, brought Faith in the office, closed the door, and asked her as gently as I could why she was acting weird around Lewis. She hadn't even been aware that she was. She was horrified when she realized how it read to him.

I sent them both down to the Coffee Stop to talk it out, hoping for the best and bracing for more awkwardness. As it turned out, though, they quickly discovered that they both love the Red Sox and don't understand the New England fascination with Tom Brady and the Patriots...all of which made for the beginning of a beautiful friendship.

Exactly the way it's supposed to work. And so rarely does.

Today, they had a project. A few months ago, a man who was moving to North Carolina to live with his daughter had sent us the cotton crochet bed cover his mother had used. It had probably once been white, but by the time it got to us, it was a yellowish mess, not improved by being rolled in a heap for decades. Cotton I knew, but crochet I didn't, so I handled the washing and (*extremely* careful!) bleaching. It had been drying in a basement room with a low fan for days. Now it was time to bring it upstairs, lay it out on a table, and let Faith see what it needed.

Lewis would help her with the layout, pins, and taking notes for the work, and get to hang out with his buddy. All good.

I made sure there was nothing in their way in the workroom that doubled as a docents' and board meeting space and left them to their fun. I had plenty of other things to do, not all of them related to the impending Invasion of the Fourth-Graders.

Noon found me in the second-floor bedroom, showing a collar with some amazing mid-nineteenth-century floral embroidery to three ladies from Town Hall, two from the Registrar of Voters' Office, and one from the Town Clerk. After spending a couple of minutes catching up, meaning my explaining to the ladies that the sirens this morning were no big deal and mutually deploring the unfortunate end of Brett Studebaker, we got down to what really mattered:

The stuff!

I love being with people who enjoy the collection as much as I do.

They were as awed as I was by the condition of the piece and probably more impressed by the quality because they actually did that kind of work. Deborah, Bethany, and Allie were three of my favorite artists (*crafters* seems dismissive of the level of work involved), and I always learned from watching them.

It wasn't really necessary to glove up to look at embroidery since it was a short period of time, and they barely touched it, but they always did, out of respect.

"It's just the quality of the work, Christian," Bethany said, her jet-black eyes wide as she gently traced the faded green line of a vine. "I've been doing this for twenty years, and I can't get my stitches this small."

"Everyone's stitches were tiny then," I said. "You've seen the seams on handmade dresses."

"Stitching away on their hope chests." Allie, a younger brunette who was getting married this summer, giggled. "I can't imagine making all of my own bedding."

"I can't imagine having the time, energy, and skill for any of that." Deborah shook her head, and the little tendrils of ash-blonde hair that had escaped her ponytail swayed. All three ladies are the absolute salt of the earth, the quiet, efficient municipal employees who keep your town going on any given day, and good friends of long standing.

One of the great things about our corner of New Haven County is that we're urban enough to have a diverse community, but small enough that everybody knows everybody else. So, you get friendships like these three, women of entirely different backgrounds and ages, but similar work and interests. Allie grew up in an old mill town in northern Connecticut, came down for college at Shoreline State, and stayed. Deborah, the Registrar herself, is from a family that's been in Unity since soon after the folks who brought the Bible. If she isn't quite one of the Town Mothers, she's close. And Bethany's a New Haven transplant like Ruby, both from families prominent in the

African-American church community.

Bethany's at least as much of a power as Deborah, even though she's not an elected official, because she's the assistant clerk in charge of deeds. So she knows quite literally every inch of town...and what people are planning to do with it. Every once in a while, I hear stuff over the embroidery silks.

Today was one of those days, because inevitably, conversation returned to Brett Studebaker. In a small town, even tiny drama is all-consuming, and when it's something that really *is* a fairly big deal, it quickly becomes the principal topic of all conversations. Be glad you didn't live in Unity the year we had a record winter after the town manager decided to gamble on putting half the snow-removal budget into renovating the offices, including his own. Needless to say, he's no longer our manager. And has gone on with his life's work with the nickname "Manager Snowbunny."

No, I did not come up with that. Might have helped it stick, though.

Anyway, soon enough, there we were, once again back to the late lamented, who would be the hot issue in town for months.

"So are they treating it as a murder?" Deborah asked me as we carefully unrolled the whole length of the wide shawl collar, which had once topped a low-shouldered evening gown. Unlike the collar, which was a fancywork-friendly cotton fabric so closely covered in embroidery that the ground was not visible, the gown had probably been made of a fine silk treated with one of the harsh dyes of the time, and it had not survived. But what mattered, the unique artistry of the woman who'd made it, had come down to us. Pretty impressive.

We all paused for a second to look at it before I spoke again.

"They're treating the death as undetermined right now." That was a matter of public record, and even if Joe Poli hadn't been the most attractive man I'd seen in years, I would not have shared anything he told me. I was married to a journalist long enough to know about keeping information close. I shrugged. "Makes sense until they look around a little."

Bethany nodded. "Especially if they're waiting for drug tests."

"Brett Studebaker?" asked Allie. "Isn't he the one who played the hot Crusader king or something back when they still did that?"

The rest of us winced. Studebaker's *Lionheart* was probably intended as an escapist swords and sandals epic, but since it was made about a year after 9/11, you can imagine where it went. I'd lasted about five minutes one late night when I couldn't sleep. Lazy stereotyping is not my thing.

"Yeah, well," Bethany said. "I heard the new movie was pretty good, though I never managed to get to the shoot."

Allie grinned. "I might have come by if I weren't working on wedding plans. Some of the camera and tech guys I saw on the Green were pretty cute."

Bethany shook her head. "Just passing through."

"No kidding." Allie laughed. "Not that there's anything wrong with that."

"Not at all." Deborah actually grinned. "Back in the day, a lot of big rock groups came through New Haven. I was a sophomore in college the year-"

"You are NOT telling the Keith Richards story again," Bethany cut in.

Even I knew the Keith Richards story. It wasn't nearly as naughty as you'd think...and Deborah probably exaggerated what there was of it for effect.

Allie just sighed. She was young enough that groupie stuff was more #MeToo than adventure. "Never mind. Is that outlet mall group nosing around in the Old Mill area again?"

Unity was resolutely opposed to any sort of strip mall development. The conventional wisdom, which Deborah and Bethany shared, and

Allie did not, was that if they allowed one good-sized grocery store into the Plaza on Route 10, the next thing you knew, there would be a Ruby Tuesday where Town Hall used to be.

Neither Deborah nor Bethany was irrational about it, but they were absolutely firm. Some of the other town leaders, particularly some of the older residents, were murderously determined to keep the stores out. Probably a bad choice of words today.

What was rather amusing, at least to me, was that most of those folks had actually liked the idea of the movie shoot. Despite Sally Birdwell's grim assessment, elected town leaders seemed to think that a wide audience seeing Unity looking cute and untouched could only improve its value.

Kind of like a Regency maiden when the wicked Duke is around, if you think about it.

Anyway, by this point, the outlet mall was practically totemic, a symbol of the horror that other towns might be forced to consider to expand the tax base, but to which our beloved Unity would never stoop. It was also an absolutely perfect change of topic for anyone who, say, didn't want to hear the Keith Richards story again.

"Not the outlet mall," Bethany said. "But there is a little talk of a zoning change to expand that small nursing home over near the Cheshire line."

"Could be months or years before it happens, though." Deborah shook her head. "Sometimes those things move really fast...but a lot of times they don't."

We all nodded.

"Depends on who's asking and how they're wired with the select board," Bethany observed. "I'm not sure who, if anyone, is the connection for the new owners."

Deborah shrugged, which meant she didn't know either. In a small town, the connection is all.

So much for that, then, at least for the moment. If those two didn't have insight, no one did.

"Anyway, I'm running out of lunch hour," Allie said, "and I want to take a closer look at that satin stitch."

"Oh, yes. Amazingly smooth," agreed Deborah.

"And the back," with her friends' eager encouragement, Bethany very, very gently turned over the collar to look at the wrong side, which was almost as neat as the front.

In theory, I understood how women did this fancy work and made it so perfect. In practice, not a clue. To me, it was very real domestic magic.

Later, as we walked to the door and the ladies plotted a trip to the specialty craft store in New Haven, Deborah took me aside. "I've heard a little concern about the temple after all of this, especially after the confusion with that bayonet this morning."

"What do you mean?"

She shook her head quickly. "Nothing bad, Christian. Not at all. Just a few friends who were worried about all of the activity and everything and not entirely sure how to let Rabbi Aaron know that they're thinking of her."

I smiled as I understood. This was the way messages were sent in a small town. We're a very diverse little community, but it's still Old New England, and people are extremely cautious about saying anything—anything at all—about someone's religious practice. Even if they want to show support for a sometimes-endangered minority.

"I'll tell her."

Deborah matched my smile, relieved. "Please do, and let her know that if there's anything she needs, people are more than ready to help."

And you thought *The Sopranos* had a subtle and careful code. Small towns make mobsters' coded language look like a public service announcement.

Looked like I was going to have to take five minutes to talk to Dina before pickup.

So much for straightening out the sheet music today.

Chapter Nine

NORM! and Garrett Too

It was a good thing I made those five minutes for Dina when I did. Once Henry and I got back from Wheatley (just us because Tiffany, Jorge, and Ava were having a catch-up family pizza night), it was one of *those* afternoons. Almost the second I waved Lewis out a little early for some writing time, the phone started ringing off the hook. For about an hour, I fielded fourth-grade teachers, parents, and school officials, each concerned in his or her own unique way about how they were going to safely herd their cherubs through the priceless artifacts on display.

I hated to tell them, but the really priceless stuff, other than the Bible, would be safely moved upstairs from the first two floors that we showed on the elementary tour. There was a reason there were pewter tankards in the dining room right now instead of someone's great-great-grandmother's wedding crystal. I'm all in favor of making history come alive for children. I'm not in favor of asking for disaster.

After reassuring the parade of anxious instructors and managing to *not* tell off one rather maddening helicopter parent, I started buttoning up the place for the night. Henry had finished his homework and was waiting for me in the foyer in the midst of a staring contest with the

Empress.

She was on one of the higher steps, and they were almost nose-to-nose. Her Imperial Majesty doesn't exactly *like* Henry, but she enjoys these little power struggles with him. Especially when she wins, which she did now when Henry turned away at the sound of my footsteps.

The Empress made a happy little ruffly noise and sprinted up the stairs.

Henry had put out food and water for the night in her spot in my office and, of course, a few of her favorite crunchy treats. (The very nice high-tech cat box in the basement—a gift from an admiring board member—was my responsibility.) Treats or no treats, she would still meet me at the door in the morning, snapping about her inadequate staff.

That was for later.

"Hey, kids. Want some company on the walk home?"

Garrett was on the porch with the dog. Not a surprise. But very pleasant.

"Norm!" called Henry, heading over for a pet.

Since we were raising him as a good little vintage TV fan, Henry was well aware that the greeting was a *Cheers* riff. Norm, not the brightest creature on earth, but very possibly the most loving, just liked the fact that every once in a while, people yelled his name appreciatively.

Like now. He wagged his tail and gave Henry a generous face-licking.

Garrett and I laughed, as we always do.

"Sounds like it was a wild day at the ranch," he said as I set the alarm and shepherded the group out the door.

"Yeah. Not as bad as it sounded." I shrugged.

Garrett's dark blue eyes narrowed a little behind his glasses. He knows me better than anyone living.

"The bayonet Donnybrook was more confusion than anything else."

"Everyone doesn't know what a Colonial bayonet is," he reminded

73

me. "Good thing you did that summer at Williamsburg."

"Never know what you'll need to know or when."

"Ain't that the truth." Garrett chuckled.

"Ain't ain't a word, Uncle Garrett!" Henry cut in.

"And right you are, young man. What did we learn at school today?"

"I had library…and they had *What Was the Battle of Gettysburg*."

"Really. How interesting…"

After a short discussion of Civil War battles (with content carefully calibrated for an eight-year-old), Garrett handed Henry the leash and let him walk Norm the rest of the way.

Well, actually, let Norm walk Henry.

It's part of our effort to safely give him some responsibility and freedom. I don't think it's entirely the Type 1, but Henry definitely has a deep need to feel that he's in charge and control—of something. I've found that giving him more responsibility for Cookie and the Empress's care, and Garrett letting him walk Norm when he's with us has helped a lot. It's good for a kid to feel that someone depends on him, the same way he depends on his family.

And the animals repay it in love. Well, maybe not the Empress, but you get the general idea.

Once Norm had pulled Henry a bit out of earshot, Garrett turned to me. "Still, the bayonet thing feels a little weird. DiBiasi told Ed about it."

I wasn't surprised. The cop gossip network was every bit as good as the Town Hall one, if better armed. "Yeah, but weird really was all. Someone was paying tribute to Studebaker's role in *Hero of the Free*."

"Silly movie." Garrett is firmly convinced that the last good film made involved Ronald Colman. He might, on rare occasions, tolerate a mob epic to please Ed, but otherwise, if it wasn't from the old studios, he wasn't interested.

"Very silly movie," I agreed. "But he had a lot of fans."

"And some of them might be a little off." Garrett shook his head. "Social media is taking an interest in all of this."

In retirement, Garrett had become a social media maven. He had more Facebook friends than anyone I knew and an active Flutter feed under the name of an obscure member of Abraham Lincoln's Cabinet. Though he has little real interest in the influencers, minor celebrities, and political trolls that populate the social media landscape, he has a finely-honed appreciation for the absurdity of it all, and he'd gained a certain following for his dry observations.

He also knew pretty much every wild theory that was flying around the Web at any given moment.

"And what does Flutter think?"

Garrett chuckled. "Thinking and Flutter do not necessarily belong in the same sentence. That said, there seems to be a good bit of speculation about the co-star leaving in a hurry."

"Olivia Carr?" I shook my head. "Flutter can probably save its energy. She left two weeks ago for a Royal Shakespeare Company production."

"Which play?"

"Hamlet. Ophelia."

He sighed. "Just once, I'd like to see a large mannish woman play Ophelia. What is it with straight men and tiny blondes?"

"When you figure it out, let me know."

We shared a small chuckle.

"So, what did you think of her?"

"I only saw her once. That night shoot when you watched Henry." I thought about it. The scene was supposed to be some kind of big confrontation between the Reverend and the Adulteress (as the character was known, presumably to avoid any awkward comparisons to previous Prynnes), but it hadn't come off as much. Part of it was Studebaker, who still had an all-consuming presence when the camera came on. But it was also the actress. The daughter of an important

British impresario, she was beautiful in that fragile, doll-like way that does indeed send some straight men over the edge. That was about it, though.

Between takes, she'd seemed bored and annoyed, smoking and complaining to anyone within range that she could not understand why they couldn't just do this on a nice soundstage in New York. Just young and petulant, though. A spoiled brat, I thought. Nothing really dangerous.

"I really don't think there's much there," I told Garrett.

"Flutter seems to think that Studebaker scared her off somehow...or she knew it was coming and bugged out."

"Best I can tell, he didn't even want to be in the room with her. You know how sometimes people say someone falls in love *at* someone, instead of with them?"

Rueful smile. "I've done it."

"Ah, haven't we all," I agreed, remembering a certain armorer in Williamsburg. We talked about cannonballs over coffee once, and that was it—though I followed him around like a baby duck for the whole summer.

"Occupational hazard of youth," Garrett said, obviously remembering his own mishaps. "But hardly the stuff of ageless romance."

"Well, exactly. But my sense was that's what the Reverend was doing. Everything was about him, and she was barely showing up. Whether that was bad direction, or her inadequacies—or some kind of creative choice, who knows?"

"What do you mean?"

"Well, at least from what I saw, the whole thing centered on the Reverend's experience. She was basically a stock character."

Garrett's brows knit, which I knew meant he was puzzling out something. "Weird choice right now."

"Anytime, I'd say."

CHAPTER NINE

"Well, yeah. But in the last few years, there's been a serious online backlash against stuff like that. You know, either ignoring a woman's experience or treating it as less important than a man's."

"True." I'd heard a lot of the same in academic circles, too.

"And this would seem to be ripe for exactly the opposite treatment. You know, taking it much more from the Adulteress's viewpoint. Maybe even raising questions about consent and power."

"I'd watch that." Alone, after Henry was in bed, of course.

"I probably wouldn't," Garrett admitted, "But a lot of people would."

"But you can't make it about the Adulteress if the Reverend is Brett Studebaker."

"Precisely. And if word got out that this production was all about the guy?" He whistled. "I'd rather walk into a nest of hornets than a Flutter mob."

"So this thing was going to tank."

"Let's just say they had to be hoping there were still a lot of Brett Studebaker fans around."

I nodded. "I wonder if they can save the film they have."

"Or if they even want to, considering."

Just then, a squirrel ran across the sidewalk, and Norm started after it.

"NORM—no!" Henry yelled, pulling hard on the leash. Garrett had to jump in and grab it, which he did, quickly restoring order.

"You do not want a squirrel, Norm!" Garrett admonished the dog and then handed the lead back to Henry.

"Yeah. Squirrels are not for you!" Henry gave the dog an equally intimidating glare as he took it back.

Norm, who genuinely loves Henry and whose entire goal of existence is to be loved by everyone, bowed his head and looked very, very sorry.

"Aw, fella. It's okay." Henry patted him and got a generous lick.

A properly chastened Norm led us the rest of the way home, with the subject firmly changed to lighter matters. We'd get back to the serious stuff soon enough.

Chapter Ten

For Whom the Phone Rings

As much as I enjoy having everyone over for a good get-together, I was glad for Tiffany and her crew that they were getting a family night—and very glad for our own, too. Pizza is a lot of carbs for Henry, so many of the usual kid standbys come up less often at our house.

My go-to when I can't think of anything else is an open-faced meatball sub for Henry and a big salad for me. If you keep good frozen meatballs and jarred sauce on hand, which everyone in New Haven County does (even if they wince at not making their own red gravy,) it's ready in a couple of minutes, and we can sit down and enjoy the meal together.

Cookie is the only member of the household who does not approve of this plan, since it does not include grilled chicken, sliced turkey, or tuna fish: the only acceptable human meals in his view—because he will happily scam a portion. Meatballs, though they definitely involve animal protein, also involve that strange, ill-smelling red stuff, which is both messy and not tasty to a cat.

He took one look at the package of frozen meatballs and howled.

If it hadn't been an unusually trying couple of days, I probably would have just left my little drama king to his misery. But I felt bad for him, so I reached in the fridge, peeled off a slice of turkey, and put it by his bowl.

Scientists say cats cannot smile. They have never seen Cookie in the presence of deli turkey.

Our small disaster averted, we settled in for dinner.

Just like we're not the classic Victorian happy family, neither is our dinner. We usually watch the news while we eat, a legacy of our life with a hard-news reporter. Frank did not consider himself properly informed if he didn't read the *New York Times* and watch a network newscast each day. I try to do the same for Henry, though I sometimes end up giving in to the call for extra time for planet documentaries. On Ur-AN-ous, obviously.

No documentaries tonight. I wanted to see if the local news had anything on the Studebaker case. Thanks to a huge, messy tractor-trailer crash near the I-91/95 split, Studebaker was relegated to the B block. Traffic always wins in Connecticut. When they did finally get to the story, though, it wasn't anything I wanted to see.

Police called to Studebaker memorial! screamed the tease before the commercial. After a couple of ads featuring various health services and people dancing about a new prescription laxative, all they had was some footage of the church, once again littered with flowers and other items, and a sound bite of Officer Tony DiBiasi explaining that a local expert had taken a look at an object of concern and determined it was no threat.

He made me sound like the damn bomb squad.

"Were you the local expert, Mom?" Henry asked when I muttered something I did not want him to repeat.

"Yeah. It really wasn't anything serious or dangerous. Somebody left a Colonial bayonet."

"Why?"

"Brett Studebaker used one in a big movie a long time ago."

"Weird."

"So weird."

Henry quickly lost interest in bayonets and Studebaker because it was time for dessert—one of the bittersweet chocolate squares he adores. We figured out early on that one chocolate square, low in sugar but high in flavor, is a manageable treat, so I always keep them in the house.

Chocolate enjoyed, Henry moved on to video game time, zooming around a racetrack lined with zombies (I didn't need or want to know more!). Cookie, now properly soothed, decided to sit on the couch beside me, just far enough away to make it clear that he was *Henry's* cat and not mine. I was giving him the permitted ear scratch when my phone rang. I picked up without looking, figuring that Garrett or Tiffany had seen the evening news. Or worse, my mom, who should have been with her knitting club in West Haven...but you never really knew with that crew.

"Hey."

"Dr. Shaw?"

Joe Poli's voice was low and distinctive, even as he said my name uncertainly.

"Sorry. Yes. I assumed it was friends or family calling."

"*I'm* sorry. It's after business hours, but your number's on the card, so-"

"I'm a working mom. There are no business hours." Since I deal with volunteers who are around at all hours, I do have to be available for them...but I realized I was glad to be a little available for my friendly neighborhood prosecutor.

He laughed. "Fair enough. I heard about the bayonet thing."

"Ah. *Hero of the Free.*"

"You're sure it's a reference to the movie?"

"As sure as I can be without being in the fan's brain. The bayonet was a major thing in the posters and all."

"Could someone get a Colonial bayonet?"

"Sure." I thought about it for a moment. I should have done an online search when I brought the thing back to the museum, but I knew a little, thanks to that armorer in Williamsburg. "They're not as rare as you think they are. Metal objects last basically forever, after all, and something like that would have been kept because it's useful."

"Useful?"

"Depending on where you're living, you might want to have a big, unwieldy blade with which to menace an intruder."

"Or to just run around with it in your teeth."

"You saw the movie poster."

"Yeah—I checked it out online." An amused little whistle. I could almost see him shaking his head. "He looked pretty silly."

"Plenty of girls thought otherwise."

"Including you?"

"Well…"

He laughed again. I really did like that laugh. "Aly is bonkers about one of those K-pop stars. Pictures of the guy all over her room and notebooks and everything. Was it like that?"

"Ah…no. Well, not for me, anyhow. Mostly, I was a history buff. But I learned pretty early that it was worse than geeky to admit you had a crush on Christopher Marlowe, and I had to have someone to talk about."

"Marlowe?"

"I was a little bit of a Renaissance poetry nerd."

"I was more of a Donne guy." He was silent for a second, then: "'She's all states, and all princes I...nothing else is.'"

Wow. *The Sun Rising.* Not just any Donne poem, but one of the sexiest ones, all about waking up in the morning with your lover. And perfectly delivered, in that very appealing voice of his. For a moment, I wasn't sure what to say. Finally offered something neutral: "Um, good memory."

I don't think it's possible to hear a blush, but when Joe spoke again, there was something awkward and adorable in his voice. "Yeah, well. I didn't think it was a good idea to quote *For Whom the Bell Tolls* right about now."

"Probably true. But I'm impressed."

"Thanks. I have a good memory for useless stuff."

"There's nothing useless about Donne."

"We agree."

A few seconds of surprisingly companionable silence. Then:

"So you really think the bayonet was just a tribute?"

"Sometimes, Dr. Freud, a cigar really is just a cigar."

Another wonderful laugh. "You know how to play, Dr. Shaw. I like that."

"You're not bad yourself."

"Something to keep in mind later, maybe."

"Just maybe."

If I hadn't been his expert and a nice widow lady, and all of this taking place much too close to the body of an unfortunate movie star, the next sentence might have been different. At least it felt that way for a couple of seconds.

But then he was back to cool acquaintanceship. "Thank you, Dr. Shaw. Have a good night."

"You too." I hit end.

Cookie climbed into my lap and started licking my face, reminding me that I was already at the service of one alpha male. Of course, he did.

Chapter Eleven

Another Fun Morning

W hen I can, I try to get up early and spend some time doing a good flow yoga video in the living room before Henry stirs. It's a great way to burn off all manner of life stress, not to mention the sheer pleasure of moving lightly in a quiet, half-dark room. Sometimes, Cookie joins me and climbs on my back while I do Child's Pose. It's our version of that trendy goat yoga thing.

I didn't make it to Child's Pose that morning because my phone rang at 6:15.

Almost fell out of Tree Pose.

My first thought was some kind of emergency involving my mother. She lives just over a half-hour away in West Haven, in a nice little senior building on the water. She finished her 30 years of teaching in Mars and retired while I was expecting Henry, becoming the grandmother she never dared to hope she'd be. I loved having her closer, but happily occupied and just far enough away that she wasn't all up in my business. Most of the time, she and her knitting buddies are busy enjoying a *very* late-adolescent rebellion, and we see her once a week or so.

But when you've had one early-morning phone call that stops your world, it's always the first thing on your mind when you pick up.

Most of my friends and family are well aware of that...and would never scare me.

I grabbed the phone. Unfamiliar number with a Unity exchange. What does that mean? "Hello?"

"Christian, dear!"

"Um, yes?"

A woman. Older and local. She swallowed the T.

"It's Mae Tillotson."

Of course, it was. "Okay."

I took a breath, tried to stop the fight-or-flight adrenaline that had started pouring into my bloodstream. So much for the serene start to the day.

"I didn't wake you, did I? I know you young mothers like to sleep in whenever you can..."

I bit my lip. She made it sound like I was somehow lying down on the job. Which one of my many jobs? I wondered. "Nope, I was up doing some yoga. Just surprised to hear the phone is all."

"Well, I wouldn't bother you except to tell you that I'm going to be late today. I have to go to the doctor."

"Oh, I'm sorry." While the docents were volunteers, most of them were quite serious about their responsibilities, and I appreciated that. Most of the time.

"Quite all right, dear. Nothing serious. Just a nasty little scratch on my arm that wants to get infected. I'll be right over after I get it cleaned up at the urgent care."

"That's fine. Take all the time you need."

"Thank you, dear. I'll just be a teensy bit late."

We were actually running on time that morning, thanks to Henry eating his breakfast with a little more dispatch than usual and not even arguing with me over wardrobe, since his favorite red polo was clean. I was feeling moderately saucy, too, wearing my favorite early 1900s tuxedo shirt under a dark green blazer with the crest of some prep school that went under before I was born. The tuxedo shirt always makes me feel a little spiffy.

If you're wondering how a busy working mom manages to maintain a collection of bright white vintage shirts that require ironing, the answer is depressingly simple: I have no life. When other people are out doing fun things on Saturday night – or just sulking about not having a date, I'm home washing, bleaching, and ironing five or six shirts for the week.

Well, at least I have something to show for my lonely evenings.

Turned out we weren't the only ones running early. As we turned down the walk, Sally Birdwell and her two kids were coming from the other direction, the McMansion part of the neighborhood.

"Oh, Christian. Where did you find that shirt? Did you buy it at the Mazzi's Formals Going-Out-of-Business Sale?"

It may—or may not—have been intended as a slap, but it happens that this particular shirt isn't just nice, it has *provenance*. "Um, no. It's from the estate sale at Eleanor Worden's."

Sally's eyes widened. Eleanor Worden, of course, had given Katharine Hepburn a run for her money as Connecticut's biggest vintage movie star. My tux shirt had probably belonged to her dad, a State Supreme Court justice. It was maybe fifteen years ago, soon after I came to Shoreline State. Everyone else had been buying up Worden's costumes and whatever—things that would certainly be auctioned at a great price now—and there was just a big pile of shirts in a corner. I bought as many as I could afford, and I still had a couple untouched ones wrapped in sheets (the safe way to preserve old textiles) in a trunk in the shed.

If I treated them right, they'd outlive me too.

Sally, I'm sure, had no concept of clothing or any other possessions as pieces of history, but she definitely recognized the name Eleanor

Worden. "Oh. That's right, you like old stuff."

"Pretty much."

"Hen-ree…" Sally's kindergartner Sheridan, a little girl with caramel hair and her father's hazel eyes, bounced up. Sheridan isn't old enough to know what a crush is, but she has one on Henry, following him like an adoring baby duck whenever he's around.

Henry, to his credit, doesn't mind in the least and just tolerates the attention.

Sally's son, Douglas, is an entirely different issue.

He's in Henry's class and one of those rough, nasty critters who give little boys a bad name. And it makes him nuts that Sheridan likes Henry.

As usual, Douglas smacked Henry on the arm, yelling, "Tag, you're it," and kept running. Also, as usual, because he hasn't yet learned to ignore these things, Henry gave chase. He's twice Douglas's size and not especially speedy, but Henry always has to try. Sheridan, of course, ran after both of them, yelling.

I sighed. Sally shrugged.

"Kids will be kids, right?"

"Yeah, well." I didn't say what I was thinking, which was that allowing too much "kids will be kids" leads to "boys will be boys"—and we all know where that has gotten us. Sally probably would not have understood or appreciated it.

She checked her watch. "Say, do you mind watching them go in the door? I have a meeting with a friend at Shady Rest."

"Um, sure." As little as I liked Sally, I didn't wish the nursing home conversation on anyone. I knew someday I was going to have to face it alone, but I kept hoping Mom would just live independently into her 120s…and die a week after me. "Sorry to hear that."

"Not for my family, silly." She looked irritated by the sympathy. "That's Malcolm's area anyway. The Shady Rest is working on the expansion project again."

"Oh, of course."

"They should get the zoning change because it's really good news for the town tax base and the adjacent property owner, who was thinking of selling anyway…but some of the other people in the neighborhood should really get out before the change."

"Why?"

"A bigger facility means more traffic, so it's harder to get a good deal…especially since you can pretty much cross off selling to any family with small children."

"Right." I nodded.

"Well, anyhow, thanks for keeping an eye on the kids." She patted my arm and attempted, not very successfully, to look sincerely appreciative. "See you later."

Door-opening went the way it always does, five minutes of watching every second crawl, followed by an unseemly rush to the entrance, while I made sure to get the visual of Henry actually passing through the frame. Not hard today, with the red polo and the fact that he was already taller than a lot of the other kids. I took the time to do the same for Sheridan and Douglas, easier than expected because Sheridan was right behind Henry, and Douglas appeared to be picking a fight with another classmate a few feet away.

That was not going to be good for Douglas, but hopefully, Henry would not be drawn into either the fight or the trouble afterwards.

I had all the trouble I could handle at the moment.

Once I saw that all three of them were physically inside the building, the signal that they were now somebody else's problem for the moment, I turned for the Society. A dad in an SUV, who was clearly in a hurry to get to wherever he was going, didn't see me until he almost hit me in the crosswalk. It happened at least once a month because the Wheatley parents are wretched drivers and rude to boot, but it never got easier.

Or less annoying. They can't see me? Me? The redheaded giant?

What if it were five-foot-nothing Bea Ling with her two-year-old?

Scary as hell, just in the parking lot. Even if they whack a grown person at slow speed, they could still fall and hit their head...or end up under a wheel and pulverize something important.

I took a couple deep breaths and walked on.

Idiots in SUVs are everywhere in Connecticut, and you just have to work around them. Full stop. I was kind of disappointed that Ed wasn't with me, though. One time, a different parent had almost hit him, and Norm...and Ed made a little phone call to make sure Tony DiBiasi was waiting for the guy at his office.

Today, I was just going to have to deal. The theme for the day.

There are two words you never want to ask the universe: What Now?

But the way things were going that morning, I was seriously tempted to do just that.

Perhaps the simple fact that I didn't ask is what earned me a very pleasant surprise.

Joe Poli was waiting for me on the Society porch, looking awkward and holding a package of excellent Italian dark-roast coffee. "I think I was inappropriate last night, and-"

I stared at him for a moment, gobsmacked. "What?"

He shrugged, and I noticed his ears were a little pink. "I didn't remember where that quote came from. I thought it was just a love sonnet – I forgot that it was about, um, you know."

"Waking up together."

"Yeah. I hope you weren't-"

"Not at all." I smiled. "I was just impressed that there was somebody who could quote Donne beyond 'No man is an island.'"

He smiled. Grinned, actually. "Okay. Just wanted to be sure. I brought you a little peace offering. It's not really better than yours, but it's Italian."

"Which wins all ties. How about you drink some of it with me now?"

"I would love to, but I have to get to the office. Rain check?"

"Absolutely."

It was middle school all the way, but I looked back as I punched in the code and started in, just in time to see him turning to look back at me. A shared smile and chuckle.

Sure, it was eighth-grade. Eighth-grade in that wonderful way where you suddenly realize you have the power to make someone look at you like you're special. Nothing wrong with that.

If I hadn't been less than a week out from the Invasion of the Fourth-Graders, I might have taken a few minutes to think about what, if anything, I planned to do about it.

But the phone was ringing as I opened the door. And my day was off to a running start, as I spent ten minutes talking down a panicked student teacher while the Empress nipped at my ankles. Her Majesty has little empathy when it's time for treats.

With proper credit to Linda Ellerbee: And so it goes.

Chapter Twelve

Jenny from the Entertainment Block

While Tiffany, like me, is a pretty serious person with relatively serious reading and viewing habits (balanced, of course, by a finely tuned sense of goofiness), her sister Jenny, who teaches art at the middle school, is a pop-culture aficionado. So it wasn't really a surprise to see them and a large box of Tiffany's world-famous chocolate chippers appear an hour or so before pickup that afternoon.

Jenny Medina Lawrence (she uses all three) could not be mistaken for anything other than Tiffany's sister or an art teacher. They're within a few inches in height, share the same fit but not skinny build, and sparkly amber eyes, which I suspect come from their mother. Jenny's hair is darker than Tiffany's highlighted caramel, and she wears it in a big soft braid, instead of her sister's snug sensible knot, which points in the art teacher direction.

Wardrobe was much more of a tell; while Tiffany is generally in her nicely-fitted navy uniform or jeans and a simple sweater topped with a leather blazer, Jenny is as artsy as they come. She had on a dress tie-dyed in the colors of the sunrise, topped with a sunshiny-yellow crochet cardigan. Her earrings and necklace, which she'd made herself, were delicate threads of different-shaped glass beads in colors to echo her outfit, and she had a couple of those nifty little energy bracelets clicking on her wrist, today tiger eye and Amazonite (good luck and gratitude).

Jenny didn't really need them. She's another one of those people who's happy in her life and her calling, and she gives off plenty of good energy on her own.

Tiffany's no slouch, either, I'd add. She'll never say it, of course, but I wouldn't be surprised if she'd pulled more than one person through just by calmly fixing her eyes on them and telling them they'd make it. I'd believe her.

Anyway, the cookies were probably intended partly as an entirely unnecessary thank you for picking up Ava and hosting dinner the other night, and mostly as an excuse to get Jenny to sit down and share her unique expertise. The middle school had an early dismissal that day, supposedly for professional development, but as a "special" teacher, i.e., anything beyond the three R's, Jenny had her professional development at different times—and was more than happy to pop over for coffee, cookies, and gossip.

Er, information-gathering.

And not Joe Poli's coffee. Speaking of gossip. I didn't want to explain that yet, and anything other than Jimmy's usual dark blue vacuum bag would occasion comment, so I'd hidden the Italian coffee in my desk drawer.

"So, what do you need to know about Studly Studebaker?" Jenny asked, taking a cookie after making the same token protests we all made about not needing to add one to our backsides. In no case was it a real concern, but it's what women do.

"They still called him that?" Tiffany asked with an explosive laugh. "Wasn't that on the movie poster for the one with the bayonet?"

"Thank goodness it was," I reminded her. "We'd still be trying to figure out if someone was threatening us. But yeah, the tag was something like '*Hero of the Free*—featuring studly Brett Studebaker standing up to the evil redcoats.'"

"Yikes." Tiffany, who was working on a memoir in between shifts, shook her head. "Terrible writing."

"No kidding," Jenny agreed. "But stars have a particular image and place in their world. So Studly Brett he was to start, and to finish, world without end, Amen."

We all chuckled.

"Any weird personal stuff with him?" I asked. I have no idea how my first cookie disappeared. There really shouldn't be a second one.

"*No* personal stuff I ever saw. Never married, always seemed to have a pretty lady on his arm, but never anything too serious."

"#MeToo?" asked Tiffany. She still had half a cookie.

"Not him. Two of the other guys who were in those teen movies with him got caught up in that—I think one's even doing time. But one of the actresses was very careful to say that he was always kind and protective of her."

"Gay." Tiffany and I said in unison.

"Almost certainly." Jenny nodded. "But that doesn't mean what you think it does these days."

We both stared at her, genuinely puzzled and concerned for a moment. What did *she* mean by *that*?

"No, gay is still gay." Jenny laughed. "Silly. I mean it wasn't the career ender it would have been thirty years ago. Do you remember Georgi Romanov?"

"Um, hot Eastern European guy?" I offered.

"Crime show, maybe?" Tiffany added.

"Close enough. He was on that *Criminal Procedure* show for about ten years. Did a bunch of movies in between – but in your living room every night. Well, not yours."

We shrugged.

"Anyway, he came out about a year ago. Said he wanted to live his truth. Got married a few months later, to absolutely ecstatic coverage from all of the shows."

"Really?" Tiffany asked.

"Really." Jenny smiled wisely. "I still can't turn on the shows or go to the websites without seeing him and his cute little hubs."

"So then..."

"If Brett Studebaker was thinking about leaving the closet, it would only be good for his career. Especially with that prestige production he was doing here."

Well, wasn't that something new to consider with the cookies.

"You think?" Tiffany ate the last bite of her cookie and made no move for another. Probably didn't even want one. One more reason she's my hero.

Jenny grinned. "If I were running his career—and I'd probably have done better than whoever he had the last few years—I would have had him do something like this but better and come out during the promo."

"Like this but better, how?" I asked.

"Like with a man in the Hester Prynne role." Jenny's grin widened. "It would have been perfect."

"It would," Tiffany agreed.

"Definitely." I nodded. "Or a rework of some other classic thing about forbidden love."

"Missed opportunity, big time, if you asked me." Jenny shrugged. "It's sad, really. Never got a chance to be who he really was."

"Or who he could really be." I held Jenny's serious gaze for a moment. "Did he even know he could?"

"Maybe, and maybe not." Jenny drank her coffee and contemplated. "I think he ran with a very macho old-school pack, and they might not have realized just how much things have changed."

"So even more of a waste." Tiffany shook her head.

"Yep. Not the only actor who never got a chance to live up to his potential, but it's too bad to watch." Jenny sighed.

We all looked into our coffee for a moment, saddened by the missed opportunity.

Jenny shook it off first. "All right, now. I've caught you two up on the entertainment world. You have to catch me up on Wheatley. Is Sally Birdwell still terrorizing the PTA by Instagram?"

"It's no joke, Jen, you're the crafty one." Tiffany shook her head. "Every damn week she posts some cute little project she does with Sheridan, and then Ava wants me to do it...and I can't get close, dammit."

Jenny laughed. "Nobody expects you to. You save lives every day. So what if you can't fold an origami frog?"

"You wouldn't ask that question if you knew Sally better," I told her, a little relieved that I wasn't the only one who felt inadequate around Sally, even as I wanted to go after her with her glue gun for messing with Tiffany. "She's perfect. And so pretty."

Jenny glared at us both.

"She's a pain in the backside, and she's not worthy to carry either of your sneakers. So chill out already."

Tiffany laughed. So did I.

"Thanks, little sis."

"Sometimes you need to remember to just brush people off."

"She's right, Christian." Tiffany raised her mug. "To brushing off Sally."

"Oh, yeah," I agreed.

"Got that."

We nibbled and joked for a few more minutes, but it was heading for pickup time at Wheatley. Jenny's kids were still in preschool, but she had to get moving too.

I hid the cookies in the drawer with the coffee, and Tiffany and Jenny nodded. Better not to leave them out for Henry to see.

Tiffany offered to drive me over, since it looked like rain. It was Ava's gymnastics day, so they'd be in a hurry on the way out, but that was fine. Anything to keep the little angels moving past the puddles on a rainy day; even at this age, there's still not much worse than cleaning up a muddy kid.

I grabbed my big old golf umbrella from the closet on my way out. Henry probably wouldn't stay under it anyway, but at least I wouldn't be a mess on the way home. Besides, it was the good kind of rain, just heavier than a mist, and it was a warm enough day that it didn't matter.

Lidia and Ruby were waiting under the portico when we walked up, both with their own pointless large umbrellas. Ruby had one of the new ones that opens backwards and supposedly makes less of a mess. She was explaining it to Lidia, with D'Andrea happily pointing out the big sunflower on the outside.

I've always been fascinated by those things, but I can't make myself spend that much money on something that I could just as easily leave at the library. Mrs. Crenshaw might get it back to me, but she might not too.

Tiffany cut her eyes to me. She and I had shared more than one amused conversation about the grandmas' ability and willingness to gear up.

"Pretty cool," I agreed with Lidia as Ruby folded it. "And I like the sunflower, too."

D'Andrea returned my smile, then ducked behind her grandma. Ruby patted her head. "At some point, we're going to get over the separation anxiety thing."

I shrugged. "Henry still sometimes climbed up the back of my shirt in first grade. Everybody gets there when they get there."

"True." Ruby looked out at the wet pavement. "No playground time

96

today."

Tiffany and I resisted the temptation to cheer. Even with the risk of mud, rain was a net positive, since it was always a challenge to get Henry back to the Society before my lunch hour expired.

"So," Lidia started, glancing to Tiffany, then turning to me with an impish little smile, "what do you think of my older boy?"

I stared at her for a second, puzzled. Then I put it together. As small a town as Unity is, sometimes you still don't realize who you know. Friends in the pen don't use last names; it's either first names or by the kid: a whole bunch of folks know me only as Henry's Mom. That's why I missed it.

Now, though, I remembered where I'd seen another pair of kind, intelligent brown eyes recently. "Joe Poli. A really good guy."

She nodded. "Decided to be a prosecutor after the driver who hit Tony got away."

"I respect that a lot," I said.

"Won a scholarship to Yale Law, you know. Made a ton of money with that big firm." Lidia smiled as she warmed to her theme, as any proud mom would. Someday I'd be doing the same about Henry. "But he likes putting away bad guys."

"I can see that." I nodded. "He's good at it, too."

"Yep." The smile widened into a grin. "You know he's single, right?" Matchmaking?

Ruby chuckled and piled on. "Pretty cute, too. I saw him at the fourth-grade Christmas concert."

Lidia beamed. "He's a good uncle. Comes out for Gia and Sophia whenever he can."

Any man who was willing to listen to a group of fourth-graders who were not his *actual* children sing was probably a candidate for sainthood. "Impressive."

Tiffany grinned. "Jenny had his daughter for art a couple years ago.

Really good dad. Involved without being a helicopter."

She exchanged an approving smile with Lidia. Tiffany and Dina had both been urging me to start thinking about dating for a while. That—and the incredible busy-ness of our lives – was probably why I hadn't told her about Joe's visits or the phone call. Or the Donne. Especially the Donne.

I was going to be paying for that in good coffee, I had no doubt.

"And you know he married Anna and Jamie," Lidia continued, beaming.

"I'm sorry?" I had no idea what she was talking about. I knew her daughter, Gia and Sophia's mom, was married to a woman, but little else. Actually, I'd just been impressed that Lidia was so completely un-bothered by the whole thing. It had made me re-think my biases about sweet Italian *nonna*'s a little.

"He's that thing, Peace Justice? So he married them because the priest couldn't."

Ruby grinned. "Justice of the Peace."

"Right."

Some local officials, including the occasional assistant state's attorney, were J.P.'s, an antiquated post that carried a few powers, like officiating at a wedding. It didn't just come with being a prosecutor, but it was probably easier for him to become one than a guy off the street. "Oh, okay. I get it. He did the wedding."

"Yep."

"Your daughter is probably the only woman outside Arkansas who can say her brother married her," teased Ruby.

We all laughed at that. Lidia may still have had the Italian accent, but after forty years here, she appreciated a good redneck joke as much as the next girl. I didn't point out that there was also a significant degree of intermarriage in my native corner of the Rust Belt because I didn't want them to think they'd offended me. All three know I'm originally a country girl, but I don't fly the flag much.

"I have no idea how you people can be so cheerful on such a horrid day."

Sally stomped up, her nude heels making her wobble a little on the wet pavement. She had a gigantic umbrella in a status plaid, matching her unnecessary slicker. Her hair would not have dared to frizz, but there was a definite hint of less smoothness. I don't need to tell you that the rain had turned me into the Cowardly Lion's copper sister, do I?

Tiffany nodded to Sally and turned back to Lidia and Ruby. In one more example of how she is so much more excellent than me, she merely acknowledges Sally's existence and otherwise ignores her. She may feel inadequate about Sally's Instagram feed, but she handles the actual woman so much better than I do.

"It's just rain," I reminded Sally. "And it's pretty warm."

She sniffed. "I guess I'm just stressed with everything that's going on."

Sympathetic nods all around.

I was the idiot who said it, though. "Violent death is pretty unnerving."

"Not that. I'm worried about what this whole mess will do to our property values."

Ruby's eyes widened. Lidia let out a small sigh. Tiffany winced, but kept her eyes firmly on the door, which I knew meant she was biting back a deep and visceral desire to explain to Sally in graphic detail that a real, live human being had just died in a particularly nasty way. I just stared.

"Oh, I know you all think it's insensitive, but when you try to sell your house and you can't, it's no joke." She glared at me. "That nice Mrs. Tillotson who works at the society is having a hard time."

"Mae?"

"Yes. She's a real sweetie. And what a nice little bungalow, though it does need a new kitchen. But I told her she'd better sell right after that shoot—because if the movie does well, more films will come here, and we'll have a real problem."

Lidia harrumphed. "Silly. Someone always buys a house in this town."

"And for a good price." Though Tiffany would not normally dignify Sally's existence, she could not resist a little smack on a topic she knew all too well. She and her husband had spent longer than they cared to admit, saving up the down payment for their home. So had Frank and I.

Ruby nodded. "She's right. Even if it takes a little while, people do buy."

"Only if a good agent convinces them to." Sally preened a bit. "Houses don't just sell themselves. Especially not now, with the Shady Rest working on the expansion again."

I'd forgotten that Mae lived a few blocks away from the Shady Rest. I doubted it mattered to her, except maybe as a grim reminder of what might be coming someday far too soon.

"Is it, really?" I asked. "I think there may be some uncertainty at Town Hall."

"I didn't hear that at all." Annoyed that she might not be as plugged in as she thought, Sally sniffed and turned for the door. "Well, I'm going to go get in line."

Lidia patted my arm. "I think Joe likes you."

Tiffany shot me a grin over her head.

"What?"

"Asked me if I knew anything about you. Smart lady, good coffee—and pretty, he said."

"Oh." I stared for a second, even as my inner eighth-grader squealed: *He thinks I'm pretty!*

Lidia gave me a wise nod. "Just keep pouring the coffee."

"Caffeine is our friend," Tiffany reminded me, with a smile that told me I owed her at least a full pot's worth of explanations.

Ruby smiled magisterially. "Nothing wrong with a cup of coffee."

Chapter Thirteen

Movie Folks Are Squirrelly

Ed and Norm arrived on the Society porch as Henry and I walked out the door. A hiss from the Empress told me that she'd seen them and was less than pleased by the presence of a canine in her sacred precincts.

She'd be over it by morning.

Ed gave the leash to Henry with a smile to me. "He chased a squirrel on the way over. Hopefully, he'll be calm enough for a while."

"Cool." We fell into a comfortable pace together. "So I talked to Jenny Medina today."

"Tiffany's sis? The art teacher? Nice girl."

"She is. Also, an entertainment buff."

"Studebaker?"

"Exactly."

"And what did you learn?"

"That Studebaker was probably gay, and—"

"You had to have somebody else tell you that, Christian? Not too smart for a Ph.D." He laughed. "Movie star in his 50s who's not married and hasn't been caught in a #MeToo? What did you think?"

"Waiting for the right girl?" I laughed, too.

"Uh-huh." He shook his head. "Garrett and I talked about this a while ago. I feel kinda bad for the poor bastard, sorry Christian."

"Why? He was rich, successful-"

"And probably miserable. Couldn't be who he really was."

Like Ed couldn't be who *he* really was at the beginning of his professional life. I might get some good insight on Studebaker here... but it was more important to just listen to Ed.

I nodded. "Probably pretty awful."

"I'm guessing from what it was like in the Staties, okay? But there were always people who suspected and made—little comments. We're all brothers; we're all behind each other when the shooting starts, no question, right? But that didn't mean there wouldn't be busting of balls."

No apology for the language this time. He was busy telling me his truth. I just made eye contact and nodded.

"So I'm thinking it was probably a lot like that with Studebaker. Only ten times worse. Some people had to kiss up to him because he was the big star, but other people would be able to kick him around. And would do it."

"Makes sense."

"You never know who's prejudiced until you come up against them," Ed said quietly. "That's the damn thing. More than once, I was terribly disappointed in someone I thought I trusted."

"Sorry."

"But more than once, I also found out that someone I never would have expected to get it, did."

"That helps."

"It does." Ed saw Henry and Norm a little too far ahead for his comfort, so he sped up a little, and I followed before he continued. "So I'm thinking he probably had all kinds of ugly stuff going on. And if that assistant knew something, he could have been blackmailing him."

"Maybe." I shrugged. "Jenny thinks that going public and living his truth would have been a terrific career move for Studebaker."

"Probably would have." Ed nodded. "That's how it is now. Honestly, I think that's almost as bad as forcing people to be down-low. You don't need a special party because you're getting gay-married. You just need a wedding."

"Yours was pretty great." Ed's kids had walked him down the aisle, I'd walked Garrett, and several dozen very happy people had danced all night at the historic inn a couple of towns over. They went there for dinner every anniversary.

"It was." Ed's wonderful, joyful smile told me he was remembering the same things I was. "And it is a much better world than it was, at least in some places. But," said the old cop, "Studebaker was a good blackmail target right up until he danced out of the closet."

"Which he hadn't done yet."

"And, Christian, my experience in blackmail cases is that nothing is more dangerous than the moment when somebody has to decide."

"Yeah?"

"Yeah. Dangerous for everyone. The target might decide to just go public with whatever he's being blackmailed over—and that would definitely have been the smart play for Studebaker."

"Sure. Then he's free—and probably looking at better career options than he's had in years."

"It would be the smart play, but not the only one. He might also decide to kill the blackmailer."

"Or," I said, meeting Ed's canny gaze, "the blackmailer might decide to kill him to keep him quiet."

"Precisely."

"And if anyone thought things were skidding out of control…"

"Good old fashioned self-fulfilling prophecy." Ed watched Henry for a moment, smiling at my boy's intense and careful walk behind the giant dog. "And you can't discount the producer, either. He might just decide to get rid of everybody."

"Maguire's still here."

"Right now, he is." Ed shrugged. "I hope the New Haven cops are keeping a close eye on everyone involved in this cuchifrito. I wouldn't put anything past these Hollywood types."

Something in his voice tipped me off that there was a story here. "Really? What's wrong with movie folks?"

"Movie folks are squirrelly, Christian. Surely, you've figured that out by now."

"Well, I was warned about making sure I had an ironclad contract and staying at a distance by another professor who does a little consulting."

"And good thing." Ed smiled. Garrett had found the professor in question when I got my first movie offer. "But they're even weirder when they're actually doing the thing."

"You've been on shoots?" Several film companies did work in Connecticut on occasion. He might have done security for one.

"Yeah. This was years ago, and it was some big fancy top-of-the-line thing at the state capitol of all places."

"Tell me." I had never heard this story.

"Well, it was when I was in Major Crimes. But this was an all-hands-on-deck, so they took folks from every department. I was on the night shift, watching the set in the rotunda."

"And…"

"Director was a freak. It was some kind of political thriller thing, and the scene involved the guy and girl arguing. And he kept yelling at them, and at the guy to throw the girl around more, even hit her. He was enjoying it. Maybe – excited – by it." Ed squirmed a little, still uncomfortable all these years later. "I finally walked past a couple of assistants and told him that unless he wanted an assault charge he could darn well back off."

"Yikes." Ed would have done it, too.

"Of course, everyone acted like I was the one who was out of line." Grin. "But I never had to do a movie again."

"That's good anyhow."

"For everyone." Ed chuckled. "Hadn't thought of that night in years. But nobody's beating up a woman on my watch. Sorry."

I patted his arm. "Damn right."

"So anyway, what I'm getting at is that these people are squirrelly. They're different than we are." He watched Henry and Norm taking the turn for our street, surprisingly smoothly.

"Different, how?"

"Well, you and I would never be comfortable telling someone to beat somebody up. Especially not somebody vulnerable." He took a breath. "And we definitely wouldn't get a kick out of it."

"True. But that's just the show, the game."

"Is it? Your work shapes you, doesn't it? Mine certainly shaped me." Ed's wise gaze held mine.

"So you think they're capable of anything because they're movie people?"

"Nah." He shook his head. "I think you have to acknowledge that people who pretend for a living may look at truth and reality differently than we do. And that might inform their behavior."

"Inform their behavior?" I asked, smiling. "You've been living with a professor for a while, haven't you?"

"Sure have." He laughed. "Tell you a secret. Sometimes, I ask Garrett a question I have no real interest in having answered just to hear him talk. It's great to sit there and listen to him explain something or tell a story."

"There is something about a man with a voice," I admitted. And suddenly, out of nowhere, I was reminded of Joe Poli's silky voice, quoting Donne. I actually startled a little at the thought.

"Christian?"

"Um, nothing," I said quickly, trying to sound neutral.

Never try to hide anything from a cop.

"Are you thinking about a guy?"

"Maybe." My voice wobbled a bit.

"Good."

I stared, eyes wide. "Good?"

"Good. You could use some company. And that little fella needs a man in his life."

"He has two," I reminded him as Henry turned down our walk, dragged by Norm.

"Not the same thing, and you know it. If you find the right man, he'd be good for both of you."

"Maybe. It's big stuff, you know."

"I know." Ed shrugged. "But at least you know what you're looking for. When my wife died, I didn't know what the hell to do with myself."

I took his arm. Ed didn't talk about that part of his life very often, and I was starting to suspect that this whole Studebaker thing was bringing up a lot of emotions that Ed didn't usually discuss. Didn't really need to, because he'd worked through it. I waited.

"So I know a lot about having stuff to figure out," he continued. "It's not easy, but nothing worth having is."

"There's that."

We were silent for a few moments, comfortably watching Henry and Norm blasting fast—but not out of control—down the walk.

"You got a particular guy in mind?" Ed asked.

"Maybe. Don't want to say much more yet."

"That's fair. Takes a while to get off square one. Better if you do your stuff first, so you're not dumping it all in the other guy's lap."

"I think so, too."

"But don't let it be an excuse." Ed returned my sharp glance. "Easy to say you're working through stuff when you're really just scared."

"But I *am* scared."

"Scared is the human condition, Christian. You don't not love someone because you might lose them. You look the risk in the eye, accept it, and keep on walking."

For a moment, we were both silent. Talk about laying down the truth.

"I think you called it, Ed."

"Of course I did. I'm always right." He grinned and smacked my arm. "Anyway, young lady, it wouldn't hurt you to go out on a date once in a while. Garrett and I would be happy to babysit."

"If you call it baby-sitting to Henry's face, he'll kill you both."

"Deservedly." Ed laughed. "They're touchy when they're medium-sized like that. Have to maintain their space and dignity."

"That they do."

"Ma! Look!" Henry was on the front step doing a little victory dance. "I made it home with Norm! Walked him all by myself!"

"Yay, you!" I called and ran down the walk to hug him. And yes, sneak a quick look at his meter to make sure he wasn't dropping after all of that running.

Ed followed with a big smile of his own. "Yay, you too."

Chapter Fourteen

Love or Money

Next morning, I was almost not surprised to hear the doorbell and see Joe Poli walking into the foyer, maybe ten minutes after drop-off. It was actually one of my favorite moments of the day, when the building was still quiet, and the scent of the first pot of good coffee was starting to fill my office.

Really good coffee. I'd made some of that Italian dark roast, and damned if it didn't smell better than the stuff Jimmy sends.

"Hope I'm not intruding. Just wanted to give you a heads-up on a couple things."

"No intrusion at all." *Please invade my space. Often.* I shook that off and gave him a friendly smile. "As it happens, I've just started a pot of your coffee."

"It's probably not as good as yours, but it's Italian."

"Italian always wins in coffee." I returned his significant little glance. "In other things, too."

"You're—what? Irish?"

"Scotch-Irish Appalachian, thanks. I'm from Mars."

His eyes widened.

"Mars, Pennsylvania. Little Rust Belt town far enough outside

Pittsburgh to miss the revitalization."

"Long trip here, huh?"

"Pretty much." I met his gaze, now warmed with a little new admiration. "Not exactly a short trip from Wooster Street to Yale Law, either."

He blinked.

"You think your mom forgets you won a scholarship to Yale? *Your* mom?"

"Nah." He nodded. "She talked me up at pickup, didn't she?"

"She's a mom. Someday, I'll be kvelling about Henry." I patted his arm. "She's a pretty cool lady."

"Yeah, she is." His face warmed with pride. "Always behind me, usually pushing."

"Mine too. Now, I do it with Henry. Yay for parenting."

"Oh, yeah."

These morning coffees could become a habit, I thought as I got out the extra mug. After the excellent Italian roast coffee was duly poured and appreciated, I brought out the container of Tiffany's chocolate chippers and opened it, holding it out. "I didn't make them, a friend did, but they're terrific."

"I had oatmeal for breakfast. I'm trying to be good."

"Oh—sorry." I started to pull back.

He grabbed a cookie with a truly adorable bad little boy expression. "Not that good."

"Okay." I handed him a napkin for the cookie. (I'm not Martha Stewart, but kids eat in that office—the downside potential is just too major!)

"I wanted to tell you that you were right about the movie people. There *was* something bad there."

"What?"

"It's online now—and it'll be on TV by noon, but it looks like the assistant was trolling for young ladies. Telling them he could bring them to Brett and um, diverting them."

"Charges?"

"Not yet. Looks like everything was consensual but skeevy. A couple of the girls talked to some entertainment website."

"Ugh." I shuddered.

"Definitely, ugh." He shook his head. "I've always been a little protective of women—Italian, you know—but now that I have a daughter..."

I nodded. "Changes your perspective a little."

"A lot. Y'know, every creep says he can't possibly abuse women because he has a daughter, but the older Aly gets, the more I want to slug some of these guys."

His jaw was tight, and his hands clenched a little. Nothing better than a standup guy who wants to protect his women...especially if he's rational enough to know that's not usually an option.

"Anyhow," he said, letting out a breath, "exploitation is a red line for me. I'm taking a look, and if that guy puts one finger over the line—never mind anything else—he'll be making new friends in the lockup."

I nodded. "Works for me."

"Sorry, Dr. Shaw. I don't mean to come off-"

"You come off as a man who wants to make sure that women aren't abused. That's never a bad thing."

Joe smiled. "You get it."

"I'm blessed to have the senior division of the very same thing looking out for me." I returned the smile. "I sure do."

"The dads you should have had?"

"Got it in one." I'd used the expression to describe Ed and Garrett in my first conversation with Joe, and I was impressed he remembered. "Anyway, I'm not really surprised that the assistant was involved in something nasty."

"There's probably a lot of creeping on movie sets."

"Probably." I shrugged. "It's not routine to us, but I'd guess it's fairly common."

"Common but ugly," he agreed.

"Very ugly. Not to mention that I don't think Studebaker would have wanted them anyway."

"No?"

"No. My sources, who have a very good sense of this stuff, are pretty sure he was gay."

"If it's Ed and his husband, I'd absolutely trust them."

"I trust them with my kid, so I can trust them on this."

"Good point. So it looks like we can eliminate jealous husbands, too." Joe Poli said, taking a sip of his coffee and contemplating his cookie. "But what about someone on the down-low?"

I shook my head. "Haven't been watching the entertainment shows much, have you?"

"What do you mean?"

"Tiffany—EMT Medina's sister explained it to me, so it's not like I'm this big authority…"

"But…"

"At least one older male star has revived his career in recent years by coming out and very publicly living his truth."

"Was Studebaker planning to do that?"

"No idea. You'd have to ask someone closer to him."

"The assistant didn't seem to know?"

"It really never came up in discussion." I shook my head. "We had a strictly business relationship, even if the business included a lot of weird detail that made no sense to me."

"And he wouldn't have been telling just anyone. No insult."

"None taken." I enjoyed his trace of a smile. "Anyway, the point, according to Jenny, is that the whole down-low thing probably isn't a consideration. I wondered, too."

"I don't feel like such a bigot, then."

"It's a reasonable question. Just because you're fair and enlightened doesn't mean that the world is."

He drank a little coffee and absorbed that. Finally picked up that cookie. Disciplined rascal, isn't he?

"Poor Studebaker," I continued.

"What do you mean?"

"Well, not to get too academic on you, but there's this statement in Ancient Egyptian tomb paintings. The soul being judged makes a list of all the horrible things he *didn't* do – explaining why he deserves to go to heaven. Kind of like what we've learned about this guy."

Joe nodded. "He didn't #MeToo any groupies, he didn't grab random boys in a New Haven bar, he didn't even trick a woman into marrying him…he actually tried to be a decent guy. Even if he was a pain in the backside."

"He was trying too hard. I should have seen it, but there's a lot of noise with movie stars."

"Sure is. I thought about #MeToo, and then when that was off the table, to his orientation. Bugs me that I'm not nearly as enlightened as I thought I was."

"You married your sister and her wife," I reminded him.

"Yeah." He smiled for a moment because he had to have figured out how I knew, but his face quickly clouded again. "And I still went right to the old anti-gay stuff with this guy. I need to think about this a lot, later."

"Later."

"Yeah, because I'm still not sure how we're going to figure out what happened here." He *finally* took a bite of his cookie. "Wow."

"In addition to being a crack EMT, Tiffany is an incredible baker."

"I want the recipe."

"You bake?"

"You know my mother." A knowing smile and more bites of cookie before he continued. "She made sure I could take care of myself. Don't marry some fool because you can't make your own cookies."

"Sounds like her."

"Absolutely." He savored the last bite, considered another cookie, and thought better of it.

"Well, this will probably sound like her, too," I said, topping off his coffee cup. "Sex is nice, but money will kill you every time."

Joe smiled. A different smile than I'd seen before, something naughty and appealing gleaming in his eyes. *Hey, now.*

I wasn't sure I remembered *Hey, now.*

"As a motive, I mean," I clarified quickly.

For a moment, he just twinkled at me over his coffee cup. I wouldn't have been surprised to see glitter drifting through the air, things suddenly felt so magical.

"You're right. Sex *is* very nice." Just enough of a pause that I knew it wasn't an accident. "But money is a terrific motive for murder. I wonder if I've been looking in the wrong direction. Time for me to spend a few hours combing over the financials."

"Good thought," I agreed, hoping I wasn't blushing.

"So as much as I would like to stay here and enjoy the best coffee outside my own kitchen..."

"I understand completely."

For a moment, our eyes held, acknowledgment that there was a hell of a lot going on here.

"Good. I'd hate to offend you, Dr. Shaw."

Somehow, the formal address was cuter than if he'd called me by name. I cleared my throat. "Take some cookies with you. Tiffany made a huge batch, and I don't want too many around with Henry."

"Yes, please." His tone was matter-of-fact, not making a big deal about Henry, just accepting it as part of life. Which, of course, it is, even if a lot of people don't get that.

A few minutes later, as we stood at the door with him holding his little plastic container of cookies, he turned back to me before he opened the door.

"Thanks for the cookies and the ideas, Dr. Shaw."

"You're quite welcome, Counselor."

"I might still need a bit more information one of these days."

"You're always welcome, and there's always good coffee."

"Nice to—"

"Young man, kindly get out of my way."

The sharp voice was a good foot below his chin. We both looked down to see Mae Tillotson marching up to the door.

"Oh, sorry, ma'am." Joe held the door for her and—well over her head—cut his eyes to me with a little twinkle. "Have a good day, Dr. Shaw."

"You too."

No need for him to know he was probably the highlight of my day.

Chapter Fifteen

Just More Stuff

"Who is *that?*" Mae asked as she walked in. I knew from the way she'd watched Studebaker and looked at the occasional strapping deliveryman that she had an eye for the boys, and of course, Joe Poli was definitely worth a look.

"Assistant State's Attorney Joe Poli. You might know his mom, Lidia—she goes to Star of the Sea."

"State's Attorney?" Mae's face tightened a little, but then she sighed. "Too bad. Way he was dressed, I thought he might be some rich guy looking to make a nice contribution for the tax deduction."

I shook my head. Even in the presence of masculine appeal, Mae *would* revert back to her default setting: fundraising is all. "No, he's still tying up loose ends from the Studebaker thing. But if he comes back, you should pitch him."

"Loose ends?"

I was already turning back to my office, my mind on neatening up the coffee mugs before the daily drip of eighth-graders working on local history projects distracted me. Nothing worse than having to wash the mug before you can have coffee. "Oh, just stuff."

Only later would I think that I should have had my attention on Mae and not the coffee mugs.

Mae went up to the second floor to continue the fourth-grader-proofing of the building, and I settled into a morning of paperwork. You'd be surprised at how much record-keeping is involved in even a very small private non-profit...especially if the private non-profit often accepts donations that are not cash, but have considerable value—like old stuff. Our accountant, G-d love her, does most of it for her own tax deduction, but I still have to make sure everything gets to her in apple-pie order.

I was writing up the donation acceptance record for what started out as somebody's great-grandmother's hideous wedding china, but was now a pretty impressive artifact because it was a hundred and fifty years old. It was also a complete set, which *never* happens with things that old. After a little time online, with museums and eBay—just about everything turns up there eventually—I came up with a reasonable number for the value and finished the form. I was moving on to the next form, an easier and faster one for a pile of old sheet music, when the mail carrier came.

Amara Bowen had graduated from the Wheatley pickup pen to middle school a year ago, but she was still a pal. She handed me a pile of envelopes and a medium-sized box with a chuckle.

"More stuff?"

"Oh, probably. People sometimes just send things out of the blue because they figure we'd want it."

The chuckle became a laugh. "Anything to get it out of the house, probably."

"Yes indeed." I laughed, too, but did not tell Amara the very quiet truth that every donation does not end up on display. Some, like most of that sheet music, end up in our archive files in the basement. And if we have duplicates of things, we'll sell them on E-Bay, of course, without being too specific as to where we got them, so no donors feel slighted. The money goes into the general fund, so they're still helping the Society, just in a slightly different way.

Once in a while, we get things that are so completely wrong for us and so completely unusable they end up at Goodwill. And you can be sure I never tell *anyone* that.

"How's Henry?" Amara asked.

"Wonderful. Terrifying. I hope he still likes me when he rules the world. How's Mali?"

"Pretty much the same."

We shared a parental laugh, and she went on to the next stop. I went back to my desk and riffled through the envelopes, none of which looked like much of anything, thankfully, then turned to the package.

It was a patient belongings box from Yale-New Haven Hospital, which was weird enough. Maybe a doc or staffer borrowed one because they didn't have the right size mailer at home? Just in case it was actually something important, I put on gloves before I picked up my miniature Scottish dirk letter opener and sliced the packing tape.

When I lifted the flap, the smell almost knocked me over.

Alcohol. Something of the whiskey family mixed with some strange chemical undertone.

That was weird enough, and then I looked down into the box to see dark metal. The Reverend's tankard.

I looked at the box again. Yale-New Haven was where they'd taken Studebaker and where he died. It must have gone with him. But then why send it back to me?

Surely, it would have made more sense to hand it over to the cops.

There was a form slipped down the side of the box, listing the Society as the owner of a piece of patient property that was now being returned. Why was I not surprised Yale had a form for everything? It still didn't make sense. The thing was evidence...wasn't it?

Well, I could find that out, anyway.

I had Joe Poli's number somewhere in my phone, and I rummaged it up, sending him a quick text to let him know the tankard was now in my hands. I didn't really want to call him because it felt personal and bother-y.

He texted right back: *Don't touch it, and lock it up. I don't know if I'm going to need it.*

Will do.

I owe you a bottle of wine. What do you like?

Well, then. I was glad he wasn't there, because I could feel a huge, horrible blush creeping over my face. *Not necessary, but Chianti is always a winner.*

Always.

I admit I waited maybe thirty seconds to see if he'd follow that by offering to help me drink it, but he didn't. No points off, I reminded myself, he's at work.

I re-closed the box and locked it in the secure drawer of my filing cabinet, then took off the gloves. It could wait for now. I had forms to fill out—and soon, to start prep for the Invasion of the Fourth-Graders.

Mae stuck her head in the door a few minutes after I finished with the tankard and returned to documenting the value of the sheet music. (Usually not much, since there was a lot of it, and plenty has survived. Most of the time, it's only valuable if the song is special for some reason.)

"How are you doing today, dear?" she asked.

"Just fine. How is your arm?"

"Healing beautifully. A silly gardening mishap, but one can't be too careful with a deep cut. Tetanus lives in soil, you know."

I did. And any number of grisly tales of what it did before vaccines, none of which Mae needed to hear. "Very true. Glad you are okay. Would you like coffee – or some of Tiffany's cookies?"

"Coffee would be quite nice. You've made more?"

119

I laughed. "I always make more. Black?"

"As the good Lord intended."

We shared a laugh. Mae, like many of the docents, is the very personification of the no-nonsense New Englander.

As I handed her the cup, I noticed her earrings, a pair of those very nice *Girl with a Pearl Earring* designs from the Met catalog. I'd been thinking about upping my accessory game in recent months, and I'd always liked the look. "Are those earrings really heavy?"

She looked surprised. "What? Oh—these. A gift from my daughter-in-law. Thought I would try them."

"Right. You usually wear plain studs like I do, right?"

A pause, and then she nodded quickly. "Diamonds. George gave them to me on our tenth anniversary."

I managed a small smile. My own diamond studs were also an anniversary gift. Our fifth. Frank and I didn't get ten. I took a breath, pulled back to the conversation. "I've been thinking about doing a little more in the earring department. Are those uncomfortable?"

She touched one gently. "Not especially. They're glass pearls, so not as light as some, but small enough to be tolerable...at least most of the time."

"Thanks." I took a sip of my coffee. "Thinking about a change."

"Not a bad idea for a young thing like you."

"Not that young."

"Young enough that you shouldn't wear the same things the same way forever." Her gaze sharpened in a way that suggested a lecture was coming. "Queen Elizabeth always wore the same outfit she did when she was thirty. The rest of us don't have to."

"Good point."

She looked me over, assessing. "I'd go hoops, though, if I were you."

"You would?"

"Small ones, maybe with a little sparkle to pick up those pins you wear."

I nodded, but whatever I might have said was drowned out by the ringing phone, as the latest wave of nervous field trip planners began. I would be really, really glad to see the backs of those kids. Even more so their chaperones.

Chapter Sixteen

Takes Direction Well

By pickup time, the sun was shining, and a wonderful, warm afternoon was underway. One that Tiffany would not get to enjoy for a while; her last call before the end of the shift turned out to be an Advanced Life Support run from Shady Rest to Yale. Which meant I was picking up Ava and (I hoped!) that Jorge was pouring Tiffany a good glass of wine later.

On the way out the door, I was slipping my phone back in my jacket pocket after texting back and forth with Tiffany, when I wasn't even a little surprised to see Garrett on the Green with Norm. I was surprised, though, by his first question.

"So, did you see what they're saying about the movie on social media today?"

"No…"

He shook his head. "You know, you could get a lot of positive attention for the Society with a Facebook page and the occasional post about things."

"I post not, neither do I spin."

"Nice biblical riff." Garrett chuckled. "But seriously, you should at least dabble a little. You don't have to go nuts. Just know what's going on out there."

"Maybe." This was not a new conversation. I associated social media with Flutter mobs canceling various projects that did not pass their particular political or societal muster and gratuitous personal abuse. But Garrett kept telling me that there were actually plenty of kind humans online, many of whom were just waiting for a chance to help a good cause, like, say, the Society.

I still wasn't sure I believed him.

"That's for another day," he continued. "Sooner or later, I will get you into social. You could just post pictures of interesting objects from the Society. Call yourself Dr. Stuff. It might be fun."

"Dr. Stuff?"

"Maybe Professor Stuff. Anyway, if you had troubled to maintain a presence, you would know that Flutter blew up today."

"Is that good or bad?"

"Very good for people who like to watch social...very bad for the movie."

Norm stopped to menace a squirrel, and we shared a light laugh.

As we went on, so did Garrett. "It's pretty much what I thought would happen...but with help from the director and costar."

"Really?"

"Oh yeah. A little background first. Remember I told you social media was wondering about her—Olivia Carr, the young British actress?"

"She left for the Royal Shakespeare Company."

"*You* know that, but apparently, plenty of folks weren't too sure that was all there was to it."

"Right." I nodded.

"Some of the comments centered on the idea that the movie was the epitome of the Bad Old Days."

"All about the guy and his experience...the woman as an appendage or stock character."

A wry, wise grin from Garrett. "Yep. Well, social media's been lit up with mourning for poor Studebaker for a couple of days, and with that, the occasional snarky shot toward the girl. At one point, there was even a hashtag #where'sOlivia."

"The thing where a lot of people are talking about it, right?"

"Yes, dear. You really—"

"I know what it is. I don't need to get involved in it."

Garrett smiled as we turned down to the Wheatley traffic circle. We had at least ten minutes before Henry would appear, and we took a bench just outside the playground. I didn't really need it, but I joined Garrett so we could talk.

"So, the hashtag?" I asked.

"Well, Olivia had finally had enough. She posted back, 'I left for the Royal Shakespeare Company. I'd rather play Ophelia than the Adulteress. Shakespeare – FIVE HUNDRED YEARS AGO – gave women more agency."

"Uh-oh."

"Oh, yeah. It was on. Lots of support for her and lots of anger at the movie people. They started with the director."

"Him?" I shook my head. "I think he was on a plane before they even pronounced Studebaker."

"Not the guy. The original director. Ellen DeWise."

"They started with Ellen DeWise, and they ended up with the scriptwriter?" Even I knew who Ellen DeWise was. Only the second or third woman to be nominated for the Best Director Oscar.

"Ellen DeWise left the project just before the shoot. Apparently, she wanted nothing to do with it, but also didn't want to ruin Studebaker's comeback because he was a friend."

"Yeah. They were in that teen detention movie when she was a young actress."

Garrett nodded. The movie, though it was a document of a generation and constantly playing on some channel somewhere, was well beyond his interest. "And now, as you know, she's considered a woman's director and actually gets films made her way."

"True."

"So when she saw Olivia Carr complaining, she wasn't going to be blamed for it."

I nodded. "I sure wouldn't."

"Right. Now she jumps in, posting that she bailed on the movie because she just couldn't make it the way Holman and the screenwriter imagined it."

"Makes sense."

"And now, we have a lovely hornet's nest of furious flutters downing on the movie, and Holman and powerful Hollywood men in general." He shrugged. "Telling us exactly what we need to know about the movie."

"Right." I patted Norm and shared a grim nod with Garrett. "That movie was a disaster waiting to happen."

"And it's also becoming pretty clear that Brett Studebaker isn't Elvis."

"Elvis?"

"You know, death as a good career move."

"It does work for a lot of stars."

"Not this guy, apparently." Garrett shrugged. "Before today's donnybrook, the tributes and all were tapering off, and it was pretty clear to me that it would be down to the occasional sad emoji soon."

"Emojis." I smiled. "Henry loves those."

"So do I."

I sighed. "I do need to figure out this online mess, don't I?"

"You surely do. If an old Lincoln scholar can do it, so can you."

The first buzzer rang inside the building.

A clatter of heels behind me. "Oh, Christian! And Professor Kenney, how nice to see you!"

Sally is aggressively nice to Garrett and Ed because it makes her feel like she is a good, open-minded citizen. Ed completely ignores her beyond a nod, much the same as Tiffany does.

"Nice to see you, sweetie." Garrett does his best Charles Nelson Reilly with her, because it amuses him.

Ruby and Lidia were walking up, too, and they exchanged eye-rolls with Garrett. Ruby and Garrett know each other from doing story-time at the Town Library, and Garrett goes to the same Mass as Lidia at Star of the Sea. Not to mention seeing each other in the pen, so they're all acquainted.

In case you're wondering, Garrett, Lidia, and most of the other Catholics in town go to services because of Father Dan, not Mother Church. Father Dan, like Dina, is one of those rare people who really feel the call and let G-d work through them. It's actually pretty amazing that we have two of them in Unity. Ultimate endorsement: Ed, who flatly refuses to darken the door of a church, has coffee with Father Dan a couple times a month.

"Enjoying the spring, Professor?" Sally asked Garrett.

"Oh, yes. I'm waiting for the new white lilac I put in last year to bloom…I may actually get some flowers this year."

"*Fab*-ulous!" cooed Sally.

They launched into a discussion of gardening that was well beyond anything I was interested in, leaving Lidia and Ruby and I to talk amongst ourselves.

"How's my nephew doing?" Ruby asked.

"I'm thinking of sabotaging his dissertation so he never leaves."

She laughed. "He's a good fella."

"That he is."

"The little old ladies are sometimes a bit much for him, though."

Something in her tone made me look sharply at her. It reminded me of the time when I'd had to send Faith and Lewis down to the Coffee Stop to work it out. I wondered if there was somebody else who needed a little help mixing with people who weren't like them.

Ruby shook her head. "Nothing bad. They're just all apparently working on strange little projects."

I chuckled, as much relieved as amused. "That's true. A couple of them write articles on various aspects of local history and post on social media or wherever."

"Apparently, one's been making him go through the sheet music looking for a song her mother taught her. And another had him climb up on a shelf and bring down a bunch of bottles."

Well, that explained the bottles I found in the workroom the other day. With a few exceptions, the docents are quite small and probably too old to be comfortable climbing up on stepstools, not that they'd ever admit it. As for the sheet music, we did have a truly impressive collection, thanks to a donation from the great-grandchildren of a vaudeville pianist. So Lewis and I both ended up in the downstairs storeroom a couple times a week tracking down some lyric that someone remembered hearing from a long-dead relative.

"Tell him not to be a hero, if you see him before I do." I smiled at Ruby. "I'll take the next sheet music run."

She joined the smile. "I think he's really just stressing about the school stuff. He has a lot of work to do this summer."

"I bet he does." I shook my head. "That last summer before my dissertation was awful."

"Poor kid," Lidia agreed. "Nice, hard-working guy."

"So nice," I said. "I am going to miss him when he finishes the doctorate, and somebody snaps him up."

"...no, dear, I really don't think you want striped petunias. They're so *flashy*."

I couldn't help turning, and neither could Lidia and Ruby, as Garrett shot us a little glance that Sally never saw.

"Well, maybe those nice purple ones."

"Much better choice." Garrett leaned over and patted my arm. "Christian here really needs to up her garden game."

I met his gaze with a lightly raised brow he knew well. "Might need to do a little digging in the backyard."

He laughed. "That's what Ed says."

Ruby, Lidia, and I got it. Sally just looked puzzled.

Probably a very good thing that the bell rang just then.

Chapter Seventeen

Lunch Ladies

Thursday midday found me with my fiber artists and the clothing collection again. The collar had inspired bride-to-be Allie to make some kind of embellishment for her gown that she could pass on to her eventual daughter, and when she shared the idea with the others, they wanted to work on it, too. So they came to the Society to look through some of our pieces for ideas.

As it happened, we had a surprisingly good collection of wedding gowns for a small museum. Wedding dresses often survive in close to their original form because they're special and usually much nicer than anything else a woman owns, though they can be re-worn by later relatives, or altered for another use if not white.

Often, they're not. The extremely expensive white gown that many, if not most, even relatively well-off brides consider their due now has only been around for about a century and a half. Even in the late 1800s, a middle-class bride might well have chosen a "best dress" in a color other than white because she wanted something she could use again.

Not to mention second marriages. Death rates were still much higher than we're used to, so a youngish widow like me didn't stand out as much, and most of those women usually remarried. When they did, it was in a simple ceremony in a pretty—but definitely *not* white—dress.

All of that to say, we have pieces and full dresses from about a dozen and a half wedding gowns in a nearly 200-year range. The oldest one is an embroidered bodice from the 1830s, which was once pale blue and decorated with lovely forget-me-nots. The newest is somebody's aunt's extravaganza from the 1980s.

(Yeah, I know. It's not even close to our time period, but the aunt's daughter died before she could wear it, and then the aunt died herself from a different and equally nasty form of cancer. The family wanted the dress to survive, and how was I going to say no to that? *Someday,* it will be an antique.)

For Allie and her friends, I'd brought out the forget-me-not bodice, an 1880s silk gown with an amazingly embellished bustle skirt, a frilly turn-of-the-century Gibson Girl style with ribbons and lace, and a beaded satin number from the late 1910s. I made a little bet with myself as to which one they'd take; I know my artists pretty well.

Allie got there first, all lit up with excitement that had little to do with the wedding and everything to do with seeing the dress collection. I felt the same; I was thrilled they'd given me the excuse to rummage in the collection. Wedding dresses are special in another way; if ordinary clothes often have some kind of special resonance for the wearer, wedding dresses seem to shimmer with her dreams and hopes.

Especially since we know how things can really turn out.

"Wow!" Allie said, bending down for a closer look at the dresses laid out on the work table. "They're so pretty."

"Just like now, women liked to go a little wild with their wedding dresses if they could."

"Maybe a little too wild." Deborah chuckled as she walked in, pointing to the 1880s bustle dress, which I'd set up on a form so they could get the full effect of the embellishments.

"This one's a bit much," I agreed, "but the work is gorgeous, and you might get some ideas for motifs. I'm NOT suggesting you copy the style."

"Poor Allie would drown in it." Bethany was chuckling, too, and I could see her relax as she left whatever was happening at Town Hall for the moment.

Deborah looked to her. "Still getting all those requests from the nursing home company?"

Bethany sighed and nodded. "They keep asking for more information on surrounding parcels. Either they're expanding their plan, or they have no idea what they're doing."

"My money's on don't know what they're doing." Deborah shook her head. "That bunch has been trying to expand for a long time, and it never seems to work out."

"No?" I asked. I vaguely remembered one previous expansion effort a few years ago, but no details.

"No." A sigh. "It's not that we couldn't use a larger and more advanced facility for seniors in town. The demographics are definitely on their side. The problem is, they're a small, rather sloppily-run company and never line everything up before they move."

"So they make everyone in the neighborhood crazy," Allie put in, "and then nothing happens. My aunt and uncle live a couple blocks away, and they were scared enough to put their house on the market right after the crash."

"Ugh." Bethany shook her head. "That's exactly how it happens. Wherever I go, people are asking me what I know about this thing, and there are no good answers, because they're so slipshod."

We shared a scowl. All of us are extremely precise people who have no patience for any form of laziness.

"Well," Deborah said, turning to the table, "I think we have much better things to talk about right now."

Allie beamed. "I think we do."

"Definitely. Let's find something special for our little bride." Bethany smiled at her pals, and I held out the gloves.

For the next half hour, it was all about the stuff. The creamy silks, the faded threads, the tiny, careful stitches. If you know how to look at it, and we do, you can see the evidence of an individual person in the way the stitches are placed and the motifs are set. Each little flower or bead is in a particular place for a reason, usually from some design in the maker's mind, and it shows how she worked, what she thought was important, and what she wanted to emphasize.

We went through each of the pieces, looking for ideas, ooh'ing and ah'ing at the quality of the work, and enjoying the beauty of things that aren't—that really can't be—made anymore.

Finally, Deborah's cell phone chimed a warning that they were nearly out of time, and all of us pulled back from the worktable with a sigh.

"Good ideas?" I asked.

They smiled.

"I think I know which one I like best," Allie said.

"So do I." Deborah and Bethany weren't trying for unison, but it happened that way.

"So…" I waited for the answer to my little bet with myself.

They all pointed to the forget-me-not bodice.

I grinned. I'd guessed right.

"You thought it would be the one." Bethany returned the grin.

"Sure did."

Allie gently touched the little blossoms. "I like the idea of putting the flowers around the neckline like this—my dress is a very simple A-line, so we can add it."

"And we could even put in a few iridescent beads like the 1910s one, if you wanted." Deborah nodded to the other dress, which had impressed them because of the intricate and careful beading.

"I like that. Maybe very pale blue for luck." Allie nodded.

"Not too much, just enough," Bethany said.

"Exactly." Allie beamed.

"Well, I need to get back to Town Hall," Deborah said. "Can we get a pattern of this?"

"I'll take a photo, and I'll use the software that lets me print up a tracing." I'd done it before, though never for something so important. Bethany nodded. "That'll work."

"Oh, I love it!" Allie looked one more time at the bodice. "What a wonderful thing to bring down the aisle with me."

Deborah and Bethany gave me a sadder-but-wiser glance, but we all smiled at Allie. Life was going to teach her the tough stuff soon enough. She didn't need us raining on her parade.

At the door, Bethany was the last one out, and I patted her on the arm. "Good luck with that nursing home mess."

"I will probably have a voicemail box full of upset neighbors. You know, I've even heard from a few of your folks."

I blinked. At least two volunteers besides Mae lived within a couple of blocks of the Shady Rest, since it was in the nicer part of town. I knew she couldn't tell me who, but I wondered what she *was* trying to tell me.

"Can't say much, but you'd probably spread a good bit of peace of mind if you mentioned around the place that you've heard the latest project at the Shady Rest isn't any better organized than the last one."

"Just a mention." I returned Bethany's small smile.

"Exactly."

"Funny what comes up between the old sheet music and Mason jars some days, isn't it?" A shared nod.

"Sure is."

Chapter Eighteen

A Good Talk

I t didn't hit me until after I'd snapped the picture of the forget-me-not dress and carefully wrapped the gowns in old cotton sheets, placing them back in their acid-free boxes. I'd moved three of the four back downstairs and was finishing up with the last one when the realization seeped through.

I hadn't thought about my own wedding once.

Let's keep it that way, I firmly reminded myself, even as I caught myself turning my wedding ring. It was a simple gold band; Frank knew I used my hands a lot in my work, and he'd wanted me to have something I could wear and not worry about. Something I wouldn't feel I had to take off.

And never would.

A hole opened up in my gut, as I remembered Frank trying three times to break the napkin-wrapped glass and finally *jumping* on it, then later yelling at his aunt at the reception because she'd used a real, if cheap, glass instead of the usual lightbulb. It's much easier to break and makes a nice big boom…but Aunt Mol hadn't darkened the door of a temple in decades and had no idea.

Dina still laughs when I tell her the story.

But I wasn't laughing just then.

I took a breath, smoothed down the gown in the last box, and gently settled the lid on it. My gown was in the shed with my extra vintage shirts, waiting for a possible granddaughter now. After Henry was born, Frank teased me every spring-cleaning season that we weren't going to need it, and I should just give it to charity. He'd say he hoped some deserving girl would get to be as beautiful and happy as I was.

Dammit. That's the suck about grief. You never know when it's going to come after you.

"Christian—" Faith saw my face as she walked into the workroom.

"Um, hi—you and Lewis can take over the table now." I picked up the last box.

"Thanks." She held my gaze. "Wedding gowns?"

"Yeah. It's a little…"

She patted my arm. "You don't know this because I don't talk about it, but I was married before."

"Oh."

"As it happened, he died in a stupid car crash, too. But we'd only been married six months, and I didn't have to bury the father of my child. Can't imagine that."

"Oh."

"Honey, you're doing great most days. Teaching the master class, actually. It's okay when stuff gets to you. It should."

"I know." I nodded, took a breath.

"Things get me even now. I didn't tell you about this because I didn't want to go there, as Lewis would say." Her voice was a little tight, and her eyes too bright.

I managed a smile. "Thanks."

"Glad to." She smiled, too. "Just have to keep going."

"Yep."

"Might want to let Joe Poli keep coming around, too."

My jaw dropped. There are no secrets in a small town, but still. "It's just-"

"It's not, and that's good. You could do a lot worse. And he deserves someone who wants him and not his checkbook."

"Oh?"

"Amber's mother goes to my church." The fact that she didn't call the woman a friend was significant. "The family is like that. Very caught up in status and stuff. In the showy sense. Amber couldn't understand the concept of enough money. Which Joe has, by the way."

"None of my business," I said quickly.

"Of course not, but it doesn't hurt." Faith smiled a little. "But it was too bad watching Amber leave, and her mother act like Joe was a horrible person because he wanted to do something good."

"That would be awful." I nodded. "I think he's a pretty good guy."

"He is, and a good dad to the girl, too. Aly, I think."

"Yes—she was Henry's Mentor Buddy at Wheatley, though I don't remember much about her. Henry does."

Faith chuckled. "Henry remembers everything. He once asked me why I was wearing my watch on the opposite wrist. I'd cut myself gardening, but what kid notices that?"

"My kid."

We shared a grin. Faith has two adult sons and a bunch of adorable grandchildren.

"Anyway, Joe Poli is definitely a good guy. And definitely single."

I took a breath. It would not have been kind to Faith to ask her to back off, especially after what she'd just revealed about her own life.

"New Hampshire!" Lewis walked in, saving me from further matchmaking.

"Hey!" She grinned and moved on to fun with her friend.

I was happy to leave them, and not just for the obvious reason; my phone was buzzing with a text from Tiffany. Another late run, and could I get both kids?

Could and glad to.

A couple of hours later, my pickup alarm went off as I was getting into a box of sheet music for another of those old song requests. At the door, Faith and Mae were talking, one leaving, one arriving.

"...and I cannot believe that the whole Shady Rest mess is back again." Mae sounded annoyed, not especially threatened. Still, I remembered that Bethany had said a couple of my folks were worried, and this seemed like an ideal opportunity to spread the word.

"I don't know what you're hearing," I started, making both turn to me.

"Oh?" Mae asked. Of course, everyone at the Society knows the Town Hall folks come here, so they know the info should be good.

"Can't tell you much, but I'm hearing that this new project isn't any better-organized or likely to go ahead than any other one."

"Really." Faith smiled. "Trudy will be glad to hear that."

"Trudy?" I asked. Trudy Wallens, a retired elementary principal, lived on the other side of town.

"Her mother's house is half a block down from the Shady Rest. The family hasn't sold it, even though it's been a couple of years."

"Why on earth not?" Mae asked.

"Not sure. None of my business. But she mentioned that she was afraid the whole Shady Rest mess would ruin everything."

"Maybe not," I said. "I really don't know much, but it doesn't sound like it's a very organized project."

"It is not a very organized business, so I'm not surprised," Mae observed with a twist to her mouth.

"But isn't there a lot of state oversight?" I asked, as it occurred to me that these disorganized people were in charge of some very vulnerable, frail elders.

"Of course." Faith patted my arm. "And the actual director of the place, Marge Ellison, is sharp as a tack. It's the people who own the company who are fools."

"Ah." I shook my head. "A lot of that going around."

"In the business world?" Faith, who'd spent much of her life watching her insurance-exec husband straighten out other people's messes, just chuckled. "You don't even want to know."

"Well," Mae said, "I need to find Lewis and take a good look at a couple more of those jars."

"Oh, yes," I said. "Those tonics and whatnot."

"Yes. You wouldn't believe what the young ladies used to do for beauty. I find the current fad for lasers almost soothing."

Fortunately, I had to get to Wheatley. I did not want to know what Mae might do with a laser.

Chapter Nineteen

Afterschool Special

School pickup is the great equalizer. No matter how great you think you are and how organized you may even be, there will be days you're running just that minute or so late and end up sprinting in like some sort of disheveled maniac.

These, of course, are always the days that Sally Birdwell is standing under the portico comparing notes with one of her besties about the best shade of beige for her mani.

And, of course, this was one of those days. Thanks to talking with the ladies, I needed every bit of my speed and determination to get there even close to time, and I still skidded in just as the kids ran down the hall. Sally, because she's Sally, marked my appearance with a fake-friendly smile that told me she was taking considerable pleasure in watching me flap around like some giant messy stork.

Fortunately, Lidia and Ruby were there too.

Lidia gave me a grin and a little "slow down" gesture. "It's fine."

"One of those days."

"Aren't they all?" Ruby chuckled. "We're all scrambling most of the time."

"...and I really prefer the matte to the shimmer..."

Some trick of the acoustics in the portico sent Sally's coo right to us, and the three of us shared a laugh.

"Most of us are, anyhow," Ruby said. "Hey, did you see the news this morning?"

"No—I usually watch it for the weather, but I overslept."

"I didn't catch it all, but it sounds like they announced that the movie shoot is over in town."

Lidia nodded. "Said they were leaving for good."

"That's a good thing," I said. "And not a surprise. The church scene was the last shoot."

"Why bother to announce it, then?" Ruby asked.

"Look like they're doing something in response to Studebaker's death, maybe?" I shrugged. "Nothing I can think of."

"Probably trying to look nice." Lidia shrugged. "Movie folks care about that whole image thing, right?"

"Yep." I nodded and waved to Henry and Ava, who were barreling my way. But I had another idea, too, which I didn't have time to discuss with Ruby and Lidia. An announcement like that would be a really good way to lay the groundwork for canceling the whole movie. Which might be what they really wanted to do, considering.

As I signed both kids out and enjoyed a nice tackle-hug from Henry, I thought about what Garrett had told me about the production and how it looked like it was going in exactly the wrong direction for the times. I wondered what the cancellation would do for the finances of everyone involved.

Not that I had a lot of time to think between herding those kids to the Society, getting them settled, and returning to the mess of my actual job, namely the current wild-goose chase through the sheet music.

The little angels were (temporarily) full of nutritious snacks and busy with homework by the time Tiffany arrived, her face a little tight and a trace of circles under her normally enviably bright eyes.

"Hey. Coffee's fresh," I said, putting down the pile of sheet music I was cataloging.

"Hey." She shrugged. "Think I'd rather have wine, but coffee will get me to wine o'clock."

I poured two cups as Tiffany slipped in my office for a moment and planted a kiss on Ava's head, in absolute affront to medium-sized kid dignity.

I knew what it meant.

"How old?"

"I'm such a mom." Sheepish shrug, faint smile. "Sixteen, actually. Fool drove his dad's Porsche into a pole. Girl with him had brown eyes."

Like Ava's. "Ah."

"Both going to be okay, but you know."

"Yeah. Some days hit harder than others." I held out the mug.

"That they do." She sat down in one of the workroom chairs, stretched a little, and took a sip.

I took one of the other chairs and just waited. Sometimes, she needed to talk it out a bit, and no wonder.

"Anyhow," she said, shaking it off slightly, "it was a pretty straightforward thing, just ugly. Not like the mess with Studebaker. Can you believe I'm *still* doing paperwork?"

"Really?"

"Really. Another post-incident report today." She drank more coffee. "There's going to be some kind of lawsuit."

"As soon as someone figures out who to sue and how." I shook my head. "Good luck with that."

"Yep. And good luck to the M.E. figuring out what happened to him."

"What do you mean? I thought it was a head injury."

"I don't think that's all it was. Remember how weird he was acting before he fell?"

"I figured drunk."

Tiffany shook her head. "Way he stopped breathing all of a sudden, I thought maybe some kind of drug. We gave him Narcan, because that's pretty standard now."

"Makes sense. Probably can't hurt, might help."

"Right. But it did nothing. We kept working on him, kept him going until we got there...and they hooked him right up to life support, but..."

She trailed off, took another long sip.

"So not an opiate." I drank a little of mine. "Somebody like him, who knows? Could have been into literally anything."

"Doesn't even have to be a drug. Some of those supplements and nutritional things, and all of that woo-hoo stuff they're into out in Hollywood—gonna be a puzzle for the M.E."

"But you guys did all you could," I reminded her. Between the kids in the crash and losing Studebaker earlier in the week, she might be feeling a little rough. It happened sometimes.

"Yeah, I know. But still. All I want is family dinner, a long bath... maybe curl up extra tight with Jorge."

"Just what you need." I agreed.

It was only after we'd both taken another long sip of coffee and the comfortable silence settled back between us that she looked up at me, eyes sharp.

"Sorry, Christian. I just realized what I said."

"Stop." I patted her arm. "I'm not so busy being poor Mrs. Widow that I can't wish you well. I really hope not."

Tiffany nodded. "I know, I just—"

"It's fine. I'm glad you have Jorge on nights like this. Really glad."

"Okay." She took another deep sip of coffee and studied me, thought about it, and then went ahead. "You know, you've been working through it, and it's been a while…"

"I'm kind of thinking about someone."

"Joe Poli."

"Yeah."

"If you're gonna, you could do a lot worse."

"I've heard that."

She smiled a little. "He's busy like us, so he's probably not going to be in any hurry."

"Hadn't thought of that," I admitted. "How does it work, anyhow?"

"What?"

"You know, going out, the getting started thing?"

She laughed, an uproarious, wonderful howl. "You think I know?"

"Maybe? You're younger than me."

"Oh, honey. I started dating Jorge when we were both in college. I haven't been on a first date since I was twenty."

"Guess you're not the one to ask, then." I started laughing, too.

"Maybe you ask Dina."

"She's been married since the 90s."

"Do we even know anyone…" Tiffany broke off in another laugh. "We are truly sad."

"Maybe I ask Garrett and Ed?"

"Maybe." She drank the last of her coffee. "Or maybe you just let it happen and figure it out when you get there."

"I could do that. If he's interested, does he formally ask me out? Or is there some other thing?"

"I think adults still go out. You're not kids hooking up at the Student Union, after all."

We shared another laugh at *that* thought.

Tiffany looked down into the empty mug. "I definitely don't want more to conflict with the wine."

"No."

"I could have Jorge find out what men do these days. Ask his pals at the house how guys make the first move so you know what to expect."

I finished the last of my coffee. "That might help. Might give Jorge a good laugh, too."

"Not the worst thing ever." She grinned.

"Nope."

Chapter Twenty

Look for the Union Label

Thursday evening found Henry and me relaxing at home, him enjoying some extra video game time, me working on a white linen suit jacket I'd bought at an estate sale months ago and planned to clean up for the summer.

It was the kind of thing men once wore with straw boaters and striped shirts, and I'd found it in a heap at the bottom of a pile of sheets that I was buying to wrap clothing in for the Society. I'd always wanted one to wear over bright t-shirts, but I'd never found one to fit, until that day. Thrilled with my find, I'd scooped it up and sprinted to the checkout with Henry following behind me, shaking his head at his crazy mom.

My glee hadn't prevented me from leaving it on a hanger, neatly wrapped, in the shed until spring. There was a very good reason: I couldn't work on it until I could wash it and hang it outside. Since the weather broke, though, I'd been taking slow steps every week.

Despite the best efforts of lemon juice and sun, it was never going to be bright white again. But it was over a hundred years old, and the creamy shade I'd ended up with was better for my coloring anyhow. It didn't need much else now, except a good pressing and new buttons.

THE STUFF OF MURDER

The buttons, vintage-look from the craft store, were pearl ones painted with flowers that would have horrified the original owner, but made me smile. I'm not doctrinaire about my reclamation projects; I'm not an old Victorian man, and I'm not going to dress like one.

Henry's infectious giggle bubbled from the computer desk as he made the most of his screen time with his current favorite racing game. It looked like he was driving a monster truck after a dinosaur, which was certainly a possibility with these things.

I'd just finished the initial press and was turning up the heat and settling the lapel into place for the crucial close work when my phone rang. Early enough in the evening that it could be anyone wanting darn near anything. I hoped it wasn't yet another minor crisis related to the fourth-graders.

"Hello?"

"Dr. Shaw?"

Not a minor crisis, but a minor...well, okay, more than minor, pleasure. "Counselor."

"Wonder if I might ask you a few questions about how movie sets work."

Joe's words were all business, but there was something I liked very much in his tone. I didn't think it was just the prosecutor being nice to an expert...but even if it was, I decided to just enjoy it.

"I've only been on a few sets," I admitted.

"But you've been contracted for several movies, so you know how the basic setup goes."

"You mean who does what, how they're paid, all that?"

"Yes." Joe paused for a second. "And which people are union members, who has to join which union, and what might happen if there's some kind of dispute."

"Ah." I vaguely remembered something about a union dispute in a production a few years ago where there'd been a bad accident. "You thinking there's something that might relate to what happened?"

"Maybe. Worth a look."

"Absolutely," I agreed. I turned down my iron so it wouldn't overheat and sat. This might take a while. "You already know about the writers' and actors' strike, of course."

"Yeah. What about the others?"

"Okay, so most of the stagehands and so on belong to their own union."

"Right," he said. "That's the one that almost walked two years ago, nearly shut down the whole industry, right?"

"Exactly. Directors, cinematographers, and some other professionals have their own groups and belong to them," I continued. "That's not just directors—an assistant director, for example, also belongs to the Director's Guild, and someone training to be a cinematographer would belong to that group."

"Are those really unions, or are they more like the bar?"

A very smart question, and one for which I didn't have a good answer. "I'm not sure...but I'm also not sure it matters that much, because people who don't belong to that group, or have some kind of special agreement with it, can't do those jobs."

"Okay. Actors are Screen Actors Guild, right?"

"Right. They usually, but not always, move in solidarity with the writers and stagehands unions...as we saw in the writers' strike. People learned very early on that the only way to make sure you get a decent living in the dream factory is to stick together."

"Just about anywhere, really." Joe chuckled. "My dad is still on the board of the Carpenters' Union pension fund."

"Good for him. Henry doesn't have to worry about working for a full scholarship to college because of Frank's Newspaper Guild pension." Not to mention the simple fact that, being from Western PA, I was a union girl through and through.

Joe was silent for a moment, and when he spoke, the question shocked me.

"But—he died in the line of duty, didn't he?"

"Yes."

"Didn't you get some kind of settlement or something for that?"

"No—I…" I took a breath. "The paper was almost going under anyway, and I didn't want my lawsuit to be the thing that killed it."

"Dr. Shaw…" Joe trailed off in an awkward sigh. "The paper wouldn't have paid the settlement unless they'd been dumb or desperate enough to drop their liability insurance."

"Oh."

"Do I assume that the very nice publisher showed up at the funeral, and someone asked you to sign a release not long after?"

"They did. I never signed." I was grieving, not stupid. I'd almost forgotten about that. The release was still in my files. The newspaper was mostly gone, but the remnants were still owned by a very large multimedia company.

"Good. We should talk about that sometime. I spent most of my business career getting companies out of their responsibilities. It would be fun for me to make someone live up to them."

"You made a very good career change," I said firmly. I couldn't think of anything I'd like to talk about *less*—especially with him—than the legal issues around Frank's death. "I respect that, and I know Frank did, too."

"He did. Stand-up guy."

"Knew one when he saw one."

"Thanks, Dr. Shaw." Joe's voice suggested a Jimmy Stewart shrug… but there was a deliberation in his next sentence that also suggested he knew exactly what I'd been doing with that subject change—and accepted it. "I just couldn't stand the idea that the guy who ruined my brother's life ended up free because of inadequate lawyering."

"I don't blame you. There are never enough good and committed people willing to work for what the State's Attorney pays."

"Exactly. I decided they could use one more...and I didn't need a new B-M-W."

"Ugh. You don't really-"

"Of course not. I know they used slave labor during the Holocaust." Joe's voice hardened a little. "Grandpop kept a list. Wouldn't let Grandma get a Chanel bag either."

"Nice." Frank had had a list, too.

"Grandpop's family ran from Mussolini. They took that stuff seriously." He paused for a moment. "I could talk to you all night, you know."

"Yeah. I wouldn't mind at all."

For a moment, we were both silent, basking in the warmth between us. A lot like my first talk with Frank; he'd learned all he needed to know about early electric fans within five minutes—but we were on the phone for an hour.

I'd never expected to feel anything like that again.

"But," Joe went on, sounding almost shy, "I bet you have things to do, and I really do need to know about how unions work on movie sets."

"Okay." I took a breath, sat up a little straighter, willed myself back into being a professional, even though I'd really enjoyed his voice wrapping around me. "So just about everyone except the producers belongs to some kind of union or affinity group, and there are very specific rules about who does what."

"Safety rules?"

"A lot of it is territorial. But some of it *is* safety. More of an issue when weapons or stunts are involved, of course."

"Of course. Climbing up in the pulpit wouldn't be a stunt?"

"I don't think so. It would have been checked by the set crew and maybe by a few people higher in the chain. But there was never any question of anyone other than Brett doing that speech from the pulpit."

"So, everyone knew that was going to be the big scene, and it was going to be done there."

"Yes. And yes, anyone who wanted to harm him in a very public and ugly way could have counted on that as a good time to do it."

Joe made a little growly noise like the one Garrett did when he was thinking. "Who was in charge of the tankard?"

"I think that was him alone. He grabbed it up like Gollum with his Precious when he saw it at the Society and just ran off with it. I was in his trailer one day early on to talk about costume logistics, and it was within his reach. I don't think I ever saw him without it."

"Costume logistics?" he asked with a little chuckle.

"Wellll," I started, then decided he might as well know. "He was concerned about how his outfit would work in the romantic scenes. I answered his questions as best I could that day, but he kept emailing me."

"Why? Was there something special about the clothes?"

I took a breath. Here we go. "Um, the zipper wasn't invented until the 19th century…"

"Oh, of course it wasn't. Buttons?"

"Or a kind of hook thing called points, or sometimes just pins."

"Ow."

"You might as well know the rest."

"There's more?"

"Uh-huh." I chuckled. "Men didn't always wear traditional under-wear. Sometimes, they just wore very long shirts and tucked the end around everything."

"Yuck. I'll take briefs any day." Joe gave a nervous chuckle as I firmly ignored the thought of his underwear drawer. "You had to explain that to him?"

"Yeah. Thankfully, by email. Eventually, I drew him a diagram."

That earned me his wonderful, sexy laugh. "A diagram."

"It apparently did the trick. No more questions about breeches after that."

"Would have backed me right off." There was a grin in his voice. "I'm having too much fun with this."

"Me too."

We laughed again, entirely inappropriately.

"Okay," Joe said. "Really, did you hear anything about union disputes or anything like that?"

"No. Other than the usual grousing that streaming services don't pay as much as the big studios."

"But nothing major."

"Not that I heard. But it wouldn't hurt you to buy the stagehands' shop steward a cup of coffee."

"Good idea." He took a breath. "Are you in one of the unions?"

"Consultants don't strictly have to join, but I joined the main stagehands union like most people on set." I chuckled. "Western PA girl. My mom would have killed me if I didn't."

Joe laughed. "My dad would kill me if I ever crossed a picket line."

"My whole hometown would kill me."

"Fly down in their little UFO's from Mars?"

"Nah. Pickup trucks."

Another shared laugh.

"I should let you get back to your evening."

"I'm ironing," I admitted. "Working on a new project."

"You iron?"

"For special things. I'm fixing up a 19th-century linen suit jacket for summer."

"I'm sorry I talked so long your iron got cold," he said.

"I'm not." But I was impressed that he knew. Especially since it suggested that he ironed his own shirts.

"Yeah, I'm not really, either, but I don't want to ruin your evening."

"You're the last thing from ruining it."

"Good. Good night, Dr. Shaw."

"Good night, Counselor."

None of his business if I found myself thinking about that voice and laugh of his after I'd hung up the jacket and tucked in Henry.

Chapter Twenty-One

Menace at the Society

By now, I recognized the sound of Joe's footsteps in the foyer... and I knew the person who walked in just after nine wasn't him. Also, that they didn't want me to know they were there, because they didn't announce themselves the way just about anyone would have.

He didn't announce himself the way just about anyone would have. I was pretty sure it was a guy: even very sturdy women don't usually have that heavy, confident male tread.

I don't think I was the least bit paranoid to grab the Colonial bayonet on my way through the workroom into the foyer. Not even a little.

No one knew what was going on here. Certainly, I didn't. And anyhow, my visitor wouldn't know what I'd been working on when they walked in. For all they knew, I'd been polishing the thing. I'd happily take a little ribbing from the delivery guy.

It wasn't the delivery guy.

I was glad I had the bayonet when I saw my visitor, and more specifically, the way he looked at me.

Chase Maguire gave it away when he met my gaze.

I wasn't married for eight years to a guy who covered homicides to not know what murderous intent looked like. Not that I'd ever seen it focused on me before, now that you mentioned it, but I was smart enough to recognize the look. I had seen just that expression a few times on the defendants when I'd slipped into the public gallery to watch a trial Frank was covering.

Frank never liked when I showed up, but I enjoyed watching him at work; he was incredibly intense, so different from the relaxed, affectionate guy I got at home.

Focus.

Retreating into the comfort of my happy memories was the worst and most dangerous thing I could do right now.

What would Frank do if a killer turned up in his office?

Probably keep them talking until the cops came. He didn't scare easily, but he wasn't stupid. And he always knew his first job was to come home to Henry and me.

Yeah, I know.

Okay. Talking.

"May I help you?" I asked, maintaining a perfectly polite demeanor, with the idea that if I was calm, he wouldn't see it coming when I hit him over the head with the bayonet. Which I was fully prepared to do.

The flat side would give him a nasty bump on the head, but it wouldn't kill him. And he wouldn't get to kill me.

Henry was not going to be an orphan.

Zero to life or death a little fast, wasn't it? I asked myself. Maybe. But I really didn't like that look.

"Hi, Dr. Shaw. Just wanted to talk to you about something."

His tone was friendly, neutral. No big deal here. Complete dissonance with the face and the body language.

"What's that?" I asked, acting as if I had no idea what was really happening.

"Do you have anything of Brett's here?"

"What do you mean?"

"Did he leave anything here when he came in for the consultation and tour?" Maguire's face was red, and he had a thin, oily sheen of sweat like he was trying to decide what he should do next. Like he wasn't sure what he'd have to do.

Maybe he wasn't such a cool killer. Maybe he hadn't quite decided to attack me.

Maybe he was still human enough that he couldn't casually come at an innocent woman with a child.

I hoped I wasn't about to find out.

"No, he didn't," I said, pulling my face into as blank an expression as I could manage. "He took the tankard, and that was all."

Maguire nodded, one of those fake acknowledgment nods, acting like he saw me and recognized my concerns. Bet he learned it in some New Age-y relationship seminar in Hollywood. "Did he have any concerns about the props?"

"No. He had a lot of questions about how he was supposed to do things and the costumes, but none about props."

"Oh. Okay."

I was starting to think that Maguire didn't really know what he was doing here other than trying to scare me. But why?

What could that possibly get him?

"I don't suppose you've heard anything about the tankard?" Maguire asked.

I had not, in fact, *heard* anything. And there was no way I was going to tell this guy what I'd seen. "Um, no. Haven't heard anything."

"Oh, well. Were any of the costumes sent back here?"

"No." I wasn't faking the blank look. He had to know all the costumes had come with the production, didn't he? "I'm sorry. No one borrowed anything from us."

"Oh, well." He stared at me for several very long seconds.

Trying to figure out what to do next. So was I.

Maguire took a step toward me. My fingers tightened on the bayonet.

The door opened.

Lewis took one look at the two of us and narrowed his eyes at Maguire. "Mr. Maguire, is there something we can do for you?"

"Um, no. I need to leave now."

I'm not a hundred percent sure if it was really the sight of a sturdy black man ready to defend his boss that sent Maguire scuttling out the door. I think it was simply the fact of a witness to whatever unpleasantness he'd been planning. But I couldn't completely discount the racial angle. A lot of those allegedly woke people behave worse to actual African Americans than less enlightened folks who've really worked with them.

At that exact moment, social politics was the least of my concerns.

I was just stupidly grateful that Lewis had walked in when he did.

As Maguire shuffled down the stairs, Lewis turned to me. "You okay?"

"Yeah. Just a little weirded out."

"No wonder. He looked like he was going to come at you."

I held up the bayonet. "Not without getting a dent or two."

Lewis smiled and took it from me. "Nice. Might as well do a callback to Studebaker's biggest movie."

"Yeah." I let out a long breath.

"What was all that about, anyway?" he asked.

"I wish I knew. He was asking me if anything of Brett's ended up here, if he'd had any concerns about the props – even if we'd gotten some costumes back."

"We didn't lend any. Wouldn't he know that?"

"I'd sure think he would."

"Do we have anything he'd want?" Lewis asked.

"I can't imagine anything. They sent the tankard back from Yale New Haven, and I've locked it in the office until Joe Poli can take a look, but..."

"Fingerprints?"

"He was Studebaker's assistant—his fingerprints could be on it for any innocent reason."

Lewis nodded. "So, no reason for him to come after you over that. Maybe there's something else we don't know about yet."

"That would be my guess."

"Very weird." He shook his head.

"Weird and scary," I agreed.

"But hey, Doc, you shouldn't be using the merch for self-defense."

"Probably right." I forced as wry a tone as his, trying to pull everything back to some kind of normal. Even though I was damn sure what I'd seen in that man's eyes just now.

"I'll find you a nice aluminum baseball bat instead." Lewis gave me a tiny smile. "How 'bout one of those blue Mets ones?"

"Much better." I took a breath and pushed back an unruly piece of hair.

"You going to call Officer DiBiasi, or am I?"

I sighed. "You're right. We have to."

"We do."

"I got this." I turned toward the office and my phone. "You just be on standby if any of the ladies get nervous later."

"I can do that."

DiBiasi was concerned enough to stop by for a cup of coffee within a half hour. On his way out, he patted my arm. "It's not that I really think the mope is going to come after you, Christian, but I don't want to miss something, and Ed would never forgive me."

I chuckled. There's something to be said for being a cop family. Something. I patted DiBiasi's arm back. "Thanks for the reassurance."

"Oh, I don't blame you for being a little freaked out. Any reasonable person would be. Too much weird stuff going on here. You see anything, hear anything weird, you call me. I'd rather you feel silly than have anything else happen, okay?"

"Okay."

As I watched DiBiasi walk to that goofy little cruiser of his, I suspected I'd be hearing from Ed and Garrett soon. I'd be lying if I said I minded.

Chapter Twenty-Two

And Ladies of the Ensemble

B y mid-morning, the scary part was over, and the annoying part of the incident was well underway.

It started after DiBiasi pulled away, as Mae watched him go with an expression of annoyance usually reserved for middle-schoolers who tread on the lawn. Of course, she buttonholed me the minute she got in.

I'd been petting the Empress in between, searching the front room for any breakables I'd missed. She was sitting in her favorite chair, a violet velvet hobnailed one with a perfect view of the front window, and as I moved pieces up to higher shelves or into a box to be hidden from the fourth-graders, I'd pass by and give her a scratch behind the ears.

Hardest-working cat in show business!

And, not for nothing, exactly the sort of serene scene I needed after that run-in with Chase Maguire. Mae, however, was not in the mood to leave me to my pleasure.

"What's happened now?" she asked, marching into the front room with an expression that was far more annoyed than concerned.

"Chase Maguire showed up and got a little menacing with me," I said, staying by the cat and stroking her fuzzy head. She nipped at my fingers.

Not exactly an emotional support animal.

"Menacing?" Mae asked. "How rude."

"Rude indeed, since I have no idea what he was after."

"None?"

I shrugged. I honestly didn't know, and I didn't want to say too much about the incident to her in case I inadvertently gave her some kind of dangerous knowledge. Bad enough that Maguire came after me. A fragile lady in her eighties didn't deserve to be in the line of fire. "I think part of the game was just scaring me away from asking any questions. I did make a few incisive observations when he and Holman came over here a few days ago."

"No doubt you did, dear." Mae smiled. She had the same dark sense of humor I did. "He may think you have something to do with the investigation, since that very nice-looking State's Attorney keeps showing up here."

I blushed. There is no upside to Irish fish-belly white skin. None.

Mae chuckled. "I've heard that he's come for coffee a couple times."

"He has, and yes, we were talking about the case and such." I actually hadn't thought about the possibility that any perceived connection with Joe could make me a target.

Not that it was going to discourage me from enjoying my next cup of coffee with him—assuming there was one. I realized that I kind of wanted the coffee to become a thing.

Kind of wanted Joe to become a thing.

Maybe.

"Of course you were." Mae grinned. "Dear, I was once quite a dish."

"You're still pretty terrific," I said. Unlike some of our ladies, who'd happily abdicated anything girly, Mae always looked like a woman who took joy in dressing and making up.

"I like to think so." She beamed. "But that's not where I'm going. If I were a healthy young single lady with a sweet little boy who needs a daddy, I would definitely look twice at that lawyer."

"Henry had a daddy," I reminded her. "And he has two wonderful honorary grandfathers."

"Indeed he does." Mae knows Garrett and Ed from Society events and likes both. "But it would be good for him to have the right man around. Good for you, too."

"If it's the right man."

Mae nodded. "Indeed. But you're not the kind of girl to trifle with some piker, and certainly, Professor Kenney and his husband will scare them off."

I laughed. "That they will."

"Now we just need to scare off those nasty movie people." She sighed. "Right now, though, I need to look in the sheet music collection."

"Oh?"

"Someone brought up the Floradora Sextette on a message board last night, and I want to see if I can find their song."

The Floradoras were a bunch of Broadway stars who are best described as the original happy gold-diggers. All nice, but not well-off, young ladies who were very pretty and decently talented, most of them went on to marry assorted robber barons. But—unlike some other chorus girls of the Gilded Age—they disappeared into domesticity once wed.

"I think there were a couple of songs," I said. "I know we have them."

"Delightful. I want to surprise my group with some obscure lyrics."

"Have at it." I chuckled and picked up my box of breakables. "I'll come downstairs with you as soon as I drop this off in my office."

Since I took over the Society and almost fell down the stairs in my first week, we had a rule that no one went down the old, pitchy stairs alone. A very sensible rule for a place with elderly volunteers with brittle hips, if you ask me. Not to mention clumsy six-foot directors!

By the time Mae had her lyrics and a victory over the other members of her group, our next contenders had arrived. Trudy's future daughter-in-law was working on ideas for her wedding tables and wanted to look at Victorian settings. I was happy to oblige…if a little less happy to field another round of questions about why the police had come this morning.

From Lewis's expression when Trudy asked, I could tell he'd been in the same Q and A all day, too. Small-town life.

As soon as I got the ladies started in the dining room, I slipped back to the workroom, where Lewis was making sure the cotton thread and needles were ready for Faith, who was due later in the afternoon.

"Hey," I said. "It's only about one—why don't you go hole up and read upstairs until I have to go over to Wheatley?"

"Yeah? I sure could use a break."

"Thought maybe. Coffee's fresh, too."

"Thanks."

We exchanged a smile. It always makes me feel good when I can look out for people who work with or for me.

Just a few seconds after Lewis reappeared, refreshed, relaxed, and at least a little ahead on the night's reading, there were more heavy footsteps on the porch.

This time, though, they were most welcome,

It will surprise no one that my two beloved protectors, plus Norm, were on the scene.

The Empress jumped up into the window and gave Norm a thorough hissing, which he didn't even notice. I'm not sure if this is strategy or obliviousness on Norm's part, but it's definitely consistent.

"DiBiasi called, didn't he?" I asked as I walked onto the porch.

"Did you really think he wouldn't?" Ed chuckled. "Cop grapevine, you know."

I hugged them both. "Well, Henry will be very glad to see you two—and the big guy."

"There's that." Garrett scowled as I patted Norm. "Would have been better if they could charge that creep with something."

Ed shot him a glare. "Didn't you just re-up with the ACLU this week?"

"Your point is?" Garrett's eyes narrowed at his husband. "These are not normal people, and they don't behave like normal folks. We don't know what they're capable of doing."

"We also know that Christian is smart and safe, and if she sees Maguire, she'll call the cops immediately." Ed's eyes narrowed at me. "Won't she?"

"She will. And all we're doing is going to *shul* tonight, and then we'll be at Mom's for the first part of the day tomorrow, so it's not like we'll be out looking for trouble."

"All right," Garrett grumbled. "We're walking you to *shul*. Ed and I need the exercise anyway. Jana and the kids are bringing pizza later."

I sighed. No point in arguing. At least a visit from Ed's daughter would mean the evening wouldn't be a complete stakeout. "Fine by me."

Ed smiled, nodded at Garrett. "He needs the exercise."

"I'm having an extra cookie." Garrett's mutinous expression dared Ed to argue.

I was just glad they were back to the safer ground of the food fight than worrying about me. Honestly, with a few hours' distance from that scary moment, I suspected that Maguire really wasn't any sort of serious trouble. But when I thought about his eyes, I wasn't completely sure I could brush it off.

Chapter Twenty-Three

An Appropriate Escort

hul was, as it always is, wonderful and comforting and just enough different from the Presbyterian services I grew up with to be fascinating. Plus, it's energizing to be in a room full of people united in worshiping and working on ways to be better to each other and the world at large.

And, of course, Dina. She shines in the way that only someone who lets the Spirit work through her can, and her words always seem to lead me to something I need at the moment. Even Henry, not noted for staying in one place for long, is drawn in by her charm, and the spirit of the place.

I'm not one of those folks who believe that there's only one Way—I think we're all talking to the same thing, and as long as it pulls us toward goodness and right, the way we talk to He, She, It, or Them isn't especially important. That said, *shul* and Shabbat really work for me.

I was feeling happy and refreshed, as I almost always did when I guided Henry out of the sanctuary. As I turned my phone back on in the vestibule, I saw a text from Garrett: *Sending you an appropriate escort.*

Well, at least my yeoman protectors were going to get a nice evening with the grandkids. Though I was pretty curious about who—or what—they might consider an appropriate escort.

Outside, it was that first really warm evening that made you start thinking about summer. After we hugged Dina and Ben, we started down the stairs, enjoying the stars coming out. It would have been nice to walk home, but I didn't really mind not being alone in the dark, considering.

"I think I can see a constellation, Ma." Henry pointed to the darkest corner of the sky.

"You will be able to by the time we get home."

"Cool."

A silver-colored sedan, *not* a BMW, but still imported and pretty high-end, pulled over and flashed its lights as we crossed to the Green. For a second, I was a little nervous, but then I saw the tag: TRUBILL.

As in a grand jury indictment. Only one person that could be.

Undoubtedly, my appropriate escort.

And indeed, Joe Poli was already unfolding himself from the driver's seat. "Hey, Dr. Shaw. Thought you folks might like a ride home."

"It's a pretty night, but why not?" I said, walking toward the car. Of course, I knew exactly what he was doing, and I wondered if he was going to admit it.

Besides, it was kind of nice to have an attractive man looking out for me again, even if he was just protecting his expert. Though it seemed to me that he was taking a rather appreciative look at the girly floral-print dress and loose updo I wore for shul.

"Ed and Garrett told me they're keeping an extra little eye on you..."

"They are. I'm not sure how necessary that is." I shrugged. "But this is nice."

"It's okay, right? You don't have some religious requirement to walk home?"

THE STUFF OF MURDER

"No, we're Reform. Only really strict Orthodox people do that." I smiled. "But it's kind of you to be concerned."

He did a Jimmy Stewart shrug. (A *much nicer* movie star, ask me!) "Just don't want to offend you. I want to get you right."

It was an interesting way of putting it, and just like that moment in the office a day ago, made me wonder if there really was something going on here. "Thanks."

I started to pat his arm, a perfectly innocent and friendly gesture and realized as I did that he wasn't wearing a jacket, and I could feel his muscles tense and the warmth of his skin through the smooth oxford of his shirt. Not innocent and friendly at all. If this had been one of those overwrought Victorian romances, I might have said I felt a jolt of electricity.

For a good second or two, both of us froze, standing there looking at each other in the dusk.

"Ma! We don't take rides from strangers, remember?" Henry said, popping up beside me. He knew full well that this was no stranger, and he was just making sure he wasn't left out.

"That's very true," I said. "Master Henry Glaser, meet Assistant State's Attorney Joe Poli."

"Nice to meet you." Henry held out a hand for a shake with the perfect manners and style that his dad had started teaching him before he was even entirely steady on his feet. *You stand up, shake hands, and say hello, Henry. It's what men do.* I see so much of Frank in him.

"You too." Joe shook, cutting his eyes to me, clearly impressed. "I'd like to talk to your mom for a few minutes about some stuff. Mind if I give you a ride home?"

"That'd be great."

He opened the back door for Henry and looked to me. "I don't have a booster seat anymore. I hope that's okay."

"Okay? It's AWESOME!" Henry had been lobbying me to get rid of the booster for weeks, but I had a hard time giving up that last safety device.

Once we were all belted in, Joe put the car in gear and smiled at Henry in the rear-view mirror. "So, what do you like to read about, Master Glaser?"

"The planets."

Oh, no.

"Astronomy is cool."

"Yep. Tonight, I'm going to get out my telescope and look for Saturn and Ur-ANUS." Henry grinned.

"Ur-AN-ous!" I snapped.

The alleged adult male in the car grinned every bit as naughtily as my son. "I don't know. I've always been partial to Cassio-PEE-a."

Henry practically exploded. So did Joe.

I sighed.

Joe glanced at me and stopped laughing.

We'd reached the stop sign for Main Street, and he stayed for a second, making very serious eye contact with Henry in the rear-view mirror. "I shouldn't have done that. It wasn't very respectful to your mom."

He turned to me. "Sorry, Dr. Shaw. I didn't mean to be inappropriate."

If the fact of an actual man who could admit to a mistake wasn't appealing enough, the adorable bad little boy expression on his face would have sealed the deal. It was a very good thing that there was a real little, er, medium-sized, boy in the back because I'm not sure *what* I might have done. "It's okay. The names really are funny."

"True, but I'm sure you're raising Henry here to be polite around ladies, and I'd never want to undermine that." He glanced back up at the mirror. "Nothing wrong with showing respect."

"Got that," Henry said. "Uncle Garrett says if you don't show respect to others, you don't respect yourself."

"I'm with Uncle Garrett," agreed Joe. "So anyway, your visitor from this morning is even more trouble than we thought."

"How so?" I asked carefully, appreciating that he was trying to talk about this without scaring Henry.

"Apparently, Studebaker filed a formal warning about Maguire with the actors' union when he found out about an earlier incident."

"Why not just fire him?"

"Assistants these days seem to have fairly significant contracts, so the warning was probably the first step in that process."

"Did he know?"

"Maybe. It would give him a good reason to harm Studebaker."

"But not..." Me.

"Unless you know something you don't think you know."

"What do you mean?"

"I'm not sure." Joe sighed and glanced back at Henry, who was busily staring at the sky as we rolled down the last dark block to the house. "Can you take another good look at that tankard and the pulpit?"

"Sure. The tankard probably tomorrow, but the pulpit will have to wait a day or two."

He nodded awkwardly, and I suspected I'd see a blush if we were in full light. "Sorry. Of course, it'll be in use tomorrow."

"Not the pulpit itself, but the sanctuary will."

"You don't use the pulpit?"

"No. It's ten feet in the air, like you're proclaiming from on high. Totally not the right vibe for Rabbi Aaron and the rest of the congregation. You've met her. She doesn't have a Moses complex."

"True. So maybe you get another look at the pulpit Sunday or Monday."

"Okay."

"And I'm going to do a little digging on that complaint Studebaker

168

CHAPTER TWENTY-THREE

filed."

I nodded. "Did you find out anything on the finances?"

"Not much. Seemed like the production was running on a shoestring, but my forensic accountant pal says that's not unusual."

"If there's a business that throws money around in this day and age, I don't know of it."

"Oh, high-end corporate law firms still do, but it's not fun anymore." He chuckled, glanced over at me in the moonlight. "Though you'd add a lot to some boring catered party."

"Thanks." I was glad it was too dark for him to know I was blushing.

"Not the time, Dr. Shaw, but don't think I'm missing that you're smart, kind, and awfully pretty in that church—temple—dress."

"You're not so bad yourself." It was the most flirtatious thing I could come up with, and I was stupidly delighted when he grinned.

"Maybe we pick up this discussion once things calm down a little?"

"I'd like that."

"Look!" Henry called from the backseat. "I see the Big Dipper!"

Joe and I shared a nervous little laugh and exclaimed over the constellations for the last couple of driveways.

It was only maybe a minute until he turned into our house. The little solar LEDs on the path had come on, and we'd left the post light and the living room lamps on so we wouldn't be returning to a dark house. It was nothing more than what we always did, but very comforting.

"We're here, pal," Joe said pointlessly. As soon as he put the car in Park, Henry had unclipped his belt.

"Thanks for the ride, Mr. Poli." He looked closely at Joe. "I thought I knew you. You're Aly's dad."

"Right. How do you know that?"

"Aly was the Mentor Buddy for my class in first grade. I saw you with her at the Reading Week Celebration."

Joe's eyes widened a little, but he just got out of the car. So did I.

169

"Thanks again!" Henry called, running toward the door.

"How does he do that?"

"He has a photographic memory. We don't make a big deal about it, but it's a real gift."

"I'll say." Joe turned back to me as Henry dashed for the door. "I understand that Team Kenney is taking an interest in your safety?"

"They are. Henry and I are visiting my mom in West Haven tomorrow morning, and we'll be close to home the rest of the weekend. Probably with a lot more Garrett and Ed time than usual."

"Good. You need anything, you can call me, too." It wasn't a come-on. It was a standup guy looking out for a lady, and I took it that way.

"I appreciate it."

"Ma!"

"Thanks," I said. I didn't hold out my hand to shake because it didn't feel right, but I wasn't sure what did.

Joe settled matters for me. He put his hands on my arms, as if he were going to pull me in for a hug, but didn't, holding eye contact so I understood what he was doing: making a somewhat intimate and protective gesture, but very deliberately not crossing any lines. "Good night. I'll wait while you go in and lock the door."

"Thanks."

If I could still feel that gentle but firm touch on my arms an hour later, after I tucked in Henry, that was my business and nobody else's.

Chapter Twenty-Four

Knit and Spin

S aturdays are always a mixed bag. We sometimes go to *shul*, especially if there's an event like a bar or bat mitzvah or if it's a religiously significant week, but if we go on Friday, we'll just as likely get up late next morning and lie around the house until we head out to visit my mom and run errands. Mom always gets one weekend morning.

She's very well aware of her place as the matriarch and expects that we will do brunch somewhere near her building, allowing her to show off her adorable grandson and her daughter, the professor who works with movies. Mom's a little demanding, but she's earned it, raising me on her own after my father left for what was supposed to be a temporary separation in Pittsburgh that became permanent when he found another woman and died a couple years later in a bad flu season. (The flu did, and does, still kill fairly young people, not that we talk about that very often.)

Despite everything, I've never heard a bad word about him from her.

Anyway, thanks to the Mars teachers' pension fund, Mom has been happily ensconced in West Haven for the last nine years, enjoying a basically happy retirement and the continuing rivalry of the Mad

Knitters and other factions in the complex. It's got all the social contours of a gang war, just thankfully without weapons.

At Saturday's brunch at Pokey's on the Water, a nice little diner with a deck less than a block away from her house, we enjoyed our eggs with the usual side of drama.

"And are you ready for this? Peggy is sneaking around with Old Man Holman," Mom said, pouring milk, but not sugar, into her coffee. She had an egg and cheese scramble for the same reason; despite a considerable sweet tooth, she didn't want to have anything dangerously tempting to Henry.

Her low-maintenance, considerate handling of his condition is one of the most wonderful things about her.

"Old Man Holman?" I couldn't help laughing over my two poached eggs on buttered toast (It's my weekend treat—I like the gooeyness, don't judge!) Old Man Holman, so-called because he'd been in the building the longest, even though he was in the same age cohort as everyone else, was surly and monosyllabic on a good day. "What on earth do they talk about?"

"They're not talking, dear. Peggy's a bit of a slut."

I put my fork down. Some things you just don't want to think about over food – if ever. "Uh-huh."

"Well, you know, there's quite the little social scene here."

"I do know. When are you going to take the Sarge up on it?"

The Sarge was a retired and widowed Marine who always seemed to appear when the Mad Knitters had packages to carry or needed a supportive hand across an icy parking lot. He seemed to take particular pleasure in helping Mom, but of course, Peggy and Suzanne might see it differently.

"Grandma! Look!" Henry pointed to a big boat out on Long Island Sound. He was having eggs over easy with extra bacon, his favorite, and guaranteed to burn off with our busy day.

"My! Isn't he big!" The alleged slut, actually one of my mother's two closest friends, and a sweet retired teacher like her, greeted us with a great big smile.

She patted Henry on the head, but resisted a hug, being a medium-sized boy gran herself, and sat down at the table. Peggy was Mom's age, but probably seen as the cute one, a petite bottle redhead where Mom's tall and frankly silver-haired.

"So, how are things over in Unity? Anything new on that dead movie star?"

Mom, to her credit, had been more interested in Henry's school projects and the fact that I was experimenting with a bright coral lipstick and hadn't asked. But now, she put her fork down and looked to me with gossip-greedy glee.

"I don't have any inside info," I said quickly. Of course, there was no way on earth I would tell her about the incident with Maguire yesterday. Never mind that I'd been drinking coffee with the Assistant State's Attorney on the case.

"Oh, but c'mon," Peggy said. "It can't have been an accident. Jealous husband? Jilted girl?"

"Me Too, maybe?" asked Mom.

"Probably not," I said. I couldn't let that go. "It's very possible that he was gay."

They snorted in unison.

"What a silly man. Why not just come out?" Peggy asked. "It's not like it matters much these days, especially with actors."

"Too bad. All of the cute ones are." Mom sighed. "But it's true. No one really cares about that anymore."

I nodded, glad that Henry was still watching the boat. Of course, he understands what gay means—his honorary grandfathers are married to each other—but we didn't need to get into why it matters or why it doesn't.

"Still, it's hard to believe it was an accident," Peggy said. "Especially after I saw the video."

"Video?"

"Don't you ever watch the morning news, Christian?" my mother asked. "It's all over the cable channels today."

"Video," I said. Mom's a cable-news junkie. Frank had considered the 24/7 cable news/infotainment cycle a perversion of the mission of *real* journalists, and while I didn't quite buy that, I also didn't have time to sit around and follow the play-by-play on the latest controversy.

"Oh, it's just awful, sweetie." Peggy shook her head. "Flailing around in the pulpit like he was high on something and then practically flying out that little door."

"It looked like there was nothing holding the door in place," Mom said. "Don't those pulpits have latches?"

"Apparently not all." I shrugged. "Some of the cabinets in the church are so well-fitted that they don't need them."

"But even the Pilgrims would want a latch for a little safety all the way up there, wouldn't they?" Peggy asked.

"I don't know." I shrugged.

"If somebody tampered with it…" my mother said.

"Oooh, a new twist in the mystery!" Peggy's eyes gleamed, and she reached in her purse. "Here, Christian, you should look at the video."

As Peggy rummaged in her phone, and I tried to come up with a way to not watch a scene I'd already lived and would never forget, a clatter of heels and a high-pitched shriek announced the arrival of the third Mad Knitter.

"Henry!" Suzanne Luciano, her aqua wrap cardigan flying behind her, descended on him with a big hug, which he tolerated from her as he did no one else, not even his own grandmother. Suzanne has six granddaughters and no grandsons, and she adores him, at least in part because of the change of pace. Henry appreciates honest adulation, and why not?

She pointed to her spiffy floral-print satchel. "I've got a new minifigure in my purse just waiting for you…"

"Cool, Aunt Suzanne!"

Once the small Lego was produced and its new owner busy marching it across his saucer, conversation quickly returned to the hot topic of the day. Suzanne, though, being the widow of an insurance salesman, had an entirely different take.

"Somebody offed him, of course," she said, adjusting the neat aqua headband in her blonde bob. "But everyone's making it too tough."

"Too tough?" I asked.

"That Hollywood thing is just noise." She shot me a canny glance over her adorable clear rhinestone reading glasses. "Find out who got his insurance policy, and I bet you have your killer."

"You think?" Mom asked.

"I know those murder mystery writers like all kinds of wild motives for murder." Suzanne cut her eyes to Peggy, the whodunnit fan of the group. "But in real life, you can't do much better than sex or money…and money's usually the winner."

"Money." Peggy smiled.

"Money." Mom nodded.

"Money is better than sex," I agreed.

Peggy let out a little chuckle that made me re-evaluate Mom's description of her. "Not really, dear."

Chapter Twenty-Five

Something Smells Here

After Mom and the Mad Knitters, the grocery run was a relief, even if it wasn't my favorite thing.

Frank was the shopper; he enjoyed comparing prices and going to three different stores for the best deal. I'm functional: make list, go to nearest large store, buy preferred items unless they're outrageously expensive, fill cupboard, forget for a week, repeat.

Any real grocery expedition requires a trip to Hamden, twenty minutes down the road, because the only supermarket in Unity is a small, independent place that charges about twenty percent more for everything. They also have a spectacular bakery, so I get Henry's birthday cake there each year, but I'd never waste the money on daily basics. We're not struggling, but I'm not stupid.

Henry was in charge of holding the list and checking off items when he and Frank did the shopping, and now he does it for me. There's always a little bittersweet echo when I hand it to him as we climb into my tiny cobalt-blue compact…but over time, it's become less pain and more warmth.

Those small daily memories are how we keep people we've loved and lost with us, after all.

Since we weren't running on a schedule that day, I decided to swing over to the Society and take a look at the tankard for Joe after we stopped at the house and put away the perishables. Henry made a token protest about the delay in video game time, but he likes bopping around, so that's all it was.

As I turned onto the little road that cuts between the Society, Beth Shalom, and the Green, I laughed. Ed, Garrett, and Norm were walking past, Garrett with a big canvas bag. The carrot and lettuce tops sticking out the top betrayed the fact that they'd been at the Farmer's Market at Town Hall.

"We really aren't following you around," I said, climbing out of the car.

Henry jumped out, hugged Garrett and Ed, and then proceeded to enjoy some quality time with Norm, who gave him a generous sniffing and face-licking.

Cookie would reverse the process with a proper re-scenting when he got home.

"You two should go to the Farmer's Market sometime," Ed observed. "Be good for Henry."

"He eats exactly three vegetables: iceberg lettuce, carrots, and peas. Sometimes corn if it's mixed in with the peas and carrots." I shook my head. "You're right, though. Seeing where it comes from might help."

"I ate that tomato salad at Uncle Ed's birthday party last year," Henry put in, a little defensively, doggie drool clearly having no effect on his hearing.

"You ate one slice of tomato and most of the mozzarella off my caprese," I reminded him.

"Yeah, but I still ate it."

I sighed and exchanged exasperated glances with the men, both all too familiar with kids and their food habits. While Henry and I live closest to them, they see a lot of Ed's oldest daughter and her two, who are just down in Fairfield, so today's turn in the Great Veggie War surprised no one.

Garrett nodded to the car. "Grocery shopping?"

"Yup. Just got back with the week's supply of turkey, peanut butter, and meatballs." I dug out the key to the Society door. "But I wanted to zip over and take a look at something. That tankard that Brett Studebaker was using."

"Why?"

"Joe Poli thinks it might be part of the reason Chase Maguire showed up on the doorstep yesterday morning."

Ed's eyes narrowed. "Then that thing should be in an evidence bag."

"Probably," I agreed. "I don't have that, but it's still in the box the hospital sent it in."

"Why on earth did the hospital send it?" Garrett asked.

I shook my head. "It has a Unity Historical Society marker on the bottom, and someone in Yale New Haven administration just sent it back to us when the movie people picked up Studebaker's things. Joe—Poli asked me to keep it in the box until they were sure if they needed it."

Both noticed that I had to quickly add Joe's last name, but neither commented.

"Okay. So why'd he ask you to look at it?" Ed asked as we walked up to the porch.

"He thinks I know something I don't know I know."

I caught a look between Garrett and Ed, but I wasn't sure what it meant. Probably some kind of protective thing.

"Well," Ed said, "Why don't I look at it with you, then."

"Great idea." Garrett handed Norm's leash to Henry. "We'll just amuse ourselves here on the Green for a couple of minutes."

"Sounds good."

I took a moment to fill Her Majesty's bowl and check her water container, the sound bringing her to the stairs. She glared at Ed with the annoyance that only the scent of canine can bring. Of course, the Empress can smell Norm, and though she's never actually met him, she's quite sure she would not want to make his acquaintance.

"Oh, calm down," Ed said. "Norm's never eaten a cat yet."

"See?" I told her.

"But he might cuddle one to death."

The cat snorted and skipped down the stairs toward her food, which was far more important than the stupid humans.

Ed and I smiled as we walked back to my office.

I'd locked the box in my file cabinet, just in case, and I put on gloves after I pulled it out. He grinned as I snapped them in place.

"You look like you're about to go into surgery."

"Close enough. I know they look silly, but they do protect everything."

"You wear them every time?"

"Oh, yeah. Most of the docents won't unless I make them, but I don't want to leave even a trace of finger oils on things this old. Plus, then I don't have to worry about wearing my favorite honey hand cream that some nice people give me every Hanukkah..."

Ed's ears turned a little pink. He and Garrett always bought me a box of really good bath products, having decided at some point that it was a personal enough, but not TOO personal gift for a young lady, probably with help from one of Ed's daughters. "Yeah, you know."

I pulled up the loose piece of packing tape I'd put down to secure the box, and Ed leaned in as I lifted the flap. I winced again at the harsh scent of alcohol, which had lingered because the tankard was closed up. Only, I noticed something else now too.

So did Ed. His jaw tightened, and he held my gaze gravely. "You *do* know something you don't think you know."

"What do you mean?"

"That chemical smell?"

"Yeah, it's awful. I'm afraid it's the booze reacting with the pewter. Lord only knows what they're going to find in the toxicology report..."

He shook his head. "I can guess one thing."

"What?"

"Synthetic marijuana."

"You mean that crazy stuff that made the guy bite someone's face off in Florida?"

A grim nod. "Exactly that. It has a strong chemical odor."

"Why would Studebaker be messing with that stuff—especially on the set? I understood the alcohol—and I wouldn't have been surprised by some kind of anti-anxiety drug. Maybe even cocaine. He's old enough and rich enough that it might have been a standing habit. But synthetic pot?"

"I don't think *he* was messing with it."

"You think Maguire gave it to him."

"I do." He shook his head. "You package that up. I'm going to call Joe Poli and just let him know what we found."

"Okay."

Ed held my gaze for a full ten seconds or so, a long time. "You still have that pepper spray I gave you for the glove compartment?"

"Yeah. It's still there."

"Good. Put it in your purse. I'll bring you a pocket one later."

"You don't really think..."

"No. But it never hurts to be safe. And if you see that Maguire kid, do not pass Go, do not collect two hundred dollars, just call the cops. I'm going to tell Tony DiBiasi, too, so he'll get the night guy to take a swing by your house a few times. Give them something to do."

"O-kay," I said slowly.

"It's fine, Christian. I'm not really worried. Just being careful because we don't know what's going on here."

CHAPTER TWENTY-FIVE

I nodded.

"It's one of those things, you know. You're extra careful because the downside is so much worse than the inconvenience." He cleared his throat and shrugged, definitively ending the discussion. "Now package that thing back up and put it away. Not in your office. That's too easy if someone would break in."

"Okay. I'll put it up on the third floor."

"Very good."

Ed waited downstairs while I took the tankard up to a third-floor bedroom. I just put the box in the bottom drawer of the bureau for now.

"So," he said when I came back, "you should come to the Farmer's Market next week."

"Yeah?" I knew exactly what was going on here, and I was happy to play.

"Absolutely." His serious expression gave way to a wicked grin. "They're going to have striped beets. I bet even Henry would be willing to reconsider his biases for that."

"If he won't, I will."

Chapter Twenty-Six

Saturday Night Iron

I t was a lovely, warm, late-spring evening, the kind where it really starts to feel like summer. Henry and I took full advantage, opening the living room windows so the flower-scented breeze could come in and the blinds so we could absorb the sunset gleam as long as it lasted.

He was curled up on the couch with his current library book, a coffee-table one on the planets, enjoying every extra second of his later weekend-night bedtime. Cookie was on the back of the couch, watching over him and periodically "helping" him turn the page. Both as happy as it's possible for a boy and cat to be.

I wasn't doing badly either, in the middle of my Saturday night ironing spree, preparing my vintage shirts for the week. It's always a treat for me, the clean scent of cotton that's been hanging outside in the sun, the warmth of the steam iron, the precise care necessary to get the collar, placket, and cuffs perfectly set. Not as much of an art as what the needlewomen from Town Hall do, but definitely a craft—and a pleasure.

The phone rang as I finished the next-to-last collar.

This time, I looked at the screen as I picked up—and laughed. "Do you *know* when I'm ironing?"

Joe laughed. "Ironing radar. I hope I didn't interrupt anything too important."

"Not hardly." I laughed, too. "I can finish later."

"Okay. As long as I didn't ruin your big Saturday night."

"Um, no. I never have big plans."

"Too bad." A pause, probably a shrug. "I don't either."

"Maybe you should take up ironing."

"I'm not into heavy metal."

"Ooh, nice catch." I was impressed with the perfect deadpan delivery.

"Always enjoyed a little witty repartee." He took a breath, was silent longer than fit the conversation, and then, speaking carefully, as if he'd rehearsed it: "So you're not dating again?"

"Um, no. Do people even date anymore?"

"I do. I mean, I would, if there was a woman..."

"You're not, either?"

"Nah." Shy chuckle. "I'm not nearly as interesting now as I was when I had the big fancy job."

"More interesting, if you ask me. You're doing something you believe in, even at a cost. Who wouldn't want to back that up?"

"Amber, among others."

"Oh." I was surprised by the honesty. "Well, my grandma always said, 'you can't fix stupid.'"

Joe laughed full-out then. So did I. He really did have a very sexy laugh.

"Anyhow," he continued, "all that to say that I'm not averse if the right woman happened by..."

"I'm not—averse—under the right circumstances either." I took a breath, chose the next words carefully, making sure Henry was focused on his book. "But you know, it's a lot, though. Not just me."

"Your boy is terrific. Probably had to learn a lot and get used to a whole new world with his condition, right?"

"Yeah. It was a scary time, but we came through. Day-to-day, once you have a routine, it's not a big thing."

"My college friend managed pretty well—I'm guessing it's even better now."

"Exactly." I thought about what he'd mentioned the other day. "I just hope he doesn't end up as much of a daredevil as your pal."

"There was a little more to it—he was also trying to push away from his mom, who was a bit smother-y. You don't seem the type."

"I try really hard not to."

"As far as I can see, you're hitting it." He took a breath. "But it's tough, isn't it? I try really hard not to be the Weekend Fun Daddy. Aly is currently watching some reality show and doing her nails because I wanted her to have a normal night at home instead of the hot new movie."

"Good for you."

"Made spaghetti with mom's red gravy, too."

"Renaissance man."

"Something like that." He chuckled, and I could almost hear the gears turning. "Anyhow, this was just supposed to be a quick call to see what you thought of the tankard."

"Ah."

"But it turned into something much nicer…which I'd like to take up again one of these days."

"So would I."

"Good." There was definitely a smile in his voice. "But I really did need to know your impressions. Ed called and told me what he thought, and I wanted your take."

"He told you it just reeked, right?"

"Right."

"Ed said it was synthetic marijuana, and he should know."

"He sure should." Joe thought for a moment. "So, who spiked the booze?"

"You don't think he was using it himself?"

"I really doubt it. Unless I'm missing something, Studebaker was apparently extremely intense about his work, very controlled."

"Right..."

"He wouldn't use something as unpredictable as synthetic pot during filming."

"I agree," I said. "If you'd told me they found cocaine in the tankard or his system, I wouldn't be so sure."

"Exactly. Plenty of stars his age got into the old 'Bolivian marching powder' to keep up the intensity on set."

I giggled. "Someone has been reading up on the entertainment scene."

"You caught me. Researching a bit—a couple of the actors who came up when he did were heavily into drugs, but I didn't find any references to Studebaker having an issue."

"Which means he either didn't use, or hid it better."

"So lovely and yet so cynical, Dr. Shaw."

I was glad he couldn't see my blush. "I was married to a journalist, remember? Their rule is 'If Mom says she loves you, get a hard confirm.'"

"Nice." Appreciative chuckle. "So, let's assume somebody spiked his alcohol. Was the tankard always with him?"

"Yes." I shook my head. "Weirdest thing ever. He saw it during a quick visit to the Society, and he scooped it up and carried it off like Gollum with his Precious. I never saw him without it within reach."

"Some kind of character thing?"

"I'm guessing."

"I did a little acting in college—it was good for moot court."

"Did you, now?"

"Never more than Spear Carrier Number One. I think I got to yell 'Hail Caesar' once." He laughed. "But we had a bunch of method types, and they did sometimes attach themselves to things."

"I've heard about that. I don't think method is cool anymore. I think now they call it something like absorbing the emotional resonance of the object." I took a breath, decided in favor of honesty. "Which I get, because sometimes I feel things, too."

"Yeah?"

"No freaky stuff, just sometimes a little echo of the person who wore or used it."

"Interesting. Is that why you do this?"

"One big reason. I like to think that I'm keeping those memories and resonances alive. In a professional and academic way, of course."

"Of course." He thought for a moment. "Did *you* get anything from the tankard?"

I laughed. "Didn't do a darn thing for me. But I wasn't playing The Reverend, either."

"Right. So all of that to say he kept the tankard with him when he was on set."

"Yes. Within reach, I'd say. But that doesn't mean somebody couldn't have come up behind him and spiked it. And there were a lot of people around, even on what was kind of a shoestring set."

"But presumably only a limited number of people would have motive."

"I thought motive only mattered on *Law & Order*, Counselor."

"Don't do that to me." Joe laughed and then tried for a serious tone. "You're right, as far as it goes. I don't have to prove motive. But without motive, we've got nowhere to go. It could be any random person."

"Good point. So let's assume it was someone who had a reason to harm Studebaker, and the opportunity to do it. We've still got a pretty big field."

CHAPTER TWENTY-SIX

"The assistant, Maguire, is almost too easy. Almost."

"I like him too."

"What, you have a thing for pretty boys?"

"As a suspect," I clarified. "I don't like boys at all, now that you mention it. I prefer men."

"Duly noted."

"Good. But he's not the only possibility. It could be a member of the crew who had some kind of beef that we don't know about yet."

"Excellent point. Shop steward said there was a lot of grumbling about the stripped-down production, and Studebaker was one of the producers."

"Right. Which makes him an easy target." I picked up the bottle of orange-flavored seltzer I'd been drinking before the phone rang, and something else hit me. "It doesn't have to be the tankard."

"What do you mean?"

"Someone could have spiked the bottle of alcohol he filled it from."

Joe sighed. "Not funny. We released the set, including the trailers, two days ago."

"Sorry."

"No, it's worth thinking about. Chain of evidence would be a problem, but we might be able to get there from another angle. I need to think about this—"

"DAD! You promised me a round of Uno!"

The off-speaker shout had to be his daughter. Aly sounded like every demanding teenager and more power to her. "Sounds like you have a more important assignment right now."

"That I do. To be continued."

"Of course. Enjoy your game."

"Enjoy your ironing."

The conversation ended with a surprisingly comfortable shared laugh. I had no problem admitting to myself—not for anyone else yet, thanks—that I could do with a lot more Joe Poli. With a lot less murder, if possible.

Chapter Twenty-Seven

Lady with a Whacker

S unday morning meant yard work this week. It's always a little amusing to be out in front of the house mowing, whacking, and sweeping when the church folks drive by in their best, especially since many of them are my volunteers or friends.

By this point in May, we'd settled into our usual summer work routine, which meant me using the power tools and Henry mostly playing and occasionally helping with some small task that was safe for him. This week, it was sweeping the grass bits off the walk.

First, though, I had to mow. And whack.

I've always liked mowing and weed-whacking. I grew up in the country, after all, and my grandparents put me to work in their garden when I was a kid, so I'm comfortable getting a little dirty. And now that I'm old enough to use the power tools, it's fun.

Frank never liked any of it; he complained extravagantly about the pains of home ownership, and within our first year in the house, I'd taken over most of it. (We evened out because he was one of those neatniks who actually *likes* scrubbing grout.) I mowed the lawn three hours before I went into labor with Henry. I still laugh at that.

Anyway, that particular afternoon, I was out in the yard with my whacker, trimming the weeds from the walk (a most satisfying enterprise), when Mae Tillotson drove up. She parked on the street and walked over to me, not something I wanted at that point when I was wearing safety goggles, Frank's old Mets cap, and an older Mars High School tee over cutoffs.

Mae, who was in a very nice pale pink shirtwaist dress, pearls, and shiny beige pumps, looked at me and sniffed. "In my day, we wore straw hats and pedal-pushers in the garden."

"I wear what I've got." I shrugged. "On your way to church?"

"Indeed. Thought I should tell you that I have heard that the movie company may be interested in making a donation to the Society in appreciation for our help."

"Really. Who suggested that?"

"Someone from Filmagic left a message in the Society email. I always check it on Saturday evenings. I suggested they contact you on Monday."

"Reasonable." I nodded. Mae and one other volunteer who also brought in a lot of donations had access to the general Society email account so they could contact prospects. No surprise that she'd been looking. But why would Filmagic, the streaming service that was buying the movie, get involved here? If it even *was* them. One more unanswered question.

"I wanted to warn you, dear, because I won't be in early tomorrow."

"No?"

"No, I have to get down to Town Hall and look at the deeds and parcels for my property. I am not going to be caught flat-footed by those nasty nursing home people again."

"But I heard it was going nowhere—"

"I heard differently from people in a position to know."

I could have argued, considering my own excellent source, but that didn't seem to be a good idea. Also, I would never get those weeds whacked if I stood here jawing with Mae. "Well, I'm sure you'll do what's best for you."

"Indeed I will."

"Then I'll see you later in the day or later in the week. It's all good."

"We can only hope." Mae took one more disparaging glance at my outfit and proceeded back to her Buick Behemoth.

I pulled the bill of my cap down, glanced back to make sure Henry was still happily stalking a grasshopper, or whatever it was he was doing in between weeding the flower bed, and dropped the choke on the whacker. My shoulder wasn't thrilled with a second pull-start, but I reminded myself that this was my exercise for the day.

I'd barely gotten back to work when I saw her.

Of course, it was her.

I honestly don't think Sally Birdwell *tries* to make us all feel inferior and unappealing. It's just a fringe benefit for her. As it had to be just then, when she appeared on the sidewalk, matchy-matchy in navy-and-pink color block tights and top, power-walking past in sneakers that cost more than I made in a month, her hair swishing in a perfectly straight ponytail that hung halfway down her back. She, too, had on a ball cap. But hers was one of those cute girly ones—it said "SPREAD JOY" in pink rhinestones.

Somehow, I doubted Sally ever spread joy.

When she saw me, she started power walking up the path.

G-d forgive me, I thought about not turning off the whacker. I wouldn't have attacked her with it—promise!—but I'm not above spraying a few fresh cuttings in the direction of those perfect pink sneakers.

"Christian!" she trilled as I reluctantly turned it off. There were still a few errant weeds, which meant I'd have to do yet another pull-start. What doesn't kill you and all that.

"Hi, Sally."

"It's so—competent—of you to do your own yard work. I can't imagine."

That's me, folks, competent as all get out. "Yeah, well. I find it relaxing."

Sally's face crinkled as much as the Botox would permit. "Relaxing?"

"The lawn doesn't argue with me, and the weeds don't offer performance notes. They just lie there and let me mow and whack them. Sometimes very pleasing."

"Um, okay."

Not a clue.

"To each her own," I observed. "You look like you're getting a good workout."

"Not bad. I need to step up the weightlifting, really, but CrossFit is a bit—much, don't you think?"

I laughed. "I think it's a lot much. I can't afford to leave all of that energy in the gym, no matter how good it would make me look."

Sally's sharp little eyes held mine. "You know, that is an excellent point. I will use that the next time my trainer suggests it."

"Glad to help. You don't even have to credit me."

A pause, as Sally took a very long moment to process that I was teasing. "Oh, it's an academic joke because you folks always have footnotes and whatnot."

I forced a smile. "Exactly."

"So, did you hear?"

"Hear what?"

"Why, that the movie is off." She gave me a sharp glance. "It's all over social media. Aren't you on Instagram?"

"The Society has accounts, but we don't do a lot with them."

She sniffed. "You should. Imagine what it would do for fundraising."

"Garrett keeps telling me we need to improve our presence."

"He's right. Everybody needs a good social media footprint."

Why did I think hers had spike heels and red soles? I just waited for her to continue.

"Anyhow, MovieBuzz is reporting that they can't finish the film without him. Apparently, they didn't get enough good footage from the church scene."

Good footage, indeed. Sally was clearly just parroting what she'd read. And I wasn't too sure what any of it meant or who might be behind it. Even with my limited movie experience, I knew entertainment people were at least as creative as politicians and cops with planting stories for their own purposes. But what I couldn't figure out here was what they'd get for it.

They'd get out of the dead weight of a movie that was likely to fail, of course, but at what cost? And would they really write off whatever box office would come from the gruesome draw of Studebaker's last film—with at least part of the scene leading to his death?

I wasn't too sure about that.

"I'll have to take a look when I finish the yard work," I said neutrally, pulling my safety glasses back down, in a big bright hint that maybe it was time for Miss Spread Joy to move on.

Fortunately (or unfortunately for anyone who might be hoping to see me fire up the whacker within clipping distance of her overpriced sneaks), Sally took the hint.

"There'll probably be lots more to look at by this afternoon," she said, adjusting her perfectly straight pony. "People are commenting all over the place about it."

Which, of course, counts as...something? Frank had had many thoughts on the comment sections, and their news value, and I tended to agree with him. The cleaned-up version is: "Opinions are like noses. Everybody's got one."

Frank, of course, did not say noses.

"Well, I'll take a look. See you at drop-off tomorrow."

"Sure. And good luck with the fourth-graders."

"Oh, that's right. Tomorrow is field trip day." I sighed. I could have done with not thinking about that for a while.

She swatted my arm with a happy grin. "It'll be fun. They're so curious and interested at that age."

"Riiiight. Have a nice walk."

"Oh, I will. *So* good for the glutes!"

You'd think that would have been quite enough interruption for one morning of yard work. You'd be wrong.

Henry was sweeping up the weed remnants, and I was picking a few of the giant violets from the patch by the hedge, planning to put them in my grandma's violet-painted china cup as I did every spring when our latest visitor arrived.

Of course, I was bent over, giving the neighborhood a lovely view of my Irish peasant backside, when I heard the voice.

"Christian, dear?"

I sighed, recognizing the voice. It was clearly just *that* day.

Not fair. I actually like Faith.

"Hey." I stood and turned.

I liked her more when I saw that she was in capri jeans and a purple t-shirt that said, "My Garden is My Happy Place," topped by a worn denim bucket hat with a big sunflower on it. I bet she'd embroidered the sunflower.

"Sorry to bug you while you're working…I had to run out and get a new trowel because mine broke, and I saw you." A rueful head shake. "How does a trowel break?"

"That's what I was going to ask you," I said, and we both laughed.

"I'd had it since we bought the house, and the blade just fell off when I pulled it out today."

"Of course it did."

"So I zipped up to Loquat's Hardware, and Trudy Wallens was in line, getting some more marigolds for her front walk. The Majeskies' damn dog fertilized them right to death again, if you can believe it."

"Ugh." The Majeskie Saint Bernard, Bertha, is the only dog in town larger than Norm...and believes that small bedding plants are a marker for a bathroom. She—don't be sexist, now—is a town legend, and the reason the Rec Department decided on simple mulch edging for the path to the dog park. "Planting up to the street is always a risk."

"Isn't that the truth. Some of those little terriers on my street are at least as bad. Anyhow," she said, moving on to business, "she was all upset about the nursing home expansion and her aunt's house again. Didn't you say that was going nowhere?"

"I thought it was." I shrugged. "I can't tell you who my source is, but they're definitely in a position to know, and they asked me to calm the waters a bit."

"I thought that's what you were getting at." She nodded, held my gaze so I understood that she wasn't the one who had not gotten it. "And I told Trudy exactly that. But she claims that someone in a position to know told *her* that it was definitely a go."

"I would guess that person is getting their info from a different direction."

"So would I."

"And probably not nearly as good a source as mine."

A slow nod from Faith as she thought about it. "Unless that person is getting their info from a good source at another side of the transaction."

"Ah. Because there are a bunch of different people involved who could be talking."

"Exactly. Property owners, real estate agents, town officials, and the business, probably other folks too."

I noted that she carefully buried what she had to know was my likely source in the middle of the list. "You're right."

"And everyone may not be as sure as you are that it isn't going to happen. Or may know something else."

"Or think they do."

"Exactly." Faith gave me an uncertain look. "Think you could nose around a little?"

"Sure." In between the fourth-graders, the dead movie star, and all my usual fun and festivity.

"Good. I figure Trudy's just borrowing trouble, as my Scottish grandmother used to say, but maybe we can help her."

"My grandmother said that too." I joined her smile. "Always glad to help."

And I was, after all, going to see a real estate agent at drop-off in the morning. About time Sally made herself useful.

Chapter Twenty-Eight

Batting Practice

I f you weren't expecting Garrett to show up at some point Sunday, you haven't been paying attention. He appeared as Faith drove off in his own version of weekend casual: jeans and the State Police Spouse sweatshirt he proudly sported at retiree events.

"Ed is putting his foot down about walking. I thought maybe I could recruit you two to keep me company."

Since Ed had been putting his foot down about walking for roughly four years now, and Garrett only intermittently followed the advice, I knew this likely had more to do with Friday's events than Garrett's cardiovascular health.

"Sure." I held up the violets. "Let me just put these in some water."

"Works for me." He turned to Henry, who'd moved on to tossing the wiffle ball and swinging at it. Henry wasn't that great a hitter, even when I threw for him, but he had fun, which is all that really matters.

"Hey, buddy! How bout I toss a few for you?"

"Sounds great, Uncle Garrett!"

I took a couple extra minutes to arrange the violets in Grandma's bone china cup and set it on the living room bookshelf to give the guys a little time.

"Base hit!" Garrett was picking up the ball as I walked out. "Do you know this kid bats left?"

"Left? He's right-handed."

"Show her, Henry." He nodded to Henry, who moved into a perfect lefty batting stance. "He sees the ball better on this side. Watch."

Garrett threw a very decent strike with the form he'd proudly shown off at Shoreline State softball games. He'd been a pitcher in college, and a good one, though he cared far more about baseball history as told by Frank Deford and Roger Kahn than the game itself.

And Henry connected. A good solid hit.

"Well, how about that." I fetched the ball this time. "Looks like we've got a southpaw."

Garrett grinned. "Bet his gym teacher's been trying to get him to hit right because he's a righty."

"I think so."

"You may want to drop the guy a note. Some teachers don't get it without help."

"Good idea." I motioned to Henry, who was beaming with the pleasure of successfully connecting with the ball. And no wonder. "Thanks for figuring it out."

Garrett beamed, too. "Kid can hold his own as long as he knows how. Much more fun that way."

"Absolutely." Said I from the experience of life as a six-footer who never learned to sink a free throw.

"Ready to walk, Uncle Garrett?" Henry asked.

"Isn't batting practice exercise?" He sighed. "All right, I did tell Ed I was going to walk with you, so…"

"And we'd never want to make you a liar," I said. "So, how about we walk you around the block so you can tell Ed you did."

"Sure." He chuckled. "And you can tell me what you think of that video of Studebaker on social media."

"I couldn't make myself watch it." And I couldn't stop the shudder.

"Me either. I just watched a second or two to see that it really was from the shoot, then paused it." He shook his head. "Pretty awful. But who put it out there?"

"Could have been anybody who was there with a smartphone. It's easy to take and post a video, right?"

"Very. Any decent phone will do it." Garrett narrowed his eyes. "Soon, young lady, we are going to spend an evening or two getting you up to speed on social media posting."

"Fine." I narrowed mine right back. "So, was there anything distinctive about the video?"

"Actually, yes. It looked like it had been taken by someone with a decent eye for composition and camera placement."

"Not just any random lookie-loo."

"Right. Maybe someone experienced with photography." He smiled. "Or, say, film."

"That's what I was thinking. But why would someone associated with the movie put it out?"

"Not to promote whatever was left of the movie, for sure."

"That's right, it's scrapped, isn't it?"

Garrett nodded. "The internet seems to think so."

"So if it's not promotion, is it just some ghoulish way to capitalize— or maybe get their next job with some other production?"

"Maybe to show what a horrible mess it was—and that everyone who raised questions was right."

"Like, say the unions, or Olivia Carr?"

"Especially Olivia Carr." Garrett gave a canny and evil smile. "She's still trending. Not bad for a woman who's doing a stage production of Hamlet in London."

"She's definitely getting more out of the movie not happening than she ever would have if it went as planned."

"And seems to be playing it very well online." Garrett's wry tone suggested he thought the lady did protest too much.

"What are you thinking?"

"I'm not sure...but I think I want to nose around tonight."

"Carefully." I didn't want Chase Maguire coming after him with that evil look in his eyes. Though, of course, Ed probably wouldn't mind taking out the creep to defend his man.

Garrett gave me a pitying gaze. "Online snooping only, thank you, Miss Analog."

"Okay."

"And I promise, if I find anything, I will take it straight to that cute Joe Poli."

The way he put it, and the gleam in his eyes stopped me for a second. I coughed. Blushed.

"Have you perhaps noticed that the State's Attorney does not look like a pair of old shoes?" Garrett asked with a teasing grin.

"Oh, I've always had an eye for the boys." I had no real hope of playing it off, and indeed, I failed miserably.

"Honey," he said, looking to make sure Henry was still a bit ahead, "you've done your mourning and your work. It's okay if you're starting to notice men again."

"But I'm not sure I'm ready to do anything about it...and a divorced guy probably expects..."

"A decent man doesn't *expect* anything. If he's worthy of you, he'll keep his hopes to himself until the appropriate time."

I swallowed a smile. Of course, I know dating rules are a good bit different in the gay community and that Garrett had a very interesting life before his marriage. But when he's talking about me, his thoughts on courtship are positively antediluvian.

When Frank and I started dating, Garrett actually demanded that the poor guy come out with him for a man-to-man drink and pass muster. (One man to man—this was fortunately before Ed.) Frank did, of course. Said he understood and respected it. Any wonder why I married him?

"Yeah?" I managed now.

"Yeah. I'm told men are pretty scared about #MeToo anyhow, so nice guys aren't putting anything out there unless they're sure it's welcome."

"Talking to Ed's daughter again?" I asked. Jana, his older stepdaughter, was very happily divorced. Not to mention a useful subject change.

"Thought you might need a little info one of these days." His ears turned pink, just like Ed's did when he was embarrassed. "Jana's family, you know. She'd be happy to buy you a martini and give you a little advice."

A year ago, I probably would have burst into tears at the very thought. Now? Especially since I did not want to get my dating tips from Jorge via Tiffany. "Make it a glass of wine, and I'm in."

"Thought maybe." He smiled. I didn't doubt that he and Ed had sounded Jana out at that Friday night pizza party. Possibly even brought up Joe Poli specifically to see if she knew anything about him.

Unlikely, since Jana taught AP English in Fairfield, but you never did know.

"You and Henry should join Ed and me next Saturday. Jana's oldest is playing in some soccer thing, and we're going out to dinner after."

"Sounds good." If Jana's oldest's soccer thing was anything like soccer things around here, she was calling in the troops to avoid crazy coach dads, cheerleader moms, and general boredom. I could support that.

"Excellent." Garrett nodded, watched my face for a moment. "Frank Glaser was a good fella."

"That he was." My throat started to close.

"But he's not here now, and you are." Garrett patted my arm. "Nobody's saying run out and get married...or anything else. Just that maybe you want to start looking around and seeing who's there."

"Ah." I took a breath.

"I've heard good things about Joe Poli."

"Yeah?"

"Yeah. Standup guy."

"That part I knew." I smiled a little, cleared my throat. "He came to Frank's wake, not because he knew us well, but because Frank always treated him with respect."

"Kind of thing Frank would do." An approving nod.

"And did." I'd walked with him into any number of wakes for people I knew slightly or not at all because Frank had respected them and their work. I took a breath.

Garrett patted my arm. "Not where I'm going."

"Good." I nodded, tried to release the tension.

"Not only is he a standup guy in the general sense," Garrett continued, resolutely pulling us back, "unlike a lot of the straight guys around here, he didn't end up divorced because he cheated. Way I heard it, the wife wanted a corporate killer, not a crime fighter, and left for somebody who could keep her in Louboutins."

"Have you been talking to Lidia?"

"Well, a little." He smiled, looking as impish as a retired history professor of a certain age could. "If you take the mom's word and subtract about fifty percent – which is the usual calculation—he's still pretty terrific."

"Knows some Donne, too."

"And you know this…"

"Because he quoted a line or two for me." I shrugged, gave in to the blush. "Pretty nice."

"Well, then, let's get this movie star mess resolved and see what we see." He patted my arm as we turned for the house. "Now that I have done my walk like a good boy, is there any possibility that you and

Master Henry would accompany me to Ice Cream Heaven? Ed is busy washing Norm, and I am told there is no-sugar-added Cocoa Almond Crunch."

"No one in their right mind would say no to that."

Chapter Twenty-Nine

Cookie and Cannoli

By early evening, our very simple dinner was over, the light was starting to fade, and Henry and I were on the couch relaxing. Cookie was dozing between us, head on Henry's leg, backside ostentatiously toward me, as his boy watched a new Nat Geo video on the Voyager mission, and neither seemed remotely interested in my presence. So happy and relaxed that they barely noticed the knock on the screen door.

I carefully got up and walked lightly to the door, trying to ignore the nervous little twist in my stomach.

Deliveries don't usually come on Sundays, and I hadn't ordered anything lately anyway—and Chase Maguire was still out there somewhere. And my son and his cat were three feet away from that door.

I almost picked up a weapon.

Even without it, I was cautious and curious as I peered out the window.

And immediately burst out laughing at the sight that greeted me. Joe Poli, in a Yale rugby and jeans, stood on the step with one of those skinny little leashes in his hand and a small black mop at his feet. The contrast of tall, manly man and tiny, fluffy dog was more than I could handle. I had to cough and clear my throat before I opened the door, because I didn't want to be rude.

He had a slightly, but adorably, uncertain smile. "Hi."

"Well, nice to see you," I said, waving him in as if he showed up at my house all the time. "Is this the famous Cannoli?"

The black mop trundled in ahead of Joe, raised its head, and sniffed around. I caught a glimpse of bright black eyes and a cute little nose before the hair fell back down. I noted that it was at least wearing a simple red nylon collar and no bows, sweater, or any of the other precious horrors people sometimes inflict upon small dogs.

Henry looked up from his video. "Hi, Mr. Poli."

"Hi, Henry."

"Cute puppy."

"Oh, Cannoli's full-grown." Joe shrugged. "He's just small."

They exchanged smiles, and for a full second, it seemed like a nice friendly moment. Then, a black streak from the couch, as Cookie flew through the air with a bloodcurdling howl, landing in front of Cannoli.

It was obviously cat for: *"What the hell are you and what are you doing in my house?"*

Not to mention a deliberate attempt to terrify the dog, who was just over half the cat's size. It worked, too.

Cannoli whimpered and tried to hide behind Joe's leg, succeeding only in nearly tripping him up with the leash.

"Whoa! Calm down, pal!" Joe may have been trying to soothe the dog, but since he was also trying not to trip over it or the leash, he failed miserably.

"Cookie!" I snapped. The cat responded with a cool, unapologetic glare.

Henry giggled.

Cannoli whimpered some more and tried to climb up Joe's leg, complicating his efforts to detangle himself.

Cookie, knowing when he'd won, favored the dog with a hiss and stalked off with a magisterial tail flip.

Joe finally managed to recover his balance and picked up the dog, which snuggled into his shoulder like an upset toddler as he patted the poor thing's back and tried to reassure him. "You're okay, fella. It's just a cat."

"Wow." Henry laughed. "I've never seen Cookie move that fast."

"Probably defending his territory," I said. "He thinks of himself as Henry's lion protector, but he never does much about it."

"Until today." Joe laughed as Cannoli expressed his thanks for being rescued with a good lick on his face. "Cannoli has no such delusions. He knows he's a wimp."

"Aw, he's cute." Henry came over. "Cannoli?"

"Yep. Want to pet him?"

Henry held out his hand to the little black mop, and as soon as the dog sniffed it, he leaned down from Joe's arms and started licking Henry's nose. That sparked a giggle, the wonderful, infectious little-boy noise that bubbled up from his tummy and made everyone else laugh, too.

Well, except Cookie.

The cat reminded us of his existence with a heartbroken howl. I didn't really blame him. He confronted the interloper, won the day, and now that strange, smelly little black thing was licking his boy. Not fair.

"Calm down, Cookie," I called. "Henry, why don't you go give the cat a treat and let him re-scent you?"

"Sure, Ma. Nice seeing you, Mr. Poli, Cannoli."

Henry walked off toward the kitchen to get some of Cookie's favorite Tuna Greens Crunchies.

Cannoli settled in on Joe's shoulder, clearly in his happy and safe place and going nowhere.

Joe shook his head. "I did not come over here to upset your cat. Or to introduce you to my dog."

"It's okay. Life's always better with pet and kid drama."

"Best kind." He smiled. Yeah, I definitely liked that smile. "I was on my way back from dropping Aly off at her mom's, and I thought I'd swing by and get your thoughts on something about the movie."

And make sure Henry and I were safe, I was sure. I was equally sure I was not supposed to acknowledge that fact.

"Fine by me. Would you like some lemonade? It's finally in season, and I made some to go with dinner."

"You make your own lemonade?"

"Only in really nice weather after I've done yard work."

It was only then that he took a good look at me. Suddenly, I wished I'd done more than slap curl cream through my hair, smear on a little face oil, and throw on a tee and leggings after my shower.

"I like the shirt," he said.

It was a long-sleeved gray jersey that proclaimed, "Well-Behaved Women Rarely Make History," the legendary line from Laurel Thatcher Ulrich. I shrugged. "I like yours."

"Off-duty, you know."

"Yup."

"You look like a college girl," he said, then bit his lip. "In a good way."

"Thanks. Not so bad yourself...but definitely not a college bro."

"An honor I dream not of," he said.

"Ooh, nice catch. Juliet."

"It is? I just remember it was Shakespeare."

I laughed. "Juliet says it when her dad's crowing about marrying her off to Tybalt. She's not wowed."

"If I remember correctly, Juliet's younger than Aly. There's nothing grownups can do to wow teenage girls."

"Isn't that the truth." I nodded. "The ninth-grade home-ec class comes every winter for their Household History unit, and they're tougher than anyone else."

"Aly's usually not tough. She's just not interested in much."

"Yeah. If only eighteenth-century cookery had involved K-Pop stars."

We shared another laugh. Cannoli licked Joe's ear and snuggled in a little closer.

"So, is that a 'no' on the lemonade?" I asked.

"I'd better not. I don't want to turn this guy loose in your house after that little incident."

"Cookie's made his point. He won't come after him again." Probably.

"Cookie?"

"As in a certain monster." I shook my head. "He thinks he's the great defender of the house, when he's really just a big ball of goo."

"He wasn't today."

"Very unusual for him."

"Yeah. Anyway, I probably need to get this fella home and calm him down fairly soon, so I'll take a rain check on the lemonade."

"Fine by me."

"So Amber's new husband is the CFO of one of the big insurance firms."

"Oh, okay."

His face tightened a little, but his voice stayed neutral. "It *is* okay. We're very civil because we just didn't belong together anymore. I was interested in principle, and she was interested in a particular lifestyle, so..."

Meaning, Amber dumped him for a seriously rich guy when he stopped being a hired gun. Not that he needed me to point that out. I just nodded.

"Anyway, Darren's a decent guy. We were making small talk about the Studebaker case today, and he just reeled off with it: 'I wonder if he was worth more dead than alive.'"

"How's that?"

"Darren's not an expert on film, but apparently, if a star dies during a production, and they can't salvage the film, the insurance company has to pay out. Do you know anything about that?"

I shook my head. "Really not my end of things."

"I'll do some digging. Darren didn't seem to know anymore—his firm is mostly financial services." And Joe clearly didn't want to ask more of the man who'd married his former wife.

"It's Connecticut," I said, staying on topic instead of trying to offer some kind of comfort. Not that I could really come up with any, anyway. "There has to be someone who knows about insuring films."

"Well, exactly. They don't call us the insurance state for nothing."

"Makes more sense than nutmegs, for sure."

"Oh, c'mon, you have to know why that is." Joe grinned.

"The way I heard it, it had something to do with Yankee peddlers."

He laughed. Wickedly. "It did. But there's a little more than that... you really don't know this?"

"No, really." I'd just assumed it was because Yankee peddlers bought nutmegs at the port and sold them all over. I wasn't especially interested in the nickname of my state.

Joe Poli looked at me with admiration. "Cool. I like that you're not giving me a freebie."

"I wouldn't. Never learned how to play dumb."

"Good. I like that in a woman."

And I like that look on a man, I thought as I basked in his appreciative gaze. "So? The peddlers?"

"We are called the Nutmeg State, my dear Dr. Shaw, because those canny Yankee peddlers were known for selling wooden nutmegs."

I laughed. "Of course we are."

"We've been sneaky bastards from the drop."

"No kidding. I love that. Thank you for enlightening me."

"My pleasure…and apparently yours too." Maybe it was the word 'pleasure,' or maybe just the wonderful fun of laughing together, but as our eyes held, there was suddenly something else there.

Something pretty darn hot.

"Anyhow," Joe said quickly, clearing his throat and looking away so I knew I wasn't the only one who'd felt it, "we do need to find some answers on movies and insurance."

Something pinged in my memory. "I do know one thing."

"Anything helps right now."

"A few years ago, I was hired to help with a Dolley Madison biopic. A famous actress was supposedly in talks to play her, and the costume designer asked me to consult on accessories and props. There were going to be a lot of feathers—turban decorations and writing quills, maybe even boas, though that wasn't to period. I wondered if they had confused Dolley Madison with Hello Dolly."

He snickered. "Stop being funny."

"Sorry. It's hard to be serious about boas."

"True enough." Joe's tight jaw, though, made it clear that he had no interest in boas. "What famous actress?"

"I never knew. They just referred to her as 'the talent.'" I stifled a chuckle. "It was actually pretty silly."

"Sounds it."

"But it fell apart in pre-production because they couldn't get insurance."

"Couldn't get insurance?"

"The way the designer explained it to me, 'the talent' overdosed during her last movie, and nobody would insure her until she'd been through rehab and spent a couple of years demonstrating that she was healthy…and safe."

"Because…"

"You'll have to check this out, of course, but the implication was that the odds were far too high that she might become very ill or die during the movie, and the insurer would be on the hook."

Joe looked puzzled. "Then why would anyone *want* to harm Studebaker? He was the star."

"What if it was a really big policy…and the film wasn't going to make a lot?" I thought about what Garrett had told me about the likely social media reaction to a *Scarlet Letter* riff all about a man's midlife crisis in the post #MeToo world. If Garrett could see that coming, so could Greg Holman.

Joe's eyes narrowed. "Might be a fast way to turn some cash."

"It might." I remembered my conversation with Sally earlier in the day. "There's apparently some buzz that the movie is off because Studebaker can't finish it. A report and a lot of social media talk, I'm told."

"You're told?"

"Someone who's a lot more social media savvy told me I should look at it…and I haven't had time yet."

Joe smiled. "I'm not very savvy either. But I'll rummage around."

"It would fit," I said. "If there is some kind of insurance payout when a movie doesn't happen…"

He nodded. "So poor Mr. Studebaker might indeed have been worth more dead than alive."

"And wouldn't that be a kick."

"Cookie didn't kick Cannoli," Henry said, jumping back into the conversation. "He just menaced him a little."

Joe gave Henry a look.

"Okay, a lot. But Cookie's never seen anything like that, and he's kind of feisty sometimes."

"He sure is."

They laughed together, and Henry carefully reached in and patted

Cannoli. "Nice dog."

"He's a good little fella. Keeps me honest."

"You can go back to your show if you want, Henry," I cut in.

Henry's eyes gleamed. "New documentary on the Voyager Mission. I'm almost to the part where they go past Ur-ANUS."

"Ur-AN-ous." I sighed as my little cherub returned to the TV. "I'll walk you two out."

"Thanks. I will take you up on that lemonade one of these days."

"Hope you do."

Chapter Thirty

Drop(off) Clues

Monday morning, Ed *just happened* to be walking Norm at drop-off time. He and Henry had a wonderful conversation about the moon mission, and the time rookie state trooper Ed and his buddies guarded Neil Armstrong and friends during a visit to New Haven.

I hoped Henry wasn't thinking of becoming an astronaut; even with all the current advances in treatment and science, he probably wouldn't be allowed to sign up. Not that I'd say any such thing to him right now.

The astronauts apparently had had a very good time, and I had just as much fun listening to Ed's careful descriptions of wine, women, and song as "very nice parties" as I did the actual stories of the visit.

"Hen-ree!"

We were just turning for Wheatley, when little Sheridan Birdwell came running up and practically tackled him, grabbing his hand and dragging him off toward her mother and brother, who were walking in from the other direction.

"Looks like he already has an admirer," Ed said.

"Her mother's a piece of work, but she's a cute kid."

Ed chuckled. "Sally? Oh, yeah. She'd sell her grandmother with the house if it would get her numbers up."

As I joined his wry chuckle, I remembered that I needed to talk to Sally about the nursing home expansion gossip. "Even so, I have to go say hi for a minute."

Ed patted Norm. "Better you than me."

Sally was, as usual, perfect in a beige twinset and slightly darker houndstooth skirt, complete with heels and headband. "Christian! I do like those vintage shirts of yours."

"Thank you." I was wearing one of the simpler ones with my favorite navy blazer from a boys' school that had been out of business for fifty years, finished with a big sparkly crescent moon pin on the lapel... and the purple gloves I'd worn to move the Bible back to the Society hanging out one pocket. I quickly scrunched them out of view.

"I wouldn't be comfortable with such a boyish look, but on you it works."

I chose to take it as a backhanded compliment. "Someone asked me about the nursing home expansion yesterday. Have you heard anything?"

"Oh, it's definitely a go. The company approached adjacent property owners months ago."

And there's the information from another angle. "So moving ahead this time?"

"I'd sure think so." She smiled. "I'm actually thinking of approaching them about a couple of my clients a little further out...see if they want to widen the footprint."

"Deep pockets."

"Exactly." Her eyes gleamed. "The good kind of deep pockets. Those movie people supposedly had all that money, and we never saw any of it."

"Some folks had fun watching the shoots."

Sally's nose wrinkled. "Not me. I don't need to see how the sausage is made."

"Even for Brett Studebaker?"

"Oh, honey, everybody knows he's gay." She trilled a laugh. "Not that there's anything wrong with that."

I kind of wanted to smack her. But I had too many good reasons to pick just one. And even if Ed vouched for me, I'd probably still be in the town lockup when the fourth-graders got there.

Saved by the kids.

"Walk me to the door, Hen-ree…" Sheridan said, pulling him along as her brother glared at them both.

"Can't." Henry gently pulled away. "Gotta go say bye to Norm."

Sheridan pouted, a perfect twenty-five-percent copy of her mother. "Boo."

"Aww, I'll see you inside later." Henry patted her arm, and Sheridan lit up.

Sally gave me an eye-roll, and I managed to smile back. Proud that I was raising a kind boy, even if he was clearly catnip to predatory females.

"Anyhow, thanks for the info," I said, keeping my tone friendly and neutral. "Have a good one. Gotta get back to prepare for the hurricane."

"Oh, you put things the funniest way."

That's me, a barrel of laughs.

As I turned away from Sally, Ed pulled back from what had clearly been a fun conversation with Lidia and brought Norm over for the promised farewell to Henry. After sending him on with good wishes and a little doggy drool, Ed, Norm, and I turned for the Society.

As soon as we were out of the school zone, Ed pulled a small canister out of his pocket and handed it to me.

"It works the same as the big one. Just keep it in your jacket pocket, okay?"

I put it in the pocket with the gloves, glad it was small enough not to show, even if it was pretty heavy. "Thanks. I don't really think it's necessary, but…"

"I don't either. If I really thought you'd ever need it, I'd be in your office with my gun until they arrested Maguire."

I didn't doubt it.

Despite the grim topic, it was hard to be too worried about anything. In New England, May does that to people. It was one of those perfect late-spring mornings when the lilacs are coming out, and the sun is burning off the mist, and no matter what is going on, a part of your soul wants to kick off its shoes and frolic in the green, green grass.

Not Ed, though. "So Joe Poli tells me he's been visiting."

"Yeah." I could feel the blush creeping up my face, and I expected Ed to laugh.

He didn't. "He's a standup guy, Christian. A really good man. But maybe not the guy for you and Henry."

"What do you mean?"

"Garrett thinks I'm wrong, but I have to say this to you. I like Joe a lot. He's as good as he seems. But you need to think hard about whether you want to be with a prosecutor."

Ed, the former state trooper, was definitely in a position to know. "Why?"

"You won't always be first. He has a job and a duty, and if you get involved with him, there are going to be times that you and Henry will be on your own because the work comes first. You deserve better than that."

"I don't think Joe Poli is all that interested anyway," I said, giving Ed a soothing pat on the arm. "But remember, I was married to a reporter. I know about the work winning out. We scheduled our wedding around the governor's impeachment. You know the story."

"Yeah." Ed shook his head. Garrett still teased me sometimes about having been the only bride who was more interested in the State Senate

216

Judiciary Committee than the gift registry. In the end, though, the gov resigned, and Frank and I got exactly the wedding we wanted: a small, sweet ceremony by the water in New Haven.

"It's just, Christian, you and that little guy have been through so much; I don't want you being second on anyone's list."

Garrett isn't my only surrogate dad. Ed is not, and never will be, much of a hugger, but he was happy to accept another pat on the arm. "I appreciate that. And I think we're having this conversation way too early. He hasn't even asked me out…if people even do that anymore."

"Joe Poli does, and he will. After I told him what we'd found in the tankard, he asked about you and if you've worked through your issues enough to date again."

And also, in a modern riff on all of that old patriarchal stuff "among men," asking for his blessing, since Ed and Garrett are essentially my dads. I wasn't sure if it was cute or maddening, and I decided to go with cute. "Did you tell him what you just told me?"

"I did. And I told him I was going to say it to you, too."

"What did he say?"

Ed smiled a little. "He said it was fair to warn you. He also said he'd learned his lessons over the years."

"Ah." I understood that Ed was an unwilling messenger. "Did you believe him?"

"Maybe."

"So what you're really saying is…"

"I don't know." He took a long breath. "I just wouldn't feel right about you going out with him without knowing that prosecutors tend to seriously neglect their families when they're in the middle of a case."

"Well, why don't I wait and see if he asks me out and then think about it."

"Start thinking now." Ed grinned and patted Norm's giant head. "He mentioned Due Fiori."

"Really." Due Fiori, just over the town line in Cheshire, is the romantic dinner spot in our corner of the county. Twentysomethings whipping out the ring, Mom and Dad's date night, not to mention Grandma's second-chance first date with the new man, all take place at Due Fiori. It's the special place. If you just want a big relaxing family and friends' night over good pasta, you go to Malina's, about a block from the Green.

"Wait and see." He shrugged. "Even though I've got my concerns, I have to tell you, you're probably not going to meet a more ethical guy, or one who'd treat you with more respect."

"Okay."

"And you probably think he's cute."

"I do."

Ed grinned. "That's all fine. Just keep in mind that if you get serious about him, you may not always be first on his list. And you need to decide if you want that."

"That may be a conversation for a little further down the road," I warned him.

"Right." He shook his head. "Keep your eyes open, okay? That's all I'm saying."

"And I appreciate it." I planted a very careful kiss on his cheek, and his ears turned pink.

"Gotta keep an eye on you young things. Never know what kind of trouble you'll get into."

"Especially in the spring," I said, making a very deliberate subject change.

"Well, it is a pretty day," Ed observed as Norm sniffed at a petunia patch.

"Just about my favorite time of the year. Warm enough to be comfortable, not sticky yet."

"Yup. Summer was no fun when I was on patrol." He chuckled,

balance restored between us. "Winter wasn't much better."

"And yard work is still fun right now." I pointed to the petunias. "I'm thinking about putting in a few plants by the walk this year."

"Something bright would be pretty—but you should ask Garrett what to pick. He's got the eye."

"Green thumb, too."

"Exactly. I'm much happier with the handy stuff."

"What's this summer's project?"

"Thinking about re-doing the deck. It needs a coat of stain, but I might just get a sander from the hardware store and start over with a new color."

"Okay."

"I'm thinking like maybe one of those new pickled-pine grays. I've never been wild about that redwood, and now there are some nice new colors."

I nodded and tried to look interested. Deck maintenance, though a consuming preoccupation for suburban males of all ages, political stripes, and sexual orientations, was not my thing.

"But I have to fix the living room floor first."

"What happened?"

He gave an exasperated nod to the dog. "This guy was attacking one of Garrett's socks and put a really nice gouge near the door."

"Not cool."

"Good doggie having a bad day." Norm gave Ed the adorable good puppy face, clearly realizing he was the topic of conversation, and Ed bent down to pat him.

"So what do you do for that?"

"Well, I'll fill it in with wood putty, so the gouge won't show, and then add a new coat of polyurethane...it's a real pain."

"Wood putty?" I asked, as his comment tripped something in my brain.

"Yeah. It comes in all kinds of colors, or you can even blend your own. You put it in the gouge or hole in the wood, and it looks like nothing ever happened."

"Do you have to put the topcoat on?" I was starting to wonder about the pulpit. Could someone have removed the latch, if there was one, and made it look like it was never there?

Someone with all the resources of a movie scene shop, maybe?

"If you want it to stay forever in a high-traffic area, you do, but if you just want to hide the damage, not as much. I used it on the side of a table once."

"It's not shiny?"

"Not really. It looks like wood. Why?"

"I think I know how someone tampered with the pulpit door."

"Meaning you think you know how they killed Brett Studebaker." Ed's jaw tightened, and he looked very sharply at me. "Are we talking Maguire again?"

"Maybe. I think Maguire has some scenery experience." I was still pretty sure Greg Holman was the main driver, because of the money, with or without Chase's help. "I need to look at the pulpit."

"Okay. Here's what we're going to do," he said, reaching for his phone as we got within a block of the Green. "I'm going to call DiBiasi and Joe Poli and come with you and the Rabbi while you look at the pulpit."

"Fine by me." There was no point in challenging Ed's protectiveness, and I actually kind of liked it. "But we've got to resolve this before the fourth-graders arrive at noon."

"Let's hope we get it done a lot sooner than that."

Chapter Thirty-One

How We Get There

I t only took ten minutes for Dina and me to prove my theory. Ed and Norm stood guard outside, and Dina watched at the base of the stairs as I climbed into the pulpit, gloved up with a magnifying glass and flashlight. I found what I was looking for pretty quickly. It was there all along. The spots where a couple of nail holes for an old latch had once been were very neatly filled in with the putty, and the whole area carefully buffed to match the rest. It was only visible with magnification, and only if you knew what you wanted to find.

Someone was really good.

I took a couple of pics with my phone, thinking.

I remembered Chase mentioning that he'd been part of the set design crew on his first movie. I was pretty sure he'd done the work, and he might flip on Holman.

"What's this?"

Joe was walking into the sanctuary.

"I know how they did it." I looked down at him, as the height made my head spin a little.

"They who?"

"Someone affiliated with the movie," Dina told him, walking over to the old communion rail. "See how this has a little latch on the door?"

Joe bent down to take a close look.

"Then come up here," I called.

From my perch in the pulpit, my voice echoed lightly in the sanctuary, and I pushed the door out as Joe climbed partway up the stairs. I handed him the magnifying glass and pointed a purple-gloved finger. "See the tiny difference in color? That's where the putty was put in after someone took off the latch."

"Someone?"

"It would have to be a person with some woodworking experience and who knew—or suspected—that Studebaker would be impaired in some way when he was up there."

"Or so out of control from his acting..."

"Because they'd seen him practicing the scene, maybe." I nodded. "Could be Maguire."

"Did Maguire know about anything woodworking?"

"Yes. Maguire was a scenic design major in college, and he told me he worked in the shop on a couple of movies before Studebaker hired him as an assistant."

Joe nodded. "And he certainly had motive."

"But so did Holman," I reminded him. "The insurance."

"Maybe Holman got Maguire to do his dirty work. And since he's in plenty of trouble on his own now, maybe he'll give it up."

"Worth a try."

"Thanks." He stepped down, looked up at me. "Need a hand?"

"I'm fine—just not very graceful." I started climbing down, slightly, but not dangerously, wobbly as always. And as I looked out over the pews, I thought of one more possibility.

I'd assumed that Sally Birdwell was the small, dark-haired woman I saw the night we set up the Bible.

But I'd always thought it was weird that she came out for the setup, considering how much she hated having the film in town. And just now at drop-off, that comment about maybe next time they'll have a shoot where it's worth going to see.

Once again, the noise.

I'd been so busy disliking Sally and letting her make me feel insecure that I missed the obvious. What if it really hadn't been her?

What if it had been somebody else with a pretty good motive to kill Studebaker?

Olivia Carr, poorly used and badly treated co-star, was also a tiny woman. We only had her word on social media that she'd left for Britain. Put a black wig on her, and it would be hard to tell her from Sally, or any other small, dark-haired female, at a distance. The distinctive thing about her was her white-blond delicacy.

And a girl who grew up backstage in her father's theatre companies would surely know something about scene shops...including quite possibly wood putty.

"What?" Joe asked as I started down the stairs.

"I don't think Holman's the only suspect. It could have been Olivia Carr. I saw a tiny woman I thought was Sally Birdwell..."

His eyes narrowed. "Carr is small, too."

"Tiny like Sally. I feel like a different species around her."

Joe's serious face gave way to a little smile. "I'll take your species any day and twice on Sunday."

"Um, thanks." I was blushing, and I busied myself climbing down in hopes that he wouldn't notice. But he was watching me closely as he put a careful and respectful, but not entirely necessary, hand on my back to help me on the stairs.

This wasn't a blush, it was an eruption. Mount Saint Freaking Helens.

Once I was down on the floor, I tried to look very interested in removing my gloves, but there was nothing for it. Joe caught my eye and held my gaze for a second.

"Most people look awful when they blush," he said. "On you, it's cute."

"Oh."

Before I could even think of a suitable riposte to that, Joe was already moving on, giving me and Dina a professionally and definitely not personally appreciative smile as we all headed for the door.

"Thank you, ladies. We've narrowed the field of suspects nicely."

"Glad to do our civic duty, Mr. Poli," Dina said with a wicked gleam in her eye. Of course, she'd seen everything.

"Always good to help the authorities," I added.

Joe's friendly smile turned into a grin. "Something like that. I'll catch up with you folks later—after I track down Maguire and figure out if Olivia Carr really did go back to Britain."

"Well," Dina reminded him, only a small note of amusement in her tone, "you *know* where to find us."

We all walked out onto the majestic portico, where there were still a few fresh bouquets. Plus, one lone blue teddy bear in a tricorne hat with a felt bayonet in its teeth. Poor Studebaker. He was trying so hard to be someone else.

Wonder what would have happened if he'd just given up and been himself?

Joe shook Ed's hand and took a second to stop at the little Unity cruiser, pulling up with DiBiasi inside.

"Nice job," Ed said with an approving smile.

Dina and I managed modest shrugs.

"No, seriously. You figured it out, and you handed it over to the authorities. Exactly what civilians are supposed to do."

"We aren't exactly Miss Marple, Sergeant Kenney." Dina always called him by his title, and he always smiled when she did.

"No, but a lot of people think they're smarter than they are. Good on you."

"You taught me well." I patted his arm.

"Do you still have the fourth grade this afternoon?" Dina asked.

"Oh, yes."

"Well, I have the building committee and the older Hebrew School kids, and it's Ben's surgery day. He's up to his eyeballs in eyeballs."

We all chuckled.

"Still his best joke," I said.

"And he knows it," Dina continued with a grin. "What do you think of meeting up at Malina's for dinner?"

Ed beamed. "Count us in too. It's too interesting a day to just go home."

"Absolutely." I agreed. "I'll see if Tiffany and Jorge want to come too."

"The more the merrier." Dina grinned. "Sometimes you just need some good pasta and red."

All of us—except Norm—exchanged happy smiles as DiBiasi walked up and Joe drove away. I'd like to say it was the pleasure of having made sure justice was done, but it was really the prospect of a good Italian dinner and plenty of good talk. It's the New Haven County way. Whether good or bad, when anything happens in life, you round up your family of blood and choice, go to your local, and talk about it over plates of classic checked-tablecloth food.

We didn't know then how much more we'd have to discuss by dinnertime.

Chapter Thirty-Two

And You Thought the Fourth-Graders Were the Scary Part

My first fourth-grade field trip at the Society left me shaking for three days. Absolute overreaction, because as I've learned over the years, they're big enough to be fairly predictable, yet small enough to do what you tell them to. And they're still cute. The ninth-grade girls in the Home Ec Household History Unit are the ones who should really keep me up at night.

These days, I know enough to deck out the main rooms with mostly kid-proof stuff, soothe down the nervous chaperones and teachers, and keep the focus on aspects of life in the past that are interesting to kids. Meaning food, clothes, and, of course, toilets. I've got a pretty good schtick by now, and I was relaxed and having fun by the time we got to the dining room, asking the kids if they'd like to eat their vegetables after they'd been boiled for an hour.

Surprisingly good day after that scary start.

But we weren't done with scary. My phone buzzed when we were about halfway through the tour. Normally, I would never check it, but after the morning we'd had, I just quickly slipped into a corner and pulled it out of my jacket pocket.

Good thing I did.

A text from Joe: *Olivia Carr has been in London for the last three weeks. The movie had a multi-million-dollar insurance policy to pay out on Studebaker's death. Holman's in it up to his eyeballs, and we can't find him. Please be careful.*

Well, wasn't that going to be fun. I sent a quick return of thanks and dove back into the crowd, just in time to rescue one of the few actually valuable things downstairs. One of Sally's soul sisters was chaperoning, and she assumed that the "please do not touch" sign didn't apply to her.

The two-hundred-year-old chinoiserie bowl from the mantel was slipping from her grip when I caught it.

"Oh, Chris, I'm so sorry. The glaze is so slick..."

Grrrr. Chris. I managed an indulgent smile instead of the scowl I was thinking. "Yes, it is. That's why we don't want *anyone* picking it up."

To her credit, she looked honestly embarrassed. "I understand now."

I left it at that. Not worth it, especially in the middle of everything else.

Maybe thirty seconds later, I was bringing up the rear as the fourth-graders trooped up the stairs when the front door slammed open. Obviously, we do not permit the slamming of a perfectly restored eighteenth-century door, and I wheeled around, expecting to admonish a late-coming chaperone to treat the building with respect, especially around the kids.

Instead, it was Greg Holman.

Now we know where he is, anyway.

And nothing adds to the fun of a fourth-grade field trip like a killer.

"I need to talk to you." He spoke with ice-cold command, clearly expecting that I would do whatever he asked.

"Please wait a moment," I said, looking up at the teacher at the top of the stairs. "Ms. Bailey, why don't you take the kids up to the 1802 bedroom, just over on the left there, and I'll be up in a minute."

The chaperone at the back of the pack, one of the hairdressers at the salon I go to, held my gaze for a long second, and I nodded to the kids. *Get them out of here. I don't know what this is, and I want them safe.*

She immediately started urging them upstairs, and I turned back to Holman. As I did, I saw Lewis in the parlor, putting things back in order, and caught his eye.

"Now, what can I do for you?"

The producer forced a smile, which was a good bit scarier than the arrogance with those dead eyes. "We're planning a memorial photo shoot in Hollywood, and I need that mug Brett was using."

"The tankard, you mean." A photoshoot with a prop from a movie that's been very publicly scrapped? I know people think academics don't have much in the way of street smarts, but this was downright insulting.

"Yeah, that. It was like his signature thing for this film, and we're going to put it alongside the bayonet from *Hero of the Free*, his pilot's helmet from *Wingman*, stuff like that."

"Oh. How interesting." I tried to look solemn.

Holman barely heard me. He just kept going in that brusque command tone. "The hospital says it was sent to you."

"They do?" Normally, I consider lying to be a grave sin, but this isn't normal. "Really? How odd. I would have thought it went to the police or the prosecutor."

Which was exactly where it would be going as soon as I got this creep out of my building. I reminded myself that he'd flown in from California, and it was highly unlikely that he was armed.

I slipped my hand in the pepper spray pocket. Just in case. Right now, it would be tough to explain why I sprayed him for slamming the door.

Even if Mae, Faith, and the rest of the board would have applauded me for that alone. They're as protective of the building as I am.

"Apparently not." Holman took a step either toward me, or toward the stairs. "Could it be in an unopened delivery?"

I managed a puzzled look. "I doubt it. I go through everything as it comes in."

"Would you mind checking?" He moved a little closer to me. If I hadn't had a couple of inches on him and a couple of years of karate (a better fit for tall girls than yoga, even though I didn't keep up with it) in my past, I might have felt menaced.

My fingers wrapped around the pepper spray.

Holman took another step closer, gave me another of those fake smiles. "Let's just take a look, Dr. Shaw, see if we can't find it..."

It could have gotten pretty ugly right about then. For him, obviously.

Well, it could have, anyway, if Tony DiBiasi hadn't just opened the screen door and walked in. He had exactly the carefully neutral face that every State Trooper cultivates on the way into a potential situation. Training never dies. "Mr. Holman, I thought I might find you here."

Holman turned.

"State Police Major Crimes is looking for you, but I'll be happy to start the process."

I managed not to sigh audibly in relief, but it was close.

"What do you mean?" Holman asked, drawing himself up in the time-honored imperious way of the allegedly important. "Do you know who I am?"

Ah, the magic words.

That's what Frank always called it. The question that damn near guarantees a police officer will arrest you, whether you use it at a traffic stop or a murder scene. Cops *hate* the implication that who you are is more important than what you may have done.

DiBiasi may have been a small-town cop at the moment, but blue is still blue. (Okay, trooper khaki, but you get the idea.) His eyes narrowed. "I sure do. Gregory Holman of Bel Air, California, wanted on a warrant in the murder of Brett Studebaker."

"What?"

"You're under arrest, Mr. Holman. You have the right to remain silent..."

Lewis walked in from the parlor, joining me at the bottom of the stairs.

"Murder? I didn't have anything to do with any murder!" Holman's voice went higher and brittle.

"Well, you can sort that out with Major Crimes and the State's Attorney. Right now, we're going down to the police station."

Holman looked at DiBiasi. DiBiasi glared back.

"I'm calling my lawyer from the car."

"Call Angelina Jolie for all I care. But you're coming with me."

Holman didn't even bother looking back at Lewis and me. That was just fine.

"Thanks for calling the cops," I said to Lewis.

"I worried for one second that I might have been wrong and you'd never forgive me."

"Nah. Never happen."

We shared a relieved smile.

A crash from upstairs.

"I told you not to touch that, Logan!"

Back to my real job.

Chapter Thirty-Three

Nope. Not Over.

Y ou'd think helping catch a killer while giving three dozen fourth-graders a taste of local history would be enough. You'd be wrong.

I did manage to finish the rest of the field trip with no harm to the children, their handlers, or any priceless artifacts...but only barely, as usual, for such things. That crash upstairs had only been one of the three Logans knocking over the warming pan: a big, gorgeous old brass round with a long wooden handle. They're pretty much indestructible, and ours already had a couple small dents, so I was only a little annoyed.

Because it was a kid. A grownup would have gotten a very nicely worded note accompanying the sizable bill from our brass restorer.

The Logans would have destroyed the whole blasted bedroom if I hadn't been smart enough to place the pan by a wall near the door, angled so that if it did fall, it would go right down without taking anything irreplaceable (say, the early nineteenth-century cosmetic jars) with it. As it was, I just picked up the thing and restored it to its spot, treating the incident as a teachable moment without being too much of the scary museum lady.

I didn't have a lot of scary left anyway.

By the time we finished the tour, I was already exhausted and thinking about going for the carbonara, in all its eggy, bacon-y, and cheesy glory, instead of my usual marinara, not to mention a sizable glass of wine after I was home and Henry was asleep.

When Lewis and I finally wrapped it up, spending a few minutes chatting brightly with teachers and chaperones who were even more in need of liquid refreshment than we were, it was heading for pickup time. Double pickup, because Tiffany had another late run. But at least this one was a guy who fell off his roof and fractured a collarbone. He was going to make it, even if the gutter he grabbed to break his fall wasn't.

In the only relatively normal part of the day, I walked over to Wheatley to get the kids, glad to be alone and free of any danger from the Studebaker mess. On the way back, I gave Henry a few candies and moved a bit faster than usual because his numbers were edging toward low. Only to find Joe on my doorstep, with an empty evidence bag in hand.

"Heard you got a visit."

"And DiBiasi got a collar."

Joe nodded, looked hard at me for a second or two, and put his hand on my arm. "You're okay?"

"Yep. Never in any danger. And the fourth-graders had a lovely visit."

He ran his hand up and down my arm as if he were thinking about pulling me in for a hug, but didn't. "As long as everyone's safe."

"We are."

"Good."

"All wrapped up on your end?" I turned to open the door, realizing as I did that, I would have been very happy to have him keep his hand on my arm.

"Maguire is singing like a nasty little birdie." His face relaxed in a big, happy smile. "Gave Holman right up, says he planned the whole thing and forced him into helping out."

"Forced him how?"

"Threatened to tell the authorities what he saw him doing with one of those would-be groupies...and put his own spin on what he witnessed."

"Blackmail."

"Probably. Creep claims he'd never be involved in anything non-consensual...but who knows." Joe shrugged. "He's still going away for a good long time, so I'm happy."

"What about Holman?"

"In it up to his eyeballs. After Studebaker filed the complaint against Maguire, Holman called him in and, instead of firing him, suggested he'd make the complaint go away in exchange for a little help."

"Adding the threat as an incentive?"

"Sold to the pretty lady in the blazer." Joe's smile widened into a grin. A grin with plenty of extra spin. "He says he put a little synthetic pot in the tankard with Studebaker's whiskey to help things along...so we're going to need to test it for residue. Holman obviously knew it was the key and hoped to make it go away."

"Hence his visit today."

"No tankard, no chemical residue. A big chunk of the case was gone."

"Still had the pulpit door."

"He may not have known we found the woodwork." Joe shrugged. "I'm still sorting it all out. He definitely knew about the mug, and he definitely wanted it."

"Yep." I nodded. "And now you do."

"But I'll sign a release."

"You bet you will."

We shared a grin as I opened the door. Ava ran right to the office, but Henry stopped at the Bible.

"I'll get you the tankard in a minute," I said. "It's in the bureau in the 1835 bedroom on the third floor. Ed had me move it from the office after we looked at it on Saturday."

"Very smart move."

Henry poked my arm.

I patted his head, but he didn't move. "Henry needs his snack, and then I'll—"

"No problem." Joe nodded, understanding why that was so important and started up the stairs, the steep pitch of the old treads emphasizing the length of his gait. "I'll get it."

"Bottom drawer, still in the Yale-New Haven Hospital box."

"Thanks."

Henry poked my arm again.

"It's all right, sweetie, let's get you that snack right now…"

"That's not it, Mom."

"Your numbers are a little low."

"In a second. Did that movie actor change the Bible?"

"What?"

"It's not the same picture as usual. It was always on a guy talking to a crowd of people."

Which is exactly how my little Jewish boy would see the Sermon on the Mount. It was the page we generally displayed, because it was quite beautiful, and also much more neutral than say, the Crucifixion. The movie director had liked the picture as some kind of echo of the Reverend's meltdown in the pulpit, so we set it up the same way.

"Okay."

He pointed to the case. "Now it looks like some comic book."

The Horsemen of the Apocalypse—the Book of Revelation. I remembered how I'd found it there in the pulpit and how enraged I'd been to see the marks from Studebaker's fingers. I hadn't thought it meant anything then.

But with everything else that had happened, I wasn't so sure now.

"Go eat your sandwich, honey. It's okay." I shooed him back toward the office, adding the mom glare for motivation, then turned for a close look at the case.

The Bible looked much as it always had. Awe-inspiringly old, an alien object from a long-dead world. So amazing in its simple existence that I might have missed something very important here.

Noise again. Not catching the key issue because I was distracted by other things.

I leaned in close.

I could see the faint crinkles where Brett Studebaker had clutched at it, and now, as the afternoon light slanted across the case, something like dust, only thicker, on the page. Not, thank G-d, chips of the ink or paint, but something whitish.

When we were laying it back out, Lewis had asked me if the Puritans used incense on Bibles, just before we were distracted by the bayonet incident. Maybe not incense.

Maybe something very unholy.

"Hey, Lewis!" I called as coolly as I could.

"Hold that thought, guys!" He was smiling as he walked into the foyer, grinning. "They want to play that stupid car game again."

"Fine. Let them." Lewis's brows flicked at that. He knew I was usually a lot stricter about screen time and homework. "Remember when we brought the Bible back. You said you smelled something."

"Yeah. It was sweet, kind of strange."

"Spicy like incense?"

He shook his head. "No...I just asked that because it was the only thing I could think of being close to a Bible. It's weird—but it was almost like Grandma's cheesecake."

"Almonds." I should have figured it out before. I didn't smell it because my grass pollen allergy was acting up that day. "Bitter almonds.

Cyanide."

"What do you mean, cyanide?"

"You smelled it, and I couldn't. Somebody put cyanide on the Bible."

"Where would they get it?"

"I think you can order it online," I said. "But it's a lot more common than you think. It was everywhere a century ago. Rat poison."

Lewis and I looked at each other.

"Those jars I brought down," he said.

"I put them back." I nodded. "One was rat poison."

"Hundred-year-old rat poison. More than a hundred years old." Lewis sounded dubious.

"Cyanide doesn't go bad." Even if it lost strength over time, cyanide is so deadly that it would still be enough. While I didn't know of anyone who'd died from old cyanide, I did know that absolutely no one would ever re-use those old jars or handle them without gloves.

"Shouldn't we have gotten sick?"

"Nope. We wore gloves. Brett Studebaker licked his finger and touched it. Twice."

"Holy hell, sorry, Doc."

"Yeah, that." I thought about it. Who was near the Bible? Who would know? "Have you seen anyone acting weird lately?"

"Mrs. Tillotson spent a lot of time talking with me about old beauty treatments and white skin last week when she saw me reading about *Birth of a Nation*. That's when we took the jars down from the kitchen shelf. Did you know they took arsenic?"

"I did, actually," I said. So, Mae took the jars out for an innocent reason…and then what? Or who? There were some movie people going through the building during the hours before the shoot. Maybe someone else in on the plot and the cyanide as a little extra insurance?

I put my hands in my jacket pockets while I thought for a second. With Holman and Maguire in custody, I could give the pepper spray back to Ed tonight. That would be nice.

I doubted Mae Tillotson and old beauty tonics were going to get us anywhere. Something jabbed at my fingertip, and I pulled it out. A tiny clear stone. The one I'd found in the pulpit the last time I wore this jacket.

I probably got it because I'd been thinking about Mae just a second ago. She had traded her usual little diamond studs for those "Girl with a Pearl Earring" ones at some point in the last week or so.

I remembered her weird, unexpectedly lame explanation when I commented on them.

Her dad had been the sexton at the Congregational church. If anyone would know how to sneak in, climb up in the pulpit, and tamper with the Bible before the shoot, it was her. She wasn't especially frail for her age, and since she was so small, it might actually have been easier for her to get up there than me.

And the bottles. What if it wasn't really the old beauty tonic, but the rat poison? She was definitely capable of distracting Lewis with a disquisition on pale skin, arsenic, and the unforeseen dangers of the obsession with white skin. Especially if it happened to be both historically accurate and interesting.

Would have gotten my attention for sure.

Not now, though. Cyanide, I reminded myself again, doesn't go bad. And it doesn't take much.

I turned to Lewis.

"Is Mrs. Tillotson here?"

"Sure." His eyes widened as he processed it. "Upstairs in the 1835 bedroom. Something about the baby quilt design for her granddaughter?"

Where Joe was getting the tankard we'd *thought* was the key part of the murder plot. Dammit. If she saw him, anything could happen. I turned for the stairs.

"Watch the kids, Lewis. Get the musket if you have to."

"Got that, Doc."

I started up the stairs, moving as quickly and quietly as I could.

Thank G-d I'm a sneaker girl and not into heels like Sally Birdwell.

"I'm not going to jail, young man."

I heard the familiar sweet voice as I slipped past the first landing.

"I don't know what you'd go to jail for." Joe's voice was calm, but brittle.

I found out why as I turned the corner. Mae Tillotson was at the top of the flight, on the landing just above me, holding a good-sized gun on Joe. So that's why she carried such a big purse. But why come armed today? She had no idea anyone was on to her.

Did she?

With everything else going on around here, I couldn't be sure.

I did know she almost certainly had no idea that Holman and Maguire had been arrested, since the announcement didn't usually go out until around arraignment time, and even if the arrests had been right after we looked at the pulpit, it was too soon for it to make the news. At least not anything Mae would watch or listen to.

New Haven's not exactly a news desert, but local media is pretty scarce these days, and Mae wouldn't follow the celeb websites. Jenny Medina, with her love for all things entertainment, had probably seen at least an unconfirmed report on the arrests, but I couldn't imagine that Mae had.

So why the gun?

For all I knew, she always had it. She always carried the big purse. Still, I remembered her reaction when she saw Joe a few days ago. The guilty flee where no man pursueth?

Nope. She figured I knew about the jars. For the second time in a week, someone's giving me credit for being smarter than I am. Like that ever happens for a Western PA girl.

238

Later, I might have to think about that.

Right now, I had to think about the gun that was aimed at Joe's midsection.

World War Two sidearm, most likely standard Army weapon. Probably a souvenir from a husband or boyfriend.

Like it mattered. A gun's a gun once it's pointed at somebody.

I slipped inside the second-floor bedroom and grabbed that warming pan Logan had knocked over a few hours ago. A weapon with reach is good.

I crept up the first two stairs, getting close enough without distracting Mae.

She was still talking, just laying it out for Joe as if she could explain away why she'd calmly murdered a man she didn't know. "That darned movie crew was bringing down property values in town. And I have to sell before the nursing home gets approval for the expansion."

"Quite a problem, Mrs. Tillotson." Joe nodded, and as he did, he made eye contact with me over her head.

"So you see, I had no choice. I couldn't let those people ruin my chance to sell and move to Florida."

"Florida?" he asked. His voice was just a tinge higher, and I knew he was probably wondering what I was waiting for.

A good angle, and a plan, to be honest.

If I just whacked her in the back, she might shoot him. If I tried to knock the gun away, it might go off when it hit the floor. You never know with old weapons.

"Yes, Florida," Mae said, her voice suddenly dreamy. "There's the sweetest little retirement village outside Naples. I'm going to buy a one-bedroom with a lanai. They're pink stucco…"

As she waxed eloquent about the condo, I noticed that her grip on the pistol was loosening a little and her focus wavering a bit. There wasn't going to be a better chance.

I brought the pan down on her gun arm, knocking the weapon to the floor. It didn't go off, but it landed with a hellacious crash…as Mae shrieked and crumpled, falling back toward me.

I let go of the warming pan as I flailed for balance. It slid down the stairs, the brass round banging hard on each tread, just like I might do next, with Mae on top of me, to make absolutely sure I got the worst of it.

For one horrible second, as I grabbed at the railing and got nothing but air, I was sure that was how it was going to end.

A stray bullet would have been better. Safer.

"Whoa!" Joe kicked the gun out of the way and grabbed for her, getting a sleeve but not the whole arm.

I finally managed to get a good grip on the railing with one hand—and put the other one up to shove Mae toward Joe before she fell on top of me. I felt the little bird bones of her spine, suddenly reminding me how fragile and elderly she really was. Joe got a better grip on her arm and yanked her up.

He glared at her for a second, breathing hard, then spoke in the coldest prosecutorial tone he could manage: "I can't arrest you, but I can sure keep you here pending charges of murder and attempted murder and threatening a public official…"

Mae started laughing.

Joe almost let go of her, he was so stunned.

"Oh, calm down. I'll go quietly. Maybe I can catch up on my reading in prison."

"Mae?" I gasped, the shock almost a physical slap as I hung onto the railing, still trying to get back on balance myself.

"What? I'm eighty-six, dear. I would have liked a few good years on the beach, but it's important to know when you're beat."

"O-kay," I said slowly, taking a closer look at her. She seemed physically all right. "You didn't hit your head?"

"I'm perfectly fine, Christian."

"And you'll be in a nice safe prison infirmary," Joe said in an impressively respectful tone. I'm not sure I could have been so nice if she'd held that gun on me.

"Doc?" Lewis called. "You okay up there?"

"All good," I said, looking down over the rail. "We do need the cops, though."

Lewis looked up at me with a relieved smile. "Already called 'em."

"Thanks."

"The kids are playing Demon Race on your computer. I hope that's okay."

I laughed. "It's perfect."

I nodded to Joe and ran down the stairs, slipping past Lewis to check on the kids. They didn't even look up, Henry brushing me off when I planted a little kiss on the top of his head. My silent prayer of thanks for their safety probably wasn't Jewishly correct, but I sure meant it.

I slipped off my jacket and hung it over my chair so the stone wouldn't fall out of the pocket before I could give it to Joe or the Staties.

When I walked back into the foyer, Joe and Mae had made it downstairs. He was holding her arm, firmly but still respectfully. She appeared to be entirely unharmed, not to mention almost cheerful. I suspected she was actually enjoying being in the clutches of such an attractive man.

And no, I wasn't projecting. I had no desire for Joe to take me into custody. Take me to Due Fiori for a nice dinner, maybe.

The man himself seemed a bit dazed. He gave me a wry scowl, tried to play it off. "You really didn't have to whack a little old lady."

"Hell, yes, she did, sonny." Mae looked up with a rueful smile. "I was ready to empty a clip into you."

I swallowed a smile at her action-hero verbiage and did not point

241

out that since her weapon was a vintage sidearm, it was a revolver and therefore had no clip to empty.

Lewis just shook his head. "You really never do know, do you?"

Joe managed a small smile. "Nope."

For a few seconds, we were all silent, stunned at how we'd ended up here.

Then there was a siren, that silly little woop-woop so much like one of Henry's toy cars.

Twice in one day for Tony DiBiasi. He walked into the foyer and looked around, just shaking his head. Whatever he was thinking, he contented himself with making the observation that the Staties were on the way too, and he'd just hold the fort till they came.

He did not manage to keep down a wry smile or a twinkle…and I knew Ed would be hearing a very colorful version of events before dinner.

Joe handed Mae off to DiBiasi, told him her gun was on the floor on the third-floor landing, and turned to me.

For a long moment, our eyes held, as he seemed to wilt a little, all the adrenaline of the last few minutes suddenly ebbing away, leaving him awkward and unexpectedly vulnerable.

"C'mere," I said, putting a hand on Joe's back for what I intended as a casual and reassuring half-hug.

He pulled me close, wrapping his arms around me, and buried his face in my hair, just hanging on for moment, his breathing raw. I knew it wasn't that much about me, and I didn't blame him. I doubted he had guns pointed at him very often, even being a state's attorney and a former corporate killer and all. I would have been pretty shaky, too. I rubbed his back, like I would with Henry. "It's okay. We're all safe."

Joe held me for what seemed like a good while, but probably wasn't more than half a minute, getting his breathing back under control. Even though it was the last thing from a romantic moment, I'd have to have been a lot further gone not to appreciate how very, very good it felt to be in his arms.

Might be worth exploring that later.

"Okay." He said it as he pulled back, still keeping a hand on my arm.

DiBiasi smiled and shot me a wink. More for the call to Ed, I was sure.

Joe's fingers burrowed into the fabric of my shirt. "Another one of those nice old oxfords."

"Yeah." Safe subject change, I knew. "You all right?"

"Sure am." His hand on my arm became less of a clutch and more of a caress, reminding me that there was really a lot going on here. "Thanks."

I nodded, and when his face relaxed at my response, what I'd intended as a little smile turned into a big, silly one. "Everybody needs a hug sometimes."

"Yeah. Might like that again, now that you mention it."

"We could arrange that."

"Good."

For a long second, we watched each other. Then I decided to just jump.

"I don't know what you're doing after you finish the paperwork, but a bunch of us are going to Malina's for dinner tonight."

Now *he* grinned. "New Haven County. All things are marked with a good Italian dinner."

"Exactly. Maybe you join us."

"Bolognese at Malina's is always a good thing." His hand on my arm again, this time a small but unmistakable caress. "If I get done in time, I will."

Chapter Thirty-Four

Denouement Bolognese

Unity, like any proper New Haven County town, has two good Italian family restaurants. Enzo's is the pizza spot where you do takeout and maybe a fast meal with the kiddies after a sporting event. Malina's is the pasta place, and that's where you go to eat a nice big dinner and discuss anything important or interesting happening in your world. That night, of course, we had plenty. Jorge was working again, but Tiffany and Ava were happy to join in, as was Dina's husband Ben, who had finished his busy day of eye surgery and didn't mind missing the first few innings of the Mets game.

Dinner was much more fun.

Ben was always happy to commiserate with Henry and Garrett and generally had more useful insight than Garrett, who came to his baseball fandom through his love of sports writing and is always more interested in the account of the game than the actual event. They are also the only three surviving Mets fans in Connecticut. Frank was the fourth, of course.

As a Western PA girl, I should have been a Pirates fan, but my only interest in baseball was reading Roger Kahn and Frank Deford. It was easy enough to suffer along with Frank when we got together, and now, it was one more way to keep a piece of him with us.

Plus, in New Haven County, between April and November, you'd better have something to say about baseball. Yankees or Sox is preferred, but anything will do; if you can't talk a little baseball, you've excluded yourself from a lot of fun social conversation. Baseball takes over when the weather stops being the principal topic.

So, it was no surprise that night when the evening began with an assessment of the season, unrealistic hopes for another Subway World Series, and equally pie-in-the-sky Sox talk.

It didn't take long, though. We were done by the time the garlic bread had arrived, and the drinks, milk for the kids, New Haven-made Italian lemon soda for the grownups who were driving (most of us), and a small bottle of chianti to share for the few who weren't, were poured. Pleasantries disposed; it was time for the serious discussion of the evening.

Ava and Henry were mostly occupied with the tic-tac-toe kids' placemats and third-grade gossip, so we were pretty safe talking about matters dangerous and deadly.

"So they've got three people for one murder?" Ben asked. Dina had probably given him a quick sketch of what happened, but by now, there was still a lot to sort out.

"It looks like two separate plots," I said. "Three people total."

"Better than that stupid movie," Ed said.

Garret took another piece of garlic bread, drawing a mild dirty look from Ed. "Sounds like anything would have been. It was basically asking Flutter to savage it."

"Sure was." Joe Poli appeared behind Garrett and took a piece of garlic bread from the basket with that naughty boy grin of his.

"Mr. Assistant State's Attorney," Ed said, shaking the non-bread hand.

"Sergeant Kenney. Dr. Shaw told me you all might end up here."

"Well, if she asked you, that's good enough for me." Garrett put in, with a squashing look to Ed.

"Fine by me, too," Ed said, kicking out a chair next to him.

Tiffany and Dina may or may not have been aware of all the subtext, but Ben got it at once, leaning over to me with a chuckle. "Nice having two dads, huh?"

"Most of the time."

Joe got it, too, and shot me a grin as he sat down. "Well, very nice of you all to invite me."

"We have ulterior motives, of course," Dina said. "We figure you know more about what happened than anyone else."

A modest shrug. "I have a good idea…and it's all in the affidavits, of course, so I'm not talking out of school."

"What are you having, Mr. Poli?" The server, probably a former schoolmate of his daughter's, bounced up with a big smile.

"What else, Brittani? Bolognese."

A laugh from Ed and Ben, who'd ordered the same.

"Well, if you can believe, Christian went for the carbonara tonight." Dina (gnocchi marinara) shook her head in mock disgust. "Good thing she walks a lot."

"I never critique a lady's pasta choice," Joe began. "And Dr. Shaw's just perfect as she is."

It was probably intended as light and teasing, but there was a faint edge of something else there, something sweet and wonderful that I hadn't heard in a very long time.

I looked up from my lemon soda, and Joe met my gaze. *Damn.* "Well, thank you."

Under the table, Tiffany kicked me.

"Very welcome." He settled into the chair Ed had given him, next to Dina, but almost perfectly opposite me.

Dina turned her big, warm smile on him. "Nice to see you again, Mr. Poli. Been a busy day, hasn't it?"

"Sure has, Rabbi."

"Ended well, though." Ed had the grim little smile I'd seen on him after reports of an arrest or verdict in a major murder case.

"Pretty much." Joe agreed. "We've got three arrests in the murder and strong cases for all."

"And everyone's safe," I said. "I'm just glad we all got to the end of this day in one piece."

"You aren't the only one." Joe took the lemon soda Brittani handed him and raised it to the table. "To making it through a bad one."

We could all drink to that. And we did.

"Hearings tomorrow?" asked Ed.

"We arraigned the movie guys just before closing time. The lady's at Yale." Which meant the hospital.

"Is she okay?" Dina asked, shocked, as eyes widened along the table.

Joe shrugged uncomfortably. "I didn't want an eighty-six-year-old woman spending the night with the hookers. I suggested her lawyer ask for a psych eval, and she took my advice."

"Who's the lawyer?" Ed asked.

"Personal injury specialist—a friend's daughter, just pitching in for the moment till they can find her someone. Do you have someone named Amelia at the Society?"

My eyes widened. "Um, Amelia's daughter isn't just some kid off the street. She's a shark, and she wrote our release for borrowing objects."

"Ah. That explains a lot." Joe nodded. "It will probably be a very thorough evaluation then."

Garrett chuckled. "You may live to regret that. I've met the daughter a couple of times."

Joe shrugged. "We'll see. Mrs. Tillotson may have held a gun on me, but she's still my grandmother's age, and that gets her something."

Ben smiled. "Being a matriarch always gets you something."

"It should," agreed Dina. She turned to Joe. "But you deserve a little relaxation, Mr. Poli. We didn't invite you here just to talk about the case."

"No?"

"Not at all," Tiffany put in smoothly. "Christian especially wanted to relax and hang out tonight."

I returned her kick from a few moments ago. She ignored it.

"Well, that's why we're here," Garrett cut in with his usual grace, ignoring our little rub. "That and the pasta."

"Always that," Tiffany agreed. "Everything's better with fresh tagliatelle."

That, intended or not, sparked a spirited discussion of the correct pasta for the correct sauce, probably the only topic capable of providing more distraction in New Haven County than Yankees versus Red Sox—or weather. Once everyone had reached the usual conclusions about the affinity between big heavy sauce and short hollow pasta and gone a round or two on the enduring fettuccine alfredo controversy, our own pasta choices had arrived, and we tucked in.

By unspoken parental agreement, which Joe clearly understood and appreciated, while the actual eating took place, dinner conversation centered on topics suitable for the entire table, including the kids. So what if we had to spend a fair amount of time talking about the misbehavior of our various pets and whether weekend homework was unfair (Kids: yes, Parents: no)—we were teaching the little, um, medium-sized ones to converse well in groups.

Joe fit in very nicely with the crew.

Dinner had mostly wound down, and the children were happily demolishing little dishes of gelato (lower in sugar than you'd think, and I'd set Henry's meter knowing he would have to have dessert with his friend), and plotting their next video racing match when the big people returned to the matter of murder.

"So I'm still trying to figure out how you get three people charged in one killing that's not something like a gang beating," Ben said, leaning back in his chair after taking the one spoonful of Dina's gelato that would satisfy him.

He's a great guy, but I'm glad she's the one who's married to him. What kind of man eats ONE SPOONFUL of gelato?

Not Joe. He'd been doing very well by a dish of Stracciatella until Ben spoke. "Well, all of them deliberately and maliciously acted to bring about the death of another person."

"Right." Dina nodded. "But are they all equally guilty?"

"The question, of course is, lethality," Joe said, putting down his spoon. "There's no doubt he was poisoned by two or three different means…but the ME can't tell me for sure which one would have been lethal—if any. But the fall definitely was."

I remembered the day Mae was late to get a bad cut on her arm dressed. "Mae was probably in the pulpit before the latch was taken off—I think she cut herself on the metal."

Joe took a spoonful of his gelato and contemplated for a moment. "So if she had a cut from the latch, it was still in place when she poisoned the Bible."

"Exactly." I took another bite of my espresso gelato. "We're going to have to have that cleaned, by the way. And I'm not sure how."

"You'll have to worry about that later, sorry." He shook his head. "I don't want to put out an evidence warrant for it until I know for sure how we can protect it while it's tested. I'm thinking I ask to have the CSIs take some very careful swabs at the Society and maybe get you and Lewis to bring it on the day of testimony. Where is Lewis, anyhow?"

"It's Monday," I said. "He goes to dinner with his grandma. I'm surprised they're not at the next table, actually."

Dina shook her head. "They wanted to try some new Indian place in Prospect."

Ben smiled. "Maybe we go next week."

Ed growled a little.

"Maybe." Dina nudged her husband and nodded to Joe, who'd taken the opportunity to return to his dessert. "Back to the Bible and the pulpit."

Joe took a breath and put down his spoon again. "Yes. The pulpit door, the clearly and obviously fatal thing, was the last one done."

"What does the ME say?" Ed asked.

"The cyanide might or might not have killed him—the medics jumped right in and kept him going for a while, and it's hard to say with the synthetic marijuana or anything from the metal. But the head injury was definitely fatal."

Tiffany nodded. "He hit the back of the head, where all of the important real estate is."

"So," Joe said, "murder and conspiracy charges for the *coup de grace*."

Ed nodded. "The Hollywood guys are the guiltiest."

"Well," Dina said, "there's the other half of it. Who deserves to pay?"

"They all deserve some punishment, of course," Joe reminded her.

"True," I said. "But it was straight money for the movie folks. No principle, no mitigating factors in play. Just cold, hard cash."

Garrett nodded grimly. "They knew the film was going to tank. Maybe spectacularly because most of the world won't pay to see some straight white guy's midlife crisis these days, and social media would burn the damn thing down."

"Probably taking Holman with it." Joe shook his head. "So he bribed and blackmailed Maguire into doing the dirty work. On a guy he'd worked closely with and allegedly liked and respected."

"Despicable." Dina scowled into her chocolate gelato. "Choosing money over a life."

"They aren't the only ones who did," Ben reminded his wife. "Mrs. Tillotson tried to kill him to protect her property values."

"Yeah, but she's old. And scared." Tiffany shrugged. "I'm not saying it's right, but it's not as evil."

"Evil's a strong word," Dina said with a small sigh. "But at one level, they were all the same: Brett Studebaker's existence as a fellow human meant less to them than their own corrupt desires for money...or a house in Florida."

"That's how people become killers, Rabbi," Joe said. "When they no longer see someone as human."

"Because then you can do anything you think you have to do," I agreed.

"Some people are less awful than others, though," Tiffany put in, "and deserve less punishment."

"I won't lose sleep over those movie men going down hard," said Ed.

"But a little old lady?" Garrett asked. "I'm not sure what we get for locking her up for whatever's left of her life."

"Some level of justice, anyway," Joe said quietly.

We all heard the intensity in his voice.

Dina was the one who spoke. "We do the best we can."

"We do, Rabbi." Joe shrugged. "She's getting an attempted murder charge to start, and it'll probably be pled down. I don't know what we do with her. As far as I know, Corrections doesn't have a good safe place for an 86-year-old female killer."

"Why do I think you'll find one?" I asked.

Joe gave me a tiny smile and picked up his spoon. "How about those Mets?"

We all knew what that meant.

Soon enough, the gelato was gone, the bill settled (Joe insisted on not only paying his part but leaving the tip because he wanted to be generous to Brittani, who was indeed one of Aly's old classmates), and the kids were starting to wilt a little, never mind the grownups, who'd had quite a dramatic day. Tiffany scooped up Ava, giving me a significant look and whispering: "Wait five minutes."

Dina caught it and smiled, but Joe, who I assumed was the subject, didn't, because he and Garrett had discovered a shared fondness for Frank Deford. They were busy parsing the difference between his sports and feature writing.

Tiffany's grin left no doubt that she'd be expecting details at pickup the next day. I wondered if I'd have anything to offer...and was surprised to realize that I hoped I would. At least a little something.

As it happened, whether by accident or Garrett's intent—he can talk about good sports writing for five minutes or five hours—it was indeed a short while later when the two reached a lull in the conversation and Joe looked over at me.

The wonderful new thing that had been in his gaze when he sat at the table was still there, so I knew I hadn't imagined it. I still didn't know what it meant, but I was starting to get a pretty good idea of what I'd like to do about it.

I did, after all, have an excellent supply of dependable and willing baby—um, medium-size kid–sitters.

"Henry and I really should be going, too," I said, diplomatically ignoring Ben and Dina's knowing smiles as I said my goodnights. Dina would want details, too.

"I'll walk you two to your car, Dr. Shaw," offered Joe as Garrett shot me a sly wink, and Ed nodded. It was the best Joe was going to get from him right now, and that was just fine.

"C'mon, fella." I helped Henry into his jacket.

"What time is it?" he asked Joe.

"A little after seven-thirty," Joe replied as he held the door for us both.

"Cool." Henry looked across the mostly dark but very safe parking lot and started zipping toward the car. "I have enough time to watch a video on Ur-ANUS and Neptune."

"Ur-AN-ous!" I snapped as I clicked the locks, and Joe started laughing.

Giggling at his boring mom's irritation, Henry climbed into the car, leaving the two grownups standing in the last purplish glow of the late spring sunset and the single streetlamp for a moment.

"A really nice evening, Dr. Shaw," Joe started.

"I think maybe you can stop calling me Dr. Shaw now."

He shook his head, took a breath, standing there looking both adorable and awkward with his hands in his pockets. "Do you know why I always call you Dr. Shaw?"

"Because I scare you?" A guess, but maybe a good one. He sure scared me.

"Well, a little." He gave a nice Jimmy Stewart shrug. "But in a good way."

"Okay." Definitely a good way.

"It's because I can't say your damn name."

"What?"

"I grew up in New Haven. It comes out all wrong."

"The Southern Connecticut T-swallowing thing."

"Yeah."

"Well, I won't glare at you if you call me Doc in the minimart."

He took my hand. A tiny, careful, old-fashioned gesture I wasn't expecting. And certainly not the surprise of the warmth of his skin, the actual intimacy of it as he idly, but not really idly, laced fingers with mine, the two of us standing there almost alone in the warm, lilac-scented May evening. "Yeah, well. I'm kind of hoping I'll get to see you again soon—on purpose."

"You are?"

"Maybe I stop over sometime for a coffee and talk about something

253

other than dead movie stars?" His voice was a little uncertain, but his eyes, dark and bottomless, held my gaze steadily. "Or maybe even some good pasta without the entire cast on hand? What do you think of Due Fiori?"

YES! He actually asked me out! Oh, hell yes, this really is eighth grade.

I managed to keep my voice steady. "I'd like that. And I promise I won't look at you funny if you swallow the T."

"All right, then." He took a breath. "Chris'shun."

"Not so bad." I'm still not sure why, but I got on tiptoe and kissed him on the cheek. For a second, we both froze, as what I'd intended as a simple, innocent gesture reminded us that there was a whole lot more going on here.

Then he spoke. Quoted, actually. *"If ever any beauty I did see, which I desired and got, 'twas but a dream of thee."*

My jaw dropped. "Damn."

"Been brushing up on my Donne a little." He met my eyes with a shy smile for a second, and then his expression changed to something very definitely not shy and perhaps even a bit wicked. "Sometime soon, I'm going to kiss you, and I'm not going to stop until you tell me to."

"I might not tell you to stop."

For one hot second, absolutely anything could have happened.

Then a squawk from the car as Henry asserted his presence, reminding the gross adults that any and all expressions of affection are icky.

We both laughed, far too familiar with kids and their ways. But he didn't let go of my hand, pulling me a little closer, even if not making a move for anything more.

"Nice, *Dottore*." In the perfect Italian he'd learned from his mother and his own silky voice, the T soft but not swallowed, it wasn't a title but an endearment.

"Works for me."

Acknowledgements

First thanks go to my editor, Verena Rose, and agent, Eric Myers, for making this book happen. A very special acknowledgement to my friend Julie von Wettberg, her son Dougal Henken, and my neighbors, Lily and Manny Felix, and their son (my son's playmate) Enzo, for their insight on life with Type-1 diabetes.

As always, deep gratitude to my families of blood, work, and choice, for all of their support. This book—and I—would not be here without you.

About the Author

Kathleen Marple Kalb likes to describe herself as an Author/Anchor/-Mom...not in that order. An award-winning radio journalist, she currently anchors on the weekend morning show at New York's #1 news station, 1010 WINS. She's the author of several mysteries, historical and contemporary. Her short stories appear in anthologies and online and have been short-listed for Derringer and Black Orchid Novella Awards. She grew up in front of a microphone and a keyboard, working as an overnight DJ as a teenager in her hometown of Brookville, Pennsylvania...and writing her first (thankfully unpublished) novel at sixteen. When her son started kindergarten, she returned to fiction, and after two failed projects, some 200 rejections, and a family health crisis, found an agent for the third book—leading to a pandemic debut. In hopes of sharing what she's learned the hard way, she's active in writers' groups, including Sisters in Crime and the Short Mystery Fiction Society, and keeps a weekly writing survival tips blog. She, her husband, and their son live in Connecticut in a house owned by their cat.

SOCIAL MEDIA HANDLES:

Facebook: https://www.facebook.com/Kathleen-Marple-Kalb-10
82949845220373/

Twitter: https://twitter.com/KalbMarple

Instagram: https://www.instagram.com/kathleenmarplekalb/

AUTHOR WEBSITE:

https://kathleenmarplekalb.com/

Also by Kathleen Marple Kalb

Ella Shane Mysteries (Kensington)
A Fatal Finale (2020)
A Fatal First Night (2021)
A Fatal Overture (2022)

Vermont Radio Mysteries – As Nikki Knight (Crooked Lane)
Live, Local and Dead (2022)

Grace the Hit Mom Mysteries – As Nikki Knight (Charade Media)
Wrong Poison (2023)

Short Stories in Anthologies and online, including:
"The New York Goodbye," *Black Cat Weekly*, September 2023
"The Telltale Request," *Mystery Magazine*, September 2023
"Second Chances are…Murder," *Malice, Matrimony, and Murder Anthology*, November 2023
"Pie a La Poison," in *The Perp Wore Pumpkin*, Misti Media, November 2023
"The Custodian of the Body," (Old Stuff Mystery), *Black Cat Weekly*, May 2023
"This Never Happened to Wolfman Jack," M2D4 Podcast August 2023, season anthology, November 2023
"Don't Mess with the Boss Cat," CatsCast Podcast by Escape Artists, June 2023
"The Annual Mud Season Homicide," *Alfred Hitchcock's Mystery Magazine*, May/June 2023
"Owl Be Damned," Mysteryrat's Maze Podcast, January 2023
"Blame it on the Blizzard," *Deadly Nightshade: Best New England*

Crime Stories 2022

"And Your Lake Monster Too," *Crimeucopia: Tales from the Back Porch,* 2022

"The Thanksgiving Ragamuffin," *Justice For All: Murder New York Style 5,* 2021 (Derringer Award Finalist)

"Snowed Under," *Dark and Stormy Night,* 2022

"It Was Our Song," *Mystery Tribune Daily Fiction,* May 2022

"Owl Be Damned," *Tough Crime Magazine,* August 2022

"The DJ Saved My Life," White Cat Publications, August 2022

Forthcoming:

A Fatal Reception, Ella Shane Mystery #4, Level Best Books, April 2024

"Caught by the Last Star" Mysteryrat's Maze Podcast, January 2024

"Sorry Not Sorry," M2D4 Season 7, podcast and anthology, 2024

Printed in the USA
CPSIA information can be obtained
at www.ICGtesting.com
JSHW080149100224
57085JS00001B/52